ANGELS WHISPER

TONY PERONA

All the best!
Tony Perona

Five Star • Waterville, Maine

First Edition
First Printing: February 2005

Published in 2005 in conjunction with Tekno Books and Ed Gorman.

Set in 11 pt. Plantin.

Printed in the United States on permanent paper.
ISBN 1-59414-265-3 (hc : alk. paper)

Dedication

To Debbie, Liz, and Katy

You make it all worthwhile!

And to the memory of my grandmothers

Catherine Agnes Peperak Bonte
(1909–1999)

and

Minnie Catherine Bertetto Perona Miller
(1907–1980)

For their love, inspiration, and faith.

ACKNOWLEDGMENTS

First of all, I'd like to thank God once again for his inspiration and his gifts. He is truly an awesome God.

Second, my agent, Lucienne Diver, for her continued faith in my ability to write and tell stories. She is a wonderful agent.

Third, a number of people who provided their expertise: Father Francis T. Cancro, St. Eugene parish, Asheville, NC, for help with the Italian; Chief Larry Brinker, Plainfield Police Department, for technical advice; Rick Sudsberry, Counselor, for help understanding post-traumatic stress disorder and its treatment; fellow Indianapolis author D. R. Schanker, for allowing me to use his creation of the *Indianapolis Standard*; State Representative Robert W. Behning and his staff, especially Paul O'Conner, Danielle Lewis, Joe McLain, and Ryan Mangus, for sharing their knowledge of the Statehouse, its lore, and providing me with a tour of places most people never see; Linda Summerlin, R.N., for help with the hospital scenes; Cheryl Devol-Glowinski with the Casino Association of Indiana, who took the time to explain current and projected legislation affecting the casino boats in Indiana; and Lisa Dawes, membership director of the Indianapolis Athletic Club, for information about private clubs. All these people are experts, and if any mistakes were made in interpreting their information or adapting it to this story, the fault lies with me and not with them.

Fourth, my writer friends who provided support and advice, especially those in the Indiana Writers Workshop who read this manuscript several times and offered critiques: Bob Chenoweth, June McCarty Clair, John Clair, Dan Fenton, Nancy Frenzel, Pat Watson Grande, Joyce Jensen, Teri Moore, Kathy Nappier, Lucy Schilling, Kitty Smock, Marjorie Stonehill, and Steve Wynalda. There is no finer group of writers anywhere.

FOREWORD

The characters in this book are fictional. I really did make them up, and any similarities to persons living or dead should be chalked up to my boffo ability to create characters so lifelike you want them to be people you know.

While the psalmist says that God has given his angels charge over us, I don't know of any article of faith in the Catholic Church that officially says each person has a single guardian angel. It's more of a tradition that has grown throughout the centuries. Therefore, when Eli talks about guardian angels in Chapter 20, it's my own take on this tradition. It might differ a little with conventional Catholic thought, but I had fun making it work for me. Angels are certainly not perfect (fallen angels prove this), only God is.

Christianity, by the way, should be defined not by the differences we see in denominations, but rather by the shared convictions we have in our Savior. Peace.

CHAPTER ONE

CHAPTER ONE

My van was the *grande dame* of the preschool fleet, a veritable humpback Chevy whale amid the Mitsubishi minnows collecting the children from St. Rita's school at three p.m. She could hold six screaming preschoolers in the back, all of them with car seats, and without a factory-installed airbag in the passenger seat, she could accommodate an extra child up front when necessary. Today, Monday, it was necessary, and that lucky child was Melissa the Motormouth. Had the incident which was about to occur been worse, my defense would have been to put Melissa on the stand for five minutes and let her talk. I contend no jury in the world would convict me of driving too fast to get her home.

"... and then Jason took off his clothes and pooped in the wastebasket," Melissa chattered, "only it was tall and he missed so it went down the side. And then he looked at it so I went to get Mommy and she said he was like Daddy 'cause he leaves messes all over the house. Mommy almost cleaned it up, but Spike chased Fluffy through it and got poop on their feet and then Mommy chased them in the kitchen and then they got poopy paw prints everywhere. Yuck! Mommy cleaned Fluffy up and threw Spike outside. She mopped the floor and said Daddy would have to give Spike a bath when he got home 'cause Spike was his dog and—Mr. Nick, watch out for that man!"

She pointed ahead to a man I'd been watching already.

11

He was staggering down the shoulder of Highway 31, every so often lurching into the right traffic lane. The sleeves had been cut out of his flannel shirt and his too-long pant legs were bunched around his feet. Wiry, ebony arms flailed as he strove to gain his balance.

"Uncle Harold walks like that and Mommy says he needs to dry out but Uncle Harold never looks wet to me . . ." Melissa was saying, but I stopped paying attention to her and slowed the van, approaching the stranger as cautiously as I could with traffic whizzing around us. I checked the rear and side mirrors to see if I could cut into the left lane. The traffic was too heavy. He moved a little farther away from me toward the far right of the shoulder. Thinking I had room to quickly scoot by him, I nudged the accelerator.

He chose that instant to stumble toward the road again. I slammed the brake pedal to the floor and inched to the left. The preschoolers screamed, all of them, all at once. The next thing I knew the man was tumbling into the ditch. I hadn't heard a thump, but I couldn't swear I'd missed him. I pulled the van over to the side and started to get out of the car.

"Where are you going, Mr. Nick? Can I come, too?" Melissa begged. Simultaneously my daughter Stephanie said, "Daddy, don't go!"

I reached into the middle row and squeezed Stephanie's hand. "It's going to be all right. I have to make sure that man is okay. No, Melissa, you can't come. Everyone stay in your seats."

I locked them in the van and ran over to the ditch.

He lay face down in a carpet of green, shaggy weeds. We hadn't had rain in a week so there wasn't much water in the ditch. Probably no chance he could inhale water and drown, I thought, but I gently moved his face to the side anyway. He was breathing but unconscious. I checked for blood. The shirt was stained, but not with blood. He smelled of body sweat unchecked too long by soap or deodorant.

The mid-May sun, still high in the sky, made the beads of ditch water in his black hair sparkle. I patted his face. "Hey, buddy, are you all right?" There was no response. "Hello?" I lifted the eyelid I could get to.

"Is he okay?" a woman shouted. I looked up and saw a blue BMW parked behind my van. A woman in her mid-thirties, dressed in a business suit, stood next to it, waving at me. "You didn't hit him. I saw it happen. He looked like he had a leg spasm or something. It made him jerk and fall. He might be one of those insurance swindlers, though. You need to be careful."

"I don't see any wounds, but he's unconscious," I shouted back. "Do you have a cell phone? Can you call nine-one-one?"

"It's in my car." She turned and started toward it, then scanned the road, one hand shielding her eyes from the sun. "Wait. There's a police car coming. I'll flag him down."

While she stopped the police car, I ran up to reassure the kids that everything was fine. I reminded them to stay in their seats while I talked to the police officer.

From the way the officer approached, one leg stiff at the knee, I knew it was Ken Roth, an ex-reserve who'd been wounded in Desert Storm. Roth's daughter Jamie and my daughter Stephanie had gymnastics classes together, so I saw him every Monday night. After a quick hello, he followed me to the ditch, listening to my story. The woman who'd flagged him down hung around; he'd asked her to stay until the ambulance came and he had a chance to get her statement.

Roth checked the man over for injuries, found none, then went up to where my van was parked. He inspected it carefully, examining it, I guessed, for evidence that I'd hit the man. After a few minutes, he returned to the trench.

"It doesn't look like he's hurt or that you hit him, Nick," Roth said. "Don't know why he fell, but, phew, he stinks. Might have been alcohol. I don't see a wallet or anything. Looks like he might be homeless."

The man and his clothes needed a good washing—that was beyond dispute—but I didn't smell alcohol on him. I didn't contradict Roth, however.

Roth stood up. "The ambulance should be here soon. I'm going up to call in. Will you stay with him?"

I said I would.

After Roth left, I took a little more time to examine the man. His hair was matted and hadn't been cut in a long time. He had a stubby beard which I estimated at a week's growth. He appeared to be in his late fifties, with age lines in his face that, minus the unkempt beard and hair, would have made him look distinguished.

I thought I saw the corner of something sticking out of his right back pocket. Roth had felt for a wallet but hadn't actually checked anything else in there. I tugged at the corner and pulled it halfway out. It looked to be the Polaroid photograph of a hotel room.

All of a sudden he twitched, pulled his left knee toward his waist, and then turned himself over, the photograph still half in his pocket. He opened his mouth in a yawn. The teeth were yellow but straight, and there were no signs of dental work. I still could not detect alcohol on his breath when he muttered, "Ugghh."

"Hello, are you okay?" I asked.

His eyes, bloodshot and yellowish, opened. The pupils were huge, dominating the flinty brown irises, and his eyes glowed like those of a cat in the dark. "Cahill wore red," he said in a hoarse voice. Then the eyes closed up tight.

Had he said "Cahill"? That name had been in the news recently.

"What?" I nudged his shoulders. "What did you say? Come back." He didn't respond.

Roth returned. "Did you turn him over?" he asked, looking at the body.

"No, he did it himself. And he talked to me. It was a little bizarre, but for a moment he came to."

"What did he say?"

I paused for a moment. If he really said "Cahill," there might be a story in him the freelance reporter in me didn't want to share yet. Now I was sorry I'd said anything. "Well, it wasn't very clear, and I'm not sure I heard him right."

"Nothing that would tell us his name or anything?"

"No, it wasn't anything like that."

"Well, there's an ambulance on the way. Don't know what's keeping them. Nick, I need to get your statement."

"I know. I've got a van full of anxious preschoolers up there, though. Can it wait until I've dropped them off?"

His mouth tightened. I could tell he wouldn't let me go, but he understood about the preschoolers. "Why don't you go see how they're doing? Maybe I can get your statement when the paramedics get here."

I scrambled up the ditch toward the van.

The kids were all out of their seats, even the three-year-olds. The older ones must've sprung them. Every child had his or her face pressed against a window. I opened the driver's door and reached for Stephanie, who was kneeling

15

on my seat. She wasn't crying but the look in her eyes told me she was scared. "It's okay," I said, hugging her.

Using my most soothing voice, I got the rest of them back in their seats. There was no use explaining what was happening, so I just reassured them we would be going shortly. They were no sooner seated when the ambulance, siren blaring, pulled up. They popped out of their seats again.

"Are you going to jail, Mr. Nick?" Melissa asked anxiously.

"No, of course not," I said, but not before the three-year-old Starner twins began crying. Then some of the others started, and suddenly I had my hands full.

Stephanie, who's four and a half but really good with the younger kids, helped, but by the time I'd finished calming the tow-headed twins, the paramedics had returned from the ditch with the man on a stretcher. All the kids watched in awe. The paramedics said something to Ken Roth, who was standing next to the BMW taking the businesswoman's statement. He nodded. They loaded the man in the ambulance and took off.

Roth closed his book, helped the woman into her car, and watched her leave. Then he walked over to me.

"Everyone okay here?" he asked.

"For the moment," I answered. I turned to my charges in the van. "This is Officer Roth, kids. Can you say hello to him?" They did, with just a bit of awe, after which Melissa started.

"Mr. Nick didn't hit the man on purpose," she said. "He ran in front of us and Mr. Nick had to run him over . . ."

"My daddy didn't hit him!" Stephanie protested loudly. "And he'd say he was sorry if he did . . ."

"It's okay, Stephanie, Melissa," I said, holding Stephanie's hand. "Officer Roth and I are going to talk for a couple of minutes, and then I'll take everyone home." To the group, I said, "Can you be real quiet so the policeman can hear me?" With wide eyes, they nodded their heads.

True to their promise, the kids were mostly silent while Roth and I stepped out of earshot and went over what had happened. Roth seemed satisfied with what I told him, though he questioned me twice about what the man had said. Each time I insisted, and it was almost the truth, that I couldn't be sure what he'd told me. Either Roth figured I was on the level or he decided I wasn't going to let on, because he didn't push it beyond the second "Are you sure?"

"Did they take him to Johnson Memorial Hospital?" I asked.

"Yeah. Do you want to be notified if they find anything?"

I nodded. "I know I didn't hit him, but I'm sure I must've scared him. I'll try to stop by the hospital after I drop the kids off. When will you have the police report filed?"

"Now that we have these laptops, we file them as soon after the fact as possible. Mine'll be transferred to headquarters by the time you get home, if you want a copy."

"Thanks," I said. We returned to our vehicles. Roth sat in his car talking on the mike.

"Everything's fine," I assured the children as I eased into traffic. "I didn't hit him, but he fell into the ditch because there's something else wrong with him."

"Why did he fall?" Stephanie asked.

"I don't know yet."

"What's his name?"

"He told me a name, but I don't think it was *his* name."

"Whose was it?"

17

"No one you would know," I replied.

No one she knew, but if I'd heard right, I could guess who he was talking about. And although I didn't know yet what any of this meant, I definitely wanted to find out.

CHAPTER TWO

As I dropped each child off, I explained to the adult at home what had happened on the highway. There was no telling what the kids might say about the incident, and no telling what the parents might believe, so I thought it best to stifle any rumors now.

Jill, Melissa's mother, invited Stephanie to stay and play for a couple of hours. For reasons that I don't understand, but suspect may have something to do with Melissa's brother's antics (like pooping in the wastebasket), Steph likes to play with Melissa. Sometimes I let her, but I could tell today was not a good day for that. She clung to my side, something she doesn't usually do. I was certain it had been the incident on the highway. After all, the image of the man tumbling into the ditch played over and over again in my mind. Stephanie, who had stared as the stretcher was put into the ambulance, was probably not over it, either. I told Jill I thought it would be best for Stephanie to be with me today, and we left.

When we got home, I sat with Steph on the couch and asked her if she was okay. She began to cry. I held her close.

"Are you upset about the accident?" I asked.

She nodded.

"Me, too," I said.

"I was scared."

"I was, too. Scared that the man was hurt. But we know we didn't hurt him. Officer Roth told us that. There was

19

something else wrong with him. He's at the hospital now, so doctors and nurses are looking after him. He'll be okay."

Steph seemed only partially reassured by my words.

"Would you like to go see the man?" I asked. "I don't know if he's still there, or if they'll let us in, but we can try. I'd like to see him again myself."

She pushed her head into the crook of my arm, and I could feel her nodding yes. I pulled her onto my lap and gave her a hug. "Then we'll see if he's there. But first I need to check my e-mail. Will you be okay?"

She said she would.

She followed me upstairs to my office where I logged on. While mail was downloading, I checked my answering machine and asked Stephanie to go out to the mail box. She loves to get the mail.

No rush jobs had come in and no immediate e-mail replies had to be written, so I took the snail mail from Steph and looked through it. A letter from Anna Veloche caught my eye. Anna was a former client who'd nearly been framed for a murder she didn't commit. She also believed she was receiving messages from an apparition of the Virgin Mary, a claim I didn't dispute, but one that made me uncomfortable. I'd been able to uncover the real murderer's identity in a way that seemed somewhat miraculous, though there were rational explanations for how it had occurred. I found that reassuring, and yet I had never felt closer to the supernatural than I had at that moment. Who knew what to believe? I sure didn't, but I had nonetheless returned to Sunday Mass on a regular basis, sometimes with my wife Joan if she would go, and Stephanie was happy at St. Rita's preschool.

I scanned Anna's letter, which was nothing more than a notice of where she would be giving talks for the next two months. She had sent no personal messages. I tossed the letter.

Next I called the police department to find out if the accident report had been filed. True to Roth's word, he'd gotten it in already. I buckled Steph in the van and took off. Our first stop was the police station to pick up a copy of the report.

The police had misspelled my last name, Bertetto, but had managed to get the name of the man I'd almost hit: Elijah Smith, no known address. He was listed as malnourished but otherwise physically healthy. There were no signs of head trauma that would cause him to be unconscious. The hospital was holding him for observation.

Something about Smith didn't feel right to me. I wanted to help him, if I could, and to figure out what it was about him that bothered me. Plus, I had to admit, I had more than just a little curiosity about any possible relationship he might have to Cahill.

I looked at my watch. It was four o'clock, only an hour since the incident. It had felt much longer. He was surely still at the hospital.

Police headquarters was south of the town square. Johnson Memorial Hospital was west of town and the Bertetto homestead was north, so it took me about twenty-five minutes in total time to make the circuit to the hospital. Actually, the hospital was not far from Stephanie's preschool; it would have been a lot more convenient for the man to have stumbled in front of me before I left the St. Rita parking lot.

Holding my hand, Stephanie walked with me into the Emergency Room waiting area, sidestepping two wheelchairs at the entrance that had drifted away from the rest of their pack. Two women receptionists were on duty, seated at desks in their respective booths. They talked through the glass partition between them until they noticed us. Both said, "May I help you?" at the same time. I chose the mid-twentyish blonde because she looked friendlier.

"I'm looking for Elijah Smith. He was brought in about an hour ago."

"Let me get the doctor," she said, eyeing Stephanie. "I'm not sure he can receive visitors yet. Please have a seat." She disappeared into the ER area.

I prepared for a lengthy stay. Like any experienced stay-at-home dad, I kept a bag in the van with things for Steph to do—coloring books, crayons, puzzles, board books, even an electronic toy that my father had bought her—but the hospital had toys in the waiting room and Steph gravitated toward a jigsaw puzzle. I was surprised but relieved that she didn't seem apprehensive.

Rummaging about the small, airport-like waiting area, I searched for an Indianapolis paper. I'd already read the *Morning Journal*, Franklin's paper, earlier in the day. While it's a good publication for a small paper, they make it a point *not* to cover Indianapolis news in depth, so they hadn't had what I was looking for—the latest on the disappearance of State Representative Calvin Cahill.

Maybe it was a reach, I thought, but Cahill wasn't too common a name, and his name had been prominent in the media since he disappeared three days ago. The man I'd almost hit had said, "Cahill wore red," or at least I'd thought so. It seemed worth checking up on.

I found a copy of the *Indianapolis Standard* under some year-old *Newsweeks*. It was the better of Indianapolis' two daily papers, but I'm biased, since I used to work for the *Standard* as an investigative reporter. I still did the occasional freelance piece for the Lifestyle editor. It's an odd turnabout to go straight from serious to fluff, but circumstances in my life had called for it.

In many ways I was still trying to make the best of what had happened. An investigation had gone sour and my wife Joan had been kidnapped, an ordeal which left her mentally fragile. After that she couldn't cope with my job and the repercussions it might have for her and Stephanie. I had been frightened, too, that it could happen again. Thinking it might be the only way to help her overcome post-traumatic stress disorder, I'd left the paper. She went back to her job as a pharmacist, and I became a freelance writer and stay-at-home dad. Two years had passed, long enough for me to see the kidnapping for the isolated incident it was, but it still haunted us. My wife hadn't gotten over her fears, and I longed to return to investigative reporting. In fact, the case involving Anna Veloche, which had taken place a year ago in my hometown of Clinton, Indiana, had involved several murders. My looking into it had made my marital problems worse. Joan and I were seeing a counselor together, but I wasn't sure we were making progress. I loved Joan, and there were times I could see she loved me, but I wondered how much longer we could go on this way.

I scanned the front page of the tabloid-sized newspaper. "Police seek leads in Cahill disappearance," screamed the headline. I checked the byline: Ryan Lockridge. Lockridge and I go back a long way. The article stated that the police had questioned everyone who had been with Cahill at the Federal Club. That was the last place he'd been seen before vanishing on Friday, May 15. They had no suspects and no leads. Unnamed sources claimed that tapes taken from the club's security cameras did not show Cahill leaving that venerable institution. The Federal Club had been thoroughly searched by police but with no results.

The rest I knew from previous reports and because Joan had a cousin who worked at the Statehouse. Cahill's wife, Cheryl, had worried when he hadn't shown up Friday night at their home in the southern Indiana town of Vincennes, but she hadn't contacted the police because he frequently spent the night in Indianapolis. Still, it had been unusual that he hadn't called. By Saturday morning her concern had increased, and she had phoned everyone she knew in the capital city. By noon she had gone to the police.

The police determined there was reason to be concerned. After questioning the staff at the Federal Club, they restricted access to the building, much to the consternation of club members, and performed a thorough search. Apparently there was little to go on.

A companion piece appeared on page three of the newspaper's first section, right next to an L. S. Ayres department store ad for some kind of skimpy underwear that, seemingly, could only be worn by muscular men with ripped abs. If you put a little padding over the abs and added about fifteen years to the twenty-year-old model, I would have looked just like him. In my dreams.

The headline read, "Reward offered in Cahill disappearance." Cheryl Cahill had now offered a thirty-five-thousand-dollar reward for information leading police to her missing husband. "I am afraid for Cal," she was quoted as saying. The article mentioned frightening statistics about the short length of time people can be missing before the likelihood is that they will be found dead. At three days, Cal's chances had decreased significantly.

A sidebar recapped the timeline. Calvin Cahill had given a luncheon speech to the Young Republicans at noon. The lunch was over by one-thirty. After a short meeting with Statehouse leaders, ending approximately at two, Cahill had told friends he was headed for the pool. No one saw him at the pool and no one saw him leave the Federal Club. His car, parked at the Capitol garage, had not been touched. I wondered, but had he worn red? Red what? Shirt, tie, suspenders, belt, shoes, socks, hat? And so what if he had?

Stephanie interrupted my train of thought, distressed that she could not find a missing piece to the Disney princesses puzzle. We looked for it together.

"It might not be here, sweetheart," I cautioned her.

She looked up from a pile of puzzle pieces. "Why not, Daddy?"

"Because sometimes kids get careless with toys that aren't theirs. It could have been broken and thrown away."

Steph thought for a moment. "Maybe a baby ate it. Jason ate one of Melissa's."

Very little surprised me about Jason. "It could happen. Why don't you color me a picture instead?" I asked, offering a coloring book from the bag I'd brought.

She went for it.

As I pulled out her crayons, I searched the bag for my cell phone and found it at the bottom. I dialed the work number for Ryan Lockridge, the reporter who'd written the article on Cahill.

"Lockridge. Start talking," he answered.

"Geez, the *Standard*'s standards are slipping if they let you answer the phone that way."

"Some of us have caller ID, so we know ahead of time when we're being connected with cranks and weirdoes."

"Now is that any way to talk to a former roommate?"

"Hey, I earned that right." He paused for a moment. I heard him take a gulp of something, probably coffee. "So whaddya need?" he asked. "I'm kinda busy, you know."

25

"Oh, yeah, an important reporter like you with front-page bylines doesn't have much time for a guy like me. What makes you think I need something?"

"Past experience."

"Well, since you put it that way," I said. "As strange as this is going to sound, Ryan, I need to know what Calvin Cahill was wearing the day he disappeared."

There was another pause. I wondered if he had covered the phone to snicker. Finally he said, "Have you been assigned an article on last-day fashions of missing persons? Is it your theory he's been abducted by the fashion police?"

"In fact, it is. So what was he wearing?"

"How the hell am I supposed to know?"

"If I remember right, Cahill was the guest speaker at the Young Republicans' luncheon that day. With all those politically involved teenagers around, you can't tell me the paper didn't send a photographer."

"Yeah, they probably did. Hang on a minute." I heard Lockridge typing away on the computer. It took longer than a minute before he said, "Okay, I pulled it up on the screen. If you tell me why you *really* need it, I'll tell you what he was wearing."

Truth is stranger than fiction, and sometimes people can't tell them apart. I decided to rely on that. "My van almost hit a homeless man down here in Franklin, and when I went to help him, he told me what Cahill was wearing. I just want to see if he was right."

"You are weird, Bertetto," he replied. "All we have is a head and shoulders shot, but he was wearing a suit."

"Color?" Most newspaper photographs are taken in color nowadays, even though it's unlikely they'll appear in anything but black and white.

"Either charcoal gray or black. White shirt."

"Hmmm. What about the tie?"

"This really is for a fashion article, isn't it? Do you know how far you've fallen?"

"I wrestle with it every day, Ryan. Now what about the tie, was it red?"

"No, it was paisley, looks like muted colors."

We bantered some more, then I hung up. I felt a little depressed. So much for Cahill wearing red. I leafed through the rest of the paper.

Somehow I got lucky. Things were slow in the ER, and within fifteen minutes a young intern with sleepy eyes came to see me.

"I'm Doctor Sheldon," she told me. I stood and shook her hand. The touch was cool and damp, as though she'd just finished scrubbing. She had blonde hair, shoulder length, and her eyes were an unusual blue-green shade that I suspected was created by colored contacts. I guessed her to be five foot five, about half a head shorter than I. "You want to see Elijah Smith?"

I indicated Stephanie. "My daughter and I do, if he can have visitors."

She fingered the end of the stethoscope hanging from her neck. "I guess you're not relatives, are you?"

"I'm the guy who found him on the roadside. I hope he's all right."

She stuffed her hands in the pockets of her white lab coat, two sizes too big for the thin body beneath it. "He's awake. Do you mind if I ask you what happened, from your perspective?"

I told her the story, leaving out the tiny detail that he'd spoken to me. As for Stephanie, I emphasized how upset she was and how I thought she needed to see that he was okay. She listened but made no comment.

"I don't know about your daughter," she said. "Is she up to date on all her vaccines? Does she have any medical conditions right now, a cold or cough? The flu?"

I told her no. "Please, doctor, my daughter saw him go into the ambulance. It shook her up."

Of course, Stephanie didn't look very shook-up coloring in her coloring book, but Dr. Sheldon smiled at her. "I can introduce you to Mr. Smith, but whether he wants to talk to you or not is up to him," she said.

She turned and indicated for me to follow. I picked up Stephanie in one arm, stuffing the crayons and coloring book into the bag with the other. I slipped out a notepad and pen, gathered up the bag, and then rushed to catch up with Dr. Sheldon. When the automatic door to the ER opened, her lab coat billowed in the breeze.

CHAPTER THREE

The ER at Johnson Memorial looked more like an intensive care unit. There were ten rooms, five on either side of the aisle. Some had their doors open and I could see empty beds. Double doors at the opposite end of the hall led to another part of the hospital.

Dr. Sheldon's tennis shoes squeaked on the tile floor as she led me to the third room on the left and opened the door. "There's someone to see you, Mr. Smith," she said, walking in. I trailed behind her, still carrying Stephanie and her travel bag.

The man looked up at me, quite calm about having a visitor. I almost thought he'd been expecting me. As we sized each other up, I took in the differences between when I'd seen him last and what he looked like now.

His hair, once wild and unkempt, was gone, no doubt shaved as they'd checked him for head wounds. The bald dome gleamed in contrast to his beard, still scraggly, which the hospital's razor hadn't touched. He also smelled of soap, and I suspected they'd had him in the shower. He was wrapped in a green hospital gown, covered by a blanket from the chest down. An IV line was attached to his left hand. I watched the drip, drip of the saline solution.

I've done scores of interviews over the years, but I found myself oddly fumbling for words. He seemed suddenly familiar, as though I had seen him many times before the incident and should know him.

"Hello," I said lamely. "My name's Nick Bertetto." I put out my hand and he tentatively offered his. After we'd shaken, he withdrew his hand slowly, looking at it curiously. He reached out to touch Stephanie and aimed a wide smile at her.

"What's your name?" he asked.

"Stephanie," I answered for her. "She's my daughter. I'm the one who found you along the side of the road. How are you doing?"

"Better," he replied. "Dr. Sheldon says they're releasing me."

The doctor turned to me. "I'm afraid I'm needed elsewhere and can't stay. Don't get settled in. I'm sending in a nurse to take out his IV and get him ready for discharge."

I set Stephanie down and placed the bag on the floor. Elijah held out his hands for her, and she surprised me by walking over to him. "You're a pretty little girl, aren't you?" he said, sounding grandfatherly. "Would you like to sit on the bed?" She climbed up to a spot near his feet.

Dr. Sheldon was gone by then, and her absence made it easier for me to be direct. "Elijah, do you remember saying anything to me out there where I found you in the ditch?"

The skin around his eyes had deep wrinkles—part weathering and part age. His eyes seemed younger. They were sharp and alert. And suspicious. "The nurses say I was shouting something when they brought me in," he said. " 'Kay Hilgore bled,' they told me."

Hmmm. Kay Hilgore bled. Cahill wore red. Close. But the way he was looking at me, I got the impression he was being cautious.

"That's not what you said, though, is it? Didn't you say something about a person named Cahill?"

There was a flash of recognition in his eyes. "Yes."

"Do you remember exactly what you said?"

He nodded his head. "Do you?" he asked.

I chuckled. "Yes, I do. But I'm not sure what it means."

He closed his eyes and laid his head back on his pillow. "I was hoping you might know," he mumbled.

"Are we talking about the same thing, Elijah?"

"Call me Eli."

"Okay, Eli. Who is Cahill?"

He opened his eyes and stared at the ceiling. "I'm supposed to know, but I don't. Maybe I used to know."

I heard an alarm buzz. A group of nurses with a doctor in tow rushed past the open door of our room, pushing an empty gurney. Eli sat up.

"Where did you hear about him?" I asked Eli.

"So it's a him, is it?" he said. "I wondered."

"Were you talking about *Calvin* Cahill?"

"They didn't say."

"Who didn't say?"

Eli studied me, searching my eyes. "I don't know," he said.

He was lying. I called him on it. "Yes, you do know."

It was a moment before he answered. "The angels," he said.

"You hear angels." I crossed my arms over my chest. Many homeless have mental problems, but Eli didn't seem delusional. I guessed it was more likely he had information from a source he couldn't, or wouldn't, divulge.

"I don't hear them all the time," he replied, "but they've been with me a lot lately."

We looked at each other. I didn't know what to say. If he had sources to protect, that was okay by me. As an investigative reporter, I'd protected sources. Or maybe he was nuts.

"Are the angels saying anything now?"

He tilted his head as if trying to hear something. "No, it comes and goes. Right now I can't hear them."

Probably needed a little cheap wine to loosen them up, I thought.

He looked at Stephanie. "Do you hear the angels?"

She gave me a quizzical look, as if she didn't know how to respond. "I don't think so," she said.

"Calvin Cahill is a state representative who disappeared on Friday," I said.

"What day is today?" Eli asked.

"It's Monday. The police don't know how or why he vanished. If you know anything about this, it would be a good idea to tell someone."

He shook his head. Then he said, "They're going to release me."

"That's right. Thankfully there's nothing wrong with you."

"Where will they take me?" he asked.

"What makes you think they're going to take you anywhere? Don't you have a relative you can call?"

"Nope," he said. "Been a long time since I had a relative looking after me."

"You could go home."

"Home," he repeated.

I nodded.

Eli laughed. "I think you know where my home is."

The nurses rushed past the door again, this time going the other way with a patient on the gurney. The doctor stayed in step with them, issuing orders.

Eli smiled, a yellowed, toothy grin. Some of him seemed the picture of a homeless man—the scraggly beard, the stained smile—but his speech was not like the homeless. And he had developed an instant rapport with Stephanie. I wondered how he had ended up this way.

A nurse entered the room and crossed to Eli's left, opposite me. She said to Stephanie, "Let me help you off the bed. I need to check this man's blood pressure."

She put out her hands and lifted Stephanie off. Then she wrapped a blood pressure cuff around Eli's arm and took a reading. After completing a few more tasks, she double-checked the paperwork. Glancing at me, she asked, "Are you with him?"

"Umm, in a way."

The nurse removed the IV from the back of Eli's hand. "Has the doctor talked to you about being discharged?" she asked him.

"Yeah, she mentioned it."

"Well, you're being discharged now. You can change back into your clothes, and then I'll review the papers with you. I'll give you a copy. After that you can leave, but you'll need to see the receptionist on your way out." She finished with the IV.

I watched her initial the paperwork. She turned to me. "You'll need to leave, too."

"Oh, I know." Once more I gathered up Stephanie and her bag. I moved to the door. "Eli, I'd like to talk more. Is it okay if we wait for you in the waiting room?"

He smiled again at Steph. "Sure. You can do whatever you like."

"I'll see you outside, then."

Did he know anything? I doubted it. But after a good night's sleep in a safe place and a couple of good meals, he might be in a better frame of mind. He might remember something useful. Then again, would he tell me if he did? Just in case, I wanted to know where he'd be after he left the hospital.

I stopped the nurse outside the door when she'd closed it so Eli could change. "You're going to release him just like that? He doesn't have anywhere to go."

"I know that. We get indigents way out here. They don't all end up in Indianapolis. I've called for social services to come down. They'll suggest he go to the men's shelter at Good Shepherd Lutheran for the night. But if he doesn't want to go . . ." She raised her hands, palms up.

The nurse walked away from me. Good Shepherd was the right place for Eli. Many of the churches in Franklin, St. Rita included, supported the shelter, as well as the women's shelter across town at Holy Cross Episcopalian.

I was getting tired of carrying Stephanie, so I put her down and held her hand as we went out the red doors of the ER to wait for Eli. A short blonde woman in street clothes, wearing a hospital ID badge, was talking to the receptionist. Figuring she must be the person from social services, I went over to talk to her.

"The homeless man who's checking out," I said after introducing myself, "I'd like to take him to the shelter."

"Are you a relative or friend?"

"I'm the guy who found him along the road. I'm just concerned about him."

"It would be nice if you would drive him there. We've called ahead and they have room for him. But I have to warn you, if he won't go with you, and he creates a scene, I'll have to call hospital security."

I knew all about hospital security at Johnson Memorial. By the time they got there, I could have moved him to Ohio. "That's fine," I said, "I'm certainly not going to push."

After a while the doors to the ER swung open and Eli appeared, carrying a folder stuffed with paperwork. He wore

his Black Watch flannel shirt with the cut-off sleeves un-
tucked over tattered jeans and carried himself with dignity.
I was just certain he had not been homeless for long.

If Eli saw me, he ignored me. The woman from social
services went over to meet him, and they sat down with the
receptionist. After they went through his folder, he signed
some papers.

I checked my watch. I had to get home and fix dinner.

Eli noticed me as he stood to leave. I walked over to
him. "Still here, huh?" he said.

"Yeah. Do you need a ride?"

"To where?" he asked, half a grin on his face, playing
with me. That might be a good sign about his mental condition, I thought.

"Where do you want to go?"

"A good night's sleep would do me good, don't you
think? And maybe a few hot meals?"

I was startled, since those had been my exact thoughts.

"Well, that's what she suggested, anyway," Eli said, indicating the woman from social services, still talking to the receptionist. "She told me about a shelter that accepts men.
Do you know where it is?"

"On the other side of town, about ten minutes away. I
could drive you there."

"That's kind," he replied.

The woman from social services looked relieved to see us
leave together. The hospital was probably not liable after he
left the grounds.

Stephanie and I walked Eli out to the van. I put Stephanie in her usual seat in the second row. Eli hopped in front
with me and buckled his seat belt. I liked that about him.

The van started easily, and I turned right onto Jefferson
Street, heading east. "Where are you from, Eli?"

"Here and there. I don't have a permanent address."

"I meant, where were you born?"

"The first place I remember was New Orleans. But that was a long time ago."

"Is that where you call home?"

"I seem to be at home about anywhere, these days."

"Let me be honest, Eli. You don't talk like a man who's been homeless all his life."

"Oh, I'm not. I had a fairly responsible job. Once."

"What happened?"

He paused to look out the window. We were passing the Johnson County courthouse, a huge, stately building of brown brick and ornate white trim, almost alpine in its use of the two colors. The time was nearing five-fifteen p.m.; we were just in time to see several lawyers striding across the street in the radiant sunshine toward their Mercedes sports cars. They carried leather briefcases and ignored the traffic while talking on their cell phones. The sight of them didn't seem to affect Eli. He looked through them as if they weren't there. I wondered if he would react to a policeman.

"I got put on a different assignment," Eli said.

"And you didn't like it? Got fired, ended up on the street?"

"You could think of it that way."

He didn't say any more.

Good Shepherd Lutheran Church is on the edge of downtown Franklin. It's an old, red-brick, steepled church with real bells in the tower, built on the corner of King and Yandes Streets. Long ago the parishioners bought the neighboring houses and turned them into church buildings. The one next to the church along Yandes was being used as the shelter. St. Rita had a good relationship with Good Shepherd, and we sometimes provided food for their pantry. I'd visited the shelter and knew they could help Eli both physically and spiritually. They might even be able to convince him to start work again. Everyone who stays at the shelter is expected to help out.

We pulled up in front of the building. The shelter was a two-story with a burgundy front door, several shades deeper than the maroon brick. I stopped the van and looked at Eli. "This is it," I said.

Eli nodded. "It looks nice," he said, as though he were an expert on shelters. He may have been.

"They're very friendly here. Are you ready to go in?"

"I'm not going to sue you, you know."

"What?"

"Sue you, for almost hitting me. It's okay. My fault."

"That's good to hear, but that's not why I'm doing this."

"I'd hoped not." He put his hand on the door handle and got out of the van.

I was surprised by Eli's frankness. Stephanie unbuckled herself, I helped her down, and we trailed him. Before he rang the doorbell, we caught up. "Look, here's my card. You're going to be fine here, but if you need anything or remember any more about Calvin Cahill, please call me." While he slipped the card in his pocket, I pressed the doorbell and waited for a response.

A man with a full head of graying hair answered the bell. "Can I help you?"

"My name is Nick Bertetto and this is Elijah Smith. Eli needs a place to stay for the night, and we're hoping you might be able to help. I think the hospital called you."

The man opened the door all the way. "Please come in," he said. He saw Stephanie and said an extra hello to her. She suddenly got shy and held onto my leg.

We walked into a front room that had been built back

37

when front rooms were elegant—hardwood floors, dark-stained woodwork, and big windows that looked out onto the street. But this room was worn. The flowered couch and wingback chairs were in need of re-upholstering, the curtains were sun-faded, and the wood floor was scarred and darkened with heavy use.

The man introduced himself and shook our hands. As he did, a second gentleman, who looked to be in his mid-seventies, came down a staircase leading up to the second floor. His thin black hair was slicked down and he had a hearing aid in his right ear.

"Is this our new guest?" he asked the shelter manager, indicating Eli.

Eli said he was, and the man offered to show Eli around. Eli looked back at me, nodded a goodbye, and followed him back up the stairs.

I checked my watch again. I really needed to get home. Pulling a twenty-dollar bill and business card out of my wallet, I handed both to the shelter manager. "I'd like to make a donation to the shelter," I said. "This is where I can be reached. I'm concerned about Eli. If he has any problems, please let me know. And if he decides to leave, would you tell me before he goes?"

The man looked at me suspiciously.

"I almost hit him when he blundered out onto the highway," I said. "I just want to make sure he's okay."

He folded the bill around my card and placed them in his pants pocket. "Sure."

I couldn't tell if he was sincere or not, but I thanked him and we left.

CHAPTER FOUR

Stephanie helped me in the kitchen as I prepared dinner. Joan got home on Mondays around six, and we ate shortly afterwards. Steph is a good-natured kid, and Joan and I had found keeping her on a regular eating and sleeping schedule made the difference. One of the advantages of being a stay-at-home dad was maintaining that schedule.

"What are we having with the biscuits, Daddy?" Stephanie asked.

I was cutting shortening into the flour, sugar, baking soda, cream of tartar, and salt mixture. Steph asked me a million times a day what we were having for supper and promptly forgot. She remembered we were having biscuits only because I was making them now. Well, and maybe because they're her favorite, too. I used to make them from a baking mix until she told me that Grandma, Joan's mom, made better biscuits. Now I make buttermilk biscuits from scratch. I will not be outdone that easily by someone of German extraction.

"We're having chicken and noodles," I said.

"I like chicken and noodles." She had been sitting on a stool at the bar but switched to a kneeling position so she could see into the bowl where I was cutting in the shortening. "Can I help?"

"You can help me knead the dough in a minute."

When the crumbly mixture was at the right consistency, I added the buttermilk and stirred it with a fork. I used my hands to finish compacting the dough. The phone rang.

I looked at the sticky stuff clinging to my fingers. "Would you get that, please, Steph?"

She's gotten a lot better on the phone in the past year, and I don't worry so much about what she's going to say. The phone hung on the wall right next to her stool, so she picked up the receiver. "Hello?"

She listened. The voice on the other end was loud enough that I could hear it was a man. Stephanie said "uh-huh," a couple of times, then she held out the phone to me. "It's Uncle Ryan."

Cantankerous though he is, Ryan Lockridge is very good with Stephanie and she adores him.

"Ask him to wait just a minute," I said, rubbing my hands together to get as much of the dough off of them and into the bowl as I could. I washed my hands quickly and took the phone from her.

"You want a job?" Ryan asked.

"What kind of job?"

"Cahill was wearing red. He had a red handkerchief in his pocket the day he disappeared."

"Really?" I said.

"What does it mean?"

"I don't know."

"Yeah. Well, I called and talked to the Lifestyle editor. You're not doing an article for him. As far as I can determine, you don't have a Cahill assignment, yet you called and asked me if he wore red. You know something."

"What's this about a job?"

"Clarisse might be willing to hire you on a freelance basis to help me with the Cahill story." Clarisse Babcock was Ryan's editor; she had also been my editor when I'd worked for the *Standard* full time. "You know she'd love to

40

get you back on the staff."

"Ryan, that's not possible right now, and you know it. But I might be able to do some work for you. What did you have in mind?"

"Depends on what you know."

"All I know right now is that I have a possible clue."

"Here's the deal. Clarisse wants us to meet you for lunch tomorrow. You tell her what you know; if it's good enough, you get a plum assignment working with me on the Cahill disappearance."

"Working with you is never a plum assignment."

"How soon we forget who taught whom to be a reporter."

"I remember perfectly. I taught you."

"That confirms what I thought. Being at home is atrophying your brain."

"Where are we meeting?"

"Bazbeaux Pizza on Mass Av at eleven."

"Early lunch."

"Bazbeaux's may have fallen out of favor with *Star* reporters since the *Standard* made it our hangout at lunch, but some still show up occasionally. Just in case, we want time to talk without eavesdroppers."

I put the phone down and immediately began to wonder whether I really did have anything in the way of information.

Stephanie interrupted. "Can Uncle Ryan have supper with us?"

"Not tonight, honey. But we'll ask him to our house soon. It's been awhile since he's been here."

"I like Uncle Ryan."

"You like the fact he gives you candy. You can't fool me," I said, giving her hand a squeeze. I checked the time.

"We need to finish this up. Come around to this side of the bar and you can knead the dough."

She got off the stool and came around to my side, climbing up on a stool in front of me. She resumed the kneeling position. I floured the surface a bit and put the dough in front of her.

"Remember, these are biscuits, so we don't want them to be mixed together too well. Only knead it about ten times."

She counted as she took hold of the dough and pushed it down on the counter and away from her body. "One . . . two . . . three . . ."

Her hands were so little that she wasn't very efficient, but the dough didn't require much work. I helped on the last couple of pushes to make sure the mixture hung together.

"Thanks for your help. Do you want to cut the biscuits?"

She nodded and I handed her the cutter after I rolled the dough out. She plopped the cutter in the middle of the dough.

"Remember, we want to make as many biscuits from this dough as we can," I said.

"Oh, yeah. I forgot."

I helped her plan her cuts and gave a little extra weight to the cutter as she pushed it through the dough. We pulled off the biscuits and kneaded the remaining dough one more time. After it yielded another couple of biscuits, we added them on a baking sheet and slid them in the oven for fifteen minutes.

Stephanie went to wash her hands, and I got to thinking about what I would say to Clarisse Babcock the next day. I definitely needed more information about Cahill. I could always call Joan's cousin Judith at the Statehouse. She had called us during the weekend to let us know she was okay, in case her colleague's disappearance had worried us. She was a cousin I wasn't particularly fond of, but then, she was the only contact I had. Perhaps I could come to like her better.

The timer buzzed and the pan of biscuits came out right as Joan arrived.

I kissed Joan in greeting and Stephanie came in right about then. Stephanie said, "We had an accident."

Joan got down on one knee so she could look her in the eyes. "You had an accident? But Stephanie, you're a big girl. You haven't an accident in a long time. Where did you have it?" I watched as Joan brushed a strand of Steph's coffee brown hair away from her face. Other than the hair and her brown eyes, which she got from me, she looked like her mother.

"No, Mommy, Daddy and me had an accident. In the van."

Suddenly I knew what Stephanie was talking about and it made my head spin. I had planned to tell Joan, but later. Since she still had the occasional anxiety attack, my goal had been to save it for tonight when she would be more relaxed. I wanted the chance to put it in perspective.

"Oh, that. No, honey, it wasn't an accident," I corrected gently. "The man that we saw fell near the van, but we didn't hit him."

Joan looked at me with alarm in her eyes. "What?"

Reminding myself that our counselor kept stressing honesty, I told Joan the whole story, at least as I had told it to the policeman. The Cahill connection I would leave out, for the time being.

When I got to the part where they put Eli in the ambulance, Stephanie spoke up again.

"The firemen took him away in the ambulance."

"Yes, they did," I replied.

"They took him to the hospital. Daddy and I saw him there. We took him to the shelter."

Joan stood next to me with her hands on her hips. "You had that man in our van?" she asked, blue eyes wide. "He could have knocked you out and stolen the car. He could have taken Stephanie!" Her face was pinched with worry.

I took a deep breath. Moments ago, when Joan had come in from work, she had a smile on her face and appeared comfortable to be home. Now she was tense, her shoulders hunched up under her powder blue blouse.

"I was just trying to help him out, Joan. And nothing happened. It's over and done with."

She stood there, clenching and unclenching her jaw as she contemplated saying something more.

I went on the offensive. "You've got to get hold of yourself, Joan. Face your fears. This is nothing to be afraid of."

She thought about that. Her eyes softened just a bit.

"And besides," I said with a wink, "I knew I could take him."

She cracked a slight smile. "Don't feed me any of those macho lines," she said. "That guy has been living on the streets. He's probably a lot tougher than you are." That's what she said, but the tone didn't have the bite it could have had. I knew she was weighing things in her mind, and it was a good sign.

I took hold of her shoulders and pulled her close to me. As I tucked her head against my chest, she gave only a token resistance.

"We take things as they are, Joan, remember? Not as they might have turned out, or how they might be to-morrow. One day at a time."

She remained still against me for a moment. I could feel

her breathing. It was measured, even. Not like mine. I was holding my breath.

She embraced me. I exhaled. We stood that way for a while. Stephanie, who had been rooted in place silently watching us, came up and held on to us both.

"Let's eat," I said eventually.

Later that night, long after Stephanie had gone to bed, I raised the issue of the possible Cahill assignment. We were sitting on the couch reading—Joan, another in her endless stream of best-selling romance novels; me, another murder mystery. I bookmarked my place and turned to her.

"I got a phone call today from Ryan. He and Clarisse want to have lunch with me tomorrow about possibly working for them on the Calvin Cahill story."

Joan quickly looked up from her book. "The missing congressman? What kind of work?"

"I don't know at this point, but I'm thinking it's probably just a profile on Cahill, the kind of stuff I do for the Lifestyle editor, only on a political personality. Since it would be freelance, I'm sure anything I did would be a supporting article and Ryan would get the main story. They know we're not ready for me to return to the paper."

She didn't look convinced. "I'm not sure about this, Nick. Hasn't Cahill been gone for three days?"

"He has. That's why Ryan is working on it."

"Why does this have to come up now? You know Mom's angiogram is Wednesday and I've got to leave tomorrow to get to Jasper. Mom and Dad need me. I can't change my plans. What about Stephanie?"

"Stephanie will be fine. You should go. If I get the assignment, it won't be different from any other assignment. I've done favors for the parents of Stephanie's friends, and we trade kids when we need free time. You need to be with your mom and dad."

"The whole thing makes me nervous. You said you wouldn't do anything dangerous. You know what our therapist says."

"Joan, I don't even know yet what it is they're considering having me do."

Her right hand shook. She tried to hide it behind the novel she was reading, but I saw it anyway. I was getting ready to say something about our therapist, something I probably would have regretted, when Joan said something very normal. "Well, I suppose we should wait to see what it is you would be doing."

"I think that's best," I said, reaching out my hand to find hers. "We don't need to get excited about it right now."

She put her book down and we held hands.

"How much did your cousin Judith tell you about this when she called yesterday?" I asked.

"Not much. She asked if we'd seen it on the news, but she didn't offer any more than to tell me she was okay."

"She works in the Ways and Means Committee office, doesn't she?"

"I think so."

"Maybe I'll talk with her tomorrow to get the inside scoop on what Cahill is like."

"If she'll give it to you. You know she doesn't like you very well."

That much I knew for sure. Several of Joan's relatives felt that way about me, especially after the kidnapping. They blamed me for what had happened and the resulting post-traumatic stress disorder.

"A guy can't help but try," I said.

★ ★ ★ ★ ★

I woke to the sound of muffled crying. The large red numbers on the bedside clock glared two-ten. I sat up and leaned over Joan, who faced away from me into her pillow.

"Joan," I called quietly, "are you all right?"

She didn't answer, and I was fairly certain she was weeping in her sleep.

"Tell me why you're crying." I was almost afraid to know. Was it something I did?

"I can't get my breath," she gasped. "I can't get away from him."

"Can't get away from whom?"

She gripped the pillow tightly.

"It's okay. It's only a dream, Joanie." I caressed her shoulder. "I'm here."

She put a hand over mine, a reaction I knew came from her subconscious, but I liked it anyway.

"You called me Joanie," she said sleepily. "I haven't been called that in a long time."

"I wasn't sure I should. Do you like it?"

"Sometimes."

"Good. I'll do it again sometime," I said.

She released the pillow, and in a minute I could hear her breathing easily.

I curled up next to her and held her until morning.

CHAPTER FIVE

At nine a.m. I sat down with Dr. Valerie Moore, the therapist Joan and I had been seeing for about a year. I had requested the session in private several weeks earlier because I was concerned. It had been two years since Joan had been kidnapped and begun exhibiting post-traumatic stress disorder, but she wasn't making the progress I had hoped.

Dr. Moore invited me to sit, and I chose the brown leather coach that Joan and I used during our every-other-week sessions. I started talking before I even touched the couch.

"Joan is an intelligent, capable woman," I said. "I still don't understand why she can't let go of this. You told me a year ago that people like Joan, once they begin therapy, are usually free of symptoms within a year. I see some progress, but it's slow. I need to understand why she's still having problems."

Dr. Moore, a thin, red-haired woman wearing a navy blue skirt and printed blouse with a Peter Pan collar, crossed her legs and placed the notebook on her lap. She took off her unfashionably large, black-framed glasses and held them in her hands as she talked.

"First," she said, waving her glasses around, "I want to caution you, as I did a year ago, that helping the mind cure itself is not an exact science. We can't give our patients something like an antibiotic to kill off invading bacteria and have it work in fourteen days. This is not that kind of ill-

ness. You understand that?"

I nodded.

"It *is* unusual that a person like Joan, a well-educated professional woman, wouldn't have put this in perspective by now. However, it may be taking longer simply because she didn't have treatment the first year after the trauma took place."

"She didn't want it."

"And you didn't try to convince her she needed it."

I gritted my teeth for a moment. I had selected Dr. Moore specifically because she was a woman; I had hoped Joan would find her easier to talk to than a man. But as I got to know her, she seemed to have a dislike for men, me in particular. "Not until later. We've been over this before, Doctor. Don't try and pin everything on me. I carry around enough guilt as it is. I recognize that if I hadn't been investigating a murder in our neighborhood, Joan would never have been kidnapped. It's why I quit my job to stay home and do freelance writing, so that Joan would be able to cope better. I tried, and continue to try, to do my part in helping her heal. But truthfully, by now I expected I would be able to do at least some investigative reporting, that she would be okay with it. I love her, and I love being home with Stephanie, but I'm not all that happy. I want to be fulfilled professionally, too. Is that too much to expect at this point?"

"You have to decide for yourself what makes you happy," she said, crossing her arms. "I can't make that decision for you."

"I feel like you're not helping me, Doctor. Look, I hate to ask this question, but is it possible that Joan is not getting better as a way to control me?"

"Control is often compensation for a lack of trust or a

feeling of insecurity. While I don't think she trusts you completely, I don't think she's doing this consciously."

"I'm getting tired of you constantly bringing up the trust issue. When I worked on that murder in Clinton a year ago, which is the only case I've been involved in since the kidnapping, I did it to demonstrate to Joan that I could go back to work without it affecting her. If you would stop implying to her that she can't trust me, maybe she could accept that what I did was motivated by a desire for her to get better."

Dr. Moore uncrossed her arms and pointed the earpiece of her glasses at me. "Whatever reason you did it, she believes you placed your needs above hers at a time when she was particularly vulnerable. She needs to know that she can tell you whatever she feels, and that you will really hear her and have empathy and compassion."

"I don't know what else I can do. I believe I am listening to her. Just last night I listened to her tell me about a nightmare. I cuddled with her and tried to reassure her."

"What was the nightmare about?"

"It went back to the kidnapping again. She was trying to escape from someone."

She thought a moment, chewing on the earpiece. "Perhaps it's symbolic. She may not be literally remembering the kidnapping as much as she's feeling kidnapped by conflicting feelings for you or for other significant people in her life."

"Here's what I think, Doctor. I think you and everybody else keep enabling her to dwell on the past. Just once I'd like for one of her relatives to tell her, 'Joan, get over it. It's been two years, and you're perfectly safe. Get on with your life.' But all anyone wants to do is look backwards. They want to talk about wounds—theirs and Joan's. How they

share hurting. Doesn't anyone want to talk about healing?"

"I do want to talk about healing with you, Mr. Bertetto. Here's what I think: I believe that the two of you won't heal as a couple until you desperately feel that you might lose her and subsequently open up to her, and she won't heal until she sees that your work gives your life meaning, and she wants to help you be fulfilled."

She leaned back in her chair.

"And why can't we seem to get there?" I asked.

She shook her head. "I don't know. I've heard you both say the right things, but whether they're just words, or not, is up to you."

We sat there for a minute. Simultaneously, we looked at our watches, realized the half hour session was over, and stood up. I shook her hand and said goodbye, but I didn't thank her. I didn't think she was helping either of us.

I'd arranged for Stephanie to spend the morning with Tom Colby, one of my stay-at-home friends, whose son Todd was in Steph's preschool class. Tom was the only other Y-chromosome in our informal group, the Throwbacks. We called ourselves that because, men or women, we felt somewhat out of place among our career-driven peers. All of us had given up the safety of full-time jobs for some measure of family life we felt we couldn't find otherwise. We weren't stay-at-home parents all the time—Tom, for instance, was an accountant who'd cut back to thirty hours a week—but we did our best to be with our kids.

On Tuesdays Tom worked in the afternoon, so I needed to take the kids to preschool at twelve-thirty. But the morning was free until eleven, when I would be meeting with Ryan and Clarisse for lunch. I decided to head downtown early to visit the Statehouse. Part of me had a hard time believing that Cahill's wearing red was a clue to anything, even if he did have a red handkerchief in his pocket the day he disappeared. On the other hand, I didn't want to pass up something that could get me an assignment. We freelancers have to scramble for jobs enough as it is. I hoped I could come up with something to tell Clarisse that would merit hiring me. Getting something good from Joan's cousin Judith at the Statehouse might bolster my cause.

I drove from Dr. Moore's office toward U.S. 31 thinking about what she had said, that Joan and I couldn't heal as a couple until we met certain conditions. I had almost no confidence in Dr. Moore, and even if she were right, I was inclined to believe those conditions would never happen, not the way she was leading us. When I'd been an investigative reporter, there'd been times when I'd just had to make things happen. I was beginning to think that, for better or worse, Joan and I needed to make things happen. We needed to react, to change directions. Dr. Moore had said that Joan and I said the right words—maybe we needed to find out, both of us, if we meant them.

On my way I passed the shelter where I'd placed Elijah Smith. Maybe I shouldn't be so interested in a possible connection between Elijah Smith and Calvin Cahill, I thought. Maybe I should stop right now before I got myself in too deep, as I had in Clinton. But even if it were more than a curiosity, I had a hard time seeing it as anything particularly dangerous. And if it did turn into something, I could hand it over to Ryan at any time. Dr. Moore would no doubt view what I was doing as a measure of my untrustworthiness and encourage Joan in that direction. But I had tired of Dr. Moore. I just wanted things to return to normal.

I took U.S. 31 straight into Indianapolis. The trip took a half hour. At Washington Street I turned west and parked at Circle Centre Mall, where parking was only a buck for three hours. The Statehouse was a short walk away at the corner of Washington and Capitol.

Indiana's state capitol is a large, rectangular, limestone building in the Renaissance Revival style, popular when the building was completed in 1888. I entered from the south door and was amazed, as always, at the lack of security. There are no metal detectors to walk through, nothing to stop anyone from carrying a gun, and no police kiosks from which visitors could be conspicuously watched. I knew there were video cameras everywhere, but it seemed almost too old-fashioned to allow people to roam about the building that housed the highest levels of government in Indiana without some kind of screening. The place was waiting for its first shooting incident. Then security would clamp down like everywhere else in the modern world.

I went up to the second floor and looked for the office of the Ways and Means Committee Chairman. The entrance to every office on the floor looked the same—heavy, well-polished double doors nine feet high with a transom window over each, a practical means to cool the offices in pre-air-conditioned days. The Ways and Means office was identified by a brass plaque attached to the door frame, situated so high above the windows that it was difficult to read without a light shining on it. Squinting, I confirmed I was in the right place.

I walked in. Cahill's office was ahead of me, his secretary's desk to my right. I saw the name plate "Judith Blackard" sitting on it. I hadn't known she was a secretary, only that she was on staff. Her chair, a standard secretary model in mottled gray cloth, was empty. I looked beyond the desk into the large L-shaped space which bracketed his office. Twenty or so support people moved about in all directions, answering phones which seemed to ring nonstop. In the eye of this storm I spotted Judith, about Joan's height, five foot six, but stockier and heavier, dressed in a no-nonsense, navy blue Brooks Brothers business suit. She appeared to be giving orders. I tried to get her attention with a little shuffling and coughing; eventually she noticed. When she saw me, she came over right away.

"Hi, Judith," I said.

"Nick," she said, concerned, "is Aunt Janine okay? I heard she was going in the hospital."

Ahh. That explained her reaction. "She's okay. She hasn't had the angiogram yet. It's tomorrow. Joan is headed down there tonight to be with them. I came to get some information. How are you? Is your mom okay?"

"I'm fine. Mom's her usual self. Reminds me constantly that if I'd have had kids, she could be a grandma like all her friends. What kind of information do you need?"

"Background on Representative Cahill."

"You and all the other media in Indiana. Is this for a story?"

"Right now I'm gathering background material for a profile."

She practically sighed. "C'mon in. I'll talk to you for little bit. But my time is short today. We're trying to keep this committee going while he's gone."

"Peter," she said aloud to one of seven men in the work area, "I'm going to use Mr. Cahill's office for a moment."

Cahill's office was not very large, but it had a window that looked onto Market Street and the Soldiers and Sailors Monument, which was definitely a plus. A small round conference table with four chairs sat on the right. Cahill's desk was on the left, cramped against a credenza which hugged the wall. There was a guest chair across from the desk. The furniture was rich mahogany wood, which gave some elegance to the room. The desk, the window ledge, and every available wall space held framed testaments to either Cahill's education or his prowess as a legislator.

Judith sat at the conference table and I sat opposite her.

"Is Joan okay with this, your working on a story about a missing representative?"

"It's just a profile."

"Oh."

"Everyone is probably asking a lot about his career," I said, taking the lead, "and while I want that information, too, I'd like to do an in-depth profile. Deeper than just the basics—you know, more than just the education, the position, the power. I'd like to know things about his personality, his likes and dislikes, how he dresses, his hobbies . . ."

Her features softened, just for a moment, when I asked about those traits. There was a slight mistiness to her eyes. Her hand came up to her eyelid, brushing the corner where a tear had formed. I noticed how heavy her makeup was, as though she were hiding age spots or something. Judith was older than Joan by nearly twenty years, but I hadn't remembered seeing age spots before.

"Just a minute," she said. She left the room and returned with a tissue, which she dabbed at the corner of one eye. She also carried a stapled set of papers and handed them to me. "We had an emergency meeting here last night so we could get prepared for the rush. I had one of the interns write this biography of Mr. Cahill."

I glanced through it. It contained all the facts I'd need for a story. The intern had done a good job.

"What else would you like to know?"

"Well, I'd like to know the real Calvin Cahill, the man behind the power. You probably know him better than anyone around here. What's he like to work for? Any light moments you can think of that would show a different side of him?"

Judith sat for a moment considering the question. She had a slight smile on her face when she finally said, "Virtually everyone who comes in contact with him loves the man. He's a fair and honest legislator. I think one of the reasons he's successful is that when he listens to his constituents, he really listens to them, gives them his undivided attention. He wants to know where they stand on the issues.

"And of course, he's just devoted to his wife," she added, emphasizing the word "devoted," which of course set off an alarm in my head. I made a note to check on the status of his marriage.

"Tell me a little about his work life, what a regular day is like when he's here."

"There's no typical day. Since he carries a lot of weight around the Statehouse, he's sought out for just about everything. He keeps us all very busy, and he's good about giving credit to the staff. He's fair to everyone. I've never heard anyone complain. Anyone on the staff, that is. Obviously as a legislator, he occasionally needs to be tough in dealing with people who disagree with him. That's just a part of being Ways and Means Chairman."

"Is he particular about the way he dresses?"

"I don't know what you would call 'particular.' He dresses well. He has his suits custom-made."

A good thing, I thought, since Cahill sported a pretty large midsection.

"He knows a lot of people," she said, indicating the photos on the wall.

"Yes, I can tell," I said. I stood and walked to a grouping of photographs.

She joined me. "He likes having his photograph taken with important people," she said.

My eyes went immediately to the photo of a much younger Cahill standing in the Oval Office with then-President Ronald Reagan and Vice President Bush. What I was most interested in, though, was the red silk handkerchief sticking out of his breast suit pocket. "Cahill wore red."

"These silk handkerchiefs, does he still wear them?" I asked, walking around the office, looking at the walls.

"Every day. They're his signature fashion statement."

"Does he have a favorite color?"

She nodded. "Blue, I think. He was a Navy man, you know."

I looked at the photographs again. Almost all had him sporting red handkerchiefs. "Red must have been *one* of his favorites, though. Look at all these photos."

She stood and came over next to me. She looked at the photos. "I guess I hadn't noticed that," she said.

"Do you remember what color he wore on Friday?"

Judith smiled. "Actually, I think it might have been red. Why do you ask?"

"No reason."

"Do you think it might be important?"

"I don't know," I said. "Do *you* think it's important?"

She shrugged. "Don't see how it could be."

"You've been asked this probably a hundred times already, but can you think of any reason he'd disappear?"

"No, he's never done anything like this. We're all very worried about him."

We were interrupted by one of the younger men in the office holding a portable phone out to her. "Judith, for you.

The governor's press secretary. Can't wait."

She turned back to me. "Look, I'm sorry, Nick, but I really need to take this phone call, and we've got a million things going on. Maybe you could interview one of the other representatives? Who's your representative in Franklin?"

"It's Frank McCutcheson."

"Oh," she said with undisguised disgust, which told me a lot about what she thought of him. "Well, you could try him. They disagreed on a lot of issues, but I know they had great respect for each other."

I tried to fit in one more question, but when Judith Blackard ushers people out the door, she ushers them out fast. "I'm glad you stopped by," she said, shaking my hand with a firm grip as she deposited me in the hall outside the office. "Keep me up to speed with what's going on with Aunt Janine, and if you need any more information, just call." The door shut behind her.

I stood in the hall and thought about my situation. Did I have anything to tell Clarisse and Ryan?

I had learned that Cahill was fond of pocket handkerchiefs, and that he wore red sometimes. He certainly seemed to favor it when he was being photographed. Judith thought he'd worn red on Friday when he disappeared, and I knew he had, thanks to Ryan.

But did this mean anything?

It would certainly help if it did. The only other thing I had was the fact sheet and a personal contact, probably not enough to get me assigned to the story. I needed a convincing theory about the red handkerchief and why it was important. Once I had the assignment, I could start interviewing people and establish who liked Cahill and who didn't. I could also look into Cahill's marriage. If there were any gossip, it would no doubt come out.

cover.

not, if wearing rec ...

least give me an insight into the man.

And maybe the assignment I wanted.

Bazbeaux Pizza is a gourmet pizza and sandwich shop on Massachusetts Avenue, which anchors the arts district of downtown Indianapolis. Bazbeaux's is roughly halfway between the *Star*'s building on Pennsylvania and the *Standard*'s building on New Jersey. As one of the pioneers that bought and located in the district before its rejuvenation, Bazbeaux had participated in the rebuilding process by luring office workers to Massachusetts Avenue with gourmet pizza sold by the slice and served in a historic building. The location had character, good food, and outdoor seating in nice weather. I opened the dark green door and stood in the wood-floored entryway, waiting for Ryan and Clarisse. The doughy smell of pizza baking was wonderful.

At exactly eleven a.m., Ryan walked in, but alone.

"Where's Clarisse?" I asked.

"Got pulled into an editorial meeting. She may be here later, but I doubt it. Not from the look on everyone's faces as they went in." Ryan examined the platters of pizza behind the counter. "You're buying, of course."

"Why would I buy your meal?"

"Because without Clarisse here, I'm empowered to decide whether or not you get the assignment. And let's just say I got up on the wrong side of the bed this morning."

"Your bed is in the corner. You get up on the same side every morning."

"Maybe that explains it. Hmmm," Ryan said, drumming his considerable stomach. "Now let's see what looks good, since you're buying."

I contemplated the pizzas while Ryan drooled. This was going to be difficult. Trying hard to stay on a muscle-building diet, I would have preferred to have something high in protein, moderate in carbs, and low in fat. That's what my bodybuilding friend Mark Zoringer always advises me to eat to add muscle to my relatively compact frame. Of course, I've been five foot ten and a buck sixty all my adult life, so I don't hold out any extraordinary hopes. The only pizza that I thought Mark would approve of was the veggie pizza, so I ordered a slice of it. A side salad was available, so I had one of those, too, with dressing on the side. They didn't have milk, so I went with water.

Ryan, taking advantage of the fact he did not have to pay, ordered three slices of some combination pizza that had a lot of pepperoni and sausage on it. I felt my arteries clog just watching the counter person slog it onto a plate. Ryan grabbed a glass and filled it with diet Coke from the fountain. What the purpose of getting a diet drink was, I had no idea.

Ryan has a round face and an even rounder body, making me think of a snowman with a stressed-out coronary artery. He'd never been much of an athlete, even in college. Though I'd liked him a lot, he was never the kind of roommate you could coerce into ice skating or playing tennis. He liked parties and games of strategy, becoming a master at chess and bridge. I always tried to get him as a partner when we got into a bridge game—he could make three no-trump out of a mediocre hand.

I paid the woman at the counter while Ryan gathered some napkins and went downstairs. Ryan hadn't taken a

61

knife and fork but I picked up a set, along with napkins, and went after him. There weren't many people downstairs. Ryan had selected a table for four hidden away in the back and was already chewing a huge bite of his first piece of pizza. I sat across from him.

The wine cellar of Bazbeaux's was probably the right place for us to talk, given that we wanted some seclusion. The cellar has a low, darkly-colored ceiling and discreet, in-direct lighting. There are two rooms in the cellar, divided by a brick wall painted black, with arched openings between the two rooms that look like windows in a castle. The temperature was cool and the atmosphere was secretive.

"So, Cahill wore red the day he disappeared," Ryan said in quiet tones. He held his pizza by the hand and took another large bite. A pepperoni and piece of sausage slid off the pizza and onto the plate, taking a gob of cheese with it.

"It wasn't the only day he wore red," I responded.

Ryan pulled a photograph out of his pocket and tossed it on the empty space between us. He swallowed. "Here's what he looked like that day. What do you mean by, 'it wasn't the only day he wore red'?"

I picked up the photograph. "I went to his office this morning and talked with the Ways and Means Committee secretary, who, by the way, happens to be Joan's cousin . . ."

"Trying to impress me with connections now?"

"Depends. Is it working?"

"Between that and the lunch, you're maybe halfway there. Keep going."

"The secretary said that, being a Navy man, Cahill mostly wore blue pocket handkerchiefs. However, in virtu-ally every one of the photographs, they were red."

"Big deal."

"Actually, I think it might be."

I examined the photograph before I continued. Nothing that I didn't expect to see. Cahill was a sharp dresser, something I already knew. The custom-made suit enhanced his appearance. It nicely disguised the fact he was overweight. Against the flattering cut and the beautiful charcoal gray pinstripe fabric, the red handkerchief stood out like a beacon. It made him look like a man of stature.

"Convince me," Ryan said.

I cut a piece of my vegetarian pizza and ate it, a delaying tactic to give me time to think. An idea had come to mind earlier. I was developing it quickly. "Let's consider this psychologically," I said. "We know Cahill craved power. Maybe red was a sign of achievement, or something that made him feel powerful or important. It would explain the photos on the wall, since in each one he was either receiving an award or meeting someone who held a powerful position."

Ryan burped. "Excuse me," he said, wiping his mouth with a napkin. "The problem is, this doesn't explain why he would wear red the day he gave that speech. It wasn't particularly significant."

"Something else must have been going on that day. We have to find out what it was and what it meant to him."

"It meant Friday was laundry day and he was out of other colors," Ryan said. He took another huge bite of pizza, nearly finishing the piece. "Not a big deal," he mumbled, his mouth full of food.

I frowned at Ryan. "Nice manners. No, what it means is, we need a bigger data base. We need to know as much as we can about when he wore red, where he was at the time, and what he was doing. At least for the past year or so."

"That's a tough order, but I'm sure you're up to the

challenge. If Clarisse will go for this. I don't know."

Ryan waved at someone. I turned around and saw a couple of *Standard* reporters step off the stairs and into the room. They sat at a table for two.

"Work with me here, Ryan," I said, turning back around. "The other thing that I have is a potential source of information, the guy who made the statement, 'Cahill wore red.' He obviously believes it has significance."

"Whoa, wait a minute. A source of information? The homeless guy?"

I ate another bite of my pizza. It was pretty good, but I'd have been happier if it hadn't had so much artichoke on it. "Well, I said 'potential.' It might be a long shot."

Both of us saw a *Star* reporter we knew sit down at a table not too far from us. She waved and we waved back. The room was starting to fill up. We both leaned forward simultaneously and lowered our voices even more.

"Can I keep the photo?" I asked.

"Tell me more about the homeless guy first," he said.

I put the photo in my pocket anyway. While we ate, I tried to make the Eli connection sound like a blockbuster.

Ryan shook his head and gave me a pitying look after I'd finished. "Nick, you've been away from hard reporting too long. 'Cahill wore red'? And from a vagrant, no less."

"Okay, look. I've still got a connection through Joan's cousin Judith, which can be a real help, and for heaven's sake I've even got a fact sheet with all the significant dates and achievements in Cahill's career." I showed him the packet Judith had given me.

He pulled out a similar set of papers which were folded up in his notebook. "Those are a dime a dozen. I've got one here." He tossed it to me. "In fact, Clarisse told me to give it to you and have you get started on a story. She wants a sidebar timeline e-mailed to her tonight, with the most important dates asterisked for editing, and she wants you to do a profile on him for Wednesday. If you've got questions, she says to call her."

"You knew all along I was going to work on this?"

"Duh, Bertetto. Clarisse wants you back on staff in the worst way. All you had to do was drop a hint and she'd start feeding you freelance stuff. Thanks for the lunch, though."

"You bastard."

"Sticks and stones . . ."

I paused to let Ryan know I was going to get serious. "Ryan, there is one thing, though. I've hinted to Joan I might be working with you on this story, but I insisted it would probably be in a supporting role. Nothing that would make her too nervous. So we've got to make sure . . ."

He interrupted me, looking me in the eyes to make sure I knew he was serious, too. "Nick, you don't know how to do supporting roles in this kind of environment. If something needs to be investigated, you'll do it. I know that about you, and it's why Clarisse wants you on board. If I have to share my byline with someone, I want it to be someone who's good and who can pull their own weight. Plus you're my friend. Otherwise I'd be fighting against having a freelancer helping me."

I didn't want the deal to die.

I thought about that for a moment while Ryan inhaled his last slice. Actually, things looked good. I had two assignments, all background, no show-stoppers. Joan had agreed it would be best to wait and see what I was assigned. These were assignments I had expected, the kind of thing I had already told her about and she seemed to accept. I didn't know what to expect in the future, but I hoped I could reason with Clarisse if the situation warranted. Plus, Joan would be leaving for her parents' house tonight. For at least the next several days I could make decisions about the work without having to justify every move with her. And maybe this would work out for the best, be a proving ground for my ability to return to investigative reporting. So far, Joan was being reasonable.

"Joan is going to Jasper tonight. Her mom is having an angiogram tomorrow. The doctors expect to find blockages in two or three arteries. It'll either be surgery or stents, but no matter what, Joan will be gone for up to a week taking care of her mom and dad."

"Ahhh," Ryan said. He took a swig of his diet cola. "That explains a lot."

"What?"

"It explains why you didn't put up a fight when I insisted that you'll be an equal partner in this. When it comes to Joan, you're non-confrontational. If you can get away with it, you'll spring any bad news to her after it's over, that you did it and nothing happened, hoping she will get the point."

I shook my head.

"That is *exactly* what you're thinking," he insisted.

I looked at my watch. I needed to get back to Franklin to pick up the kids for preschool. "Do you know anything about the relationship between Cahill and Frank Mc-Cutcheson? I'm thinking about seeing McCutcheson this afternoon. Judith suggested I talk to my state representative, but when she found out who mine was, she almost backpedaled. I figured there must be some kind of animosity."

"Both of them are classified as Republicans, but only Cahill is the real thing. McCutcheson switched parties because Democrats never get elected from Johnson County. Their views on issues can be radically different sometimes."

66

I finished my water. "I have to go," I said, "but just for the record, if the same set of circumstances happened to you—the near-accident with Eli, the hint about Cahill—I know you'd be working this thing like Fabio at a romance readers' convention."

He grinned. "Just like him. Only I'm better-looking."

"Right."

"Does McCutcheson know you personally?" Ryan asked.

"I know who he is. I'm an occasional customer at the plant farm his family owns, but that's it. I'm sure he doesn't know me from Adam."

Ryan stood and cleared away his trash. "Well, he will after this. You might want to watch your step with him. I've heard that to those who cross his path, he can be a mean, vindictive little S.O.B."

CHAPTER SEVEN

Seeing Frank McCutcheson was actually beginning to sound appealing. He and Cahill didn't get along, had opposing views but were both from the same party, and they both served on the Ways and Means Committee. Plus, McCutcheson was an S.O.B. That might get me an interesting view of Cahill.

But fitting in an interview with McCutcheson would be tight. He wasn't at the Statehouse; I'd checked that. Indiana has a citizen legislature that is not in session year round, so the legislators have regular jobs. McCutcheson was taking advantage of the disruption caused by Cahill's absence to tend to his family business back in Franklin. If I wanted to see him, I'd have to do it there.

To further complicate matters, I had already scheduled an interview at three-thirty p.m. with the new vegetarian chef at the Tabouleh Café in Broad Ripple for *Healthful Living* magazine. That was a part of my regular freelance business, and I was bound by contract to get that story done.

In order to make the afternoon work, it was important to get the kids to preschool on time. I didn't have to look at my watch to know I was behind schedule. But Melissa, fortunately, was providing motivation for me to get them there in a hurry.

"Daddy says we eat out a lot, and Mommy's home all day and he don't know why she can't get dinner ready. But she says he can trade places anytime and find out what it's like to be home with us kids," Melissa the Motormouth said, sitting up front again. "But I like eating pizza and it's my favorite food—don't you like pizza, Mr. Nick?—why can't we have pizza every night? Daddy says he'd like to have roast beef, mashed 'tatoes, and gravy like Mammaw makes. I like mashed 'tatoes okay but gravy is yucky. Mommy said something to Daddy and I couldn't hear it but she said I should mind my own business and . . . what's that noise?"

My cell phone had never rung before with the kids in the van, so when it began playing Beethoven's *Fifth*, it made even Melissa take a breath.

"That's my cell phone, Melissa," I said, fumbling for it with my right hand while I drove with my left. I had moved the phone out of Steph's bag of toys and into the pocket between the two front seats, where it was now nestled with essential items like Tom Chapin CDs and tissues, not to mention the baby wipes I kept for the accidents which seemed to spontaneously erupt in the van.

The phone sang again just as the tow-headed Starner twins, Dustin and Justin, simultaneously dropped the cups of Cheerios they were holding. Suddenly there were Cheerios everywhere. I grabbed three CDs and a Raffi tape, but not the phone. Finally, on the third ring, I pulled to the side of the road and dug out the cell phone.

"Hello?"

There was a pause and a man's voice said, "Is this Nick Bertetto?"

The voice sounded like Elijah's. "Yes, is this Eli?"

"Nick, can you come see me?" He sounded scared. "The police are here asking questions, and I don't know what to say. They think I had something to do with that man's disappearance, and . . ."

"My Cheerios!" squealed one of the twins. I looked back to see Todd Colby, unbuckled and out of his seat, eating what cereal bits he could find on the floor.

"I want some, too," said Melissa.

"Eli, I'm tied up at the moment but I'll be over as soon as I can. You don't have to answer any of their questions, you know that, don't you? It might be best not to say anything. I'll be there in fifteen minutes." Eli said it was okay and broke the connection.

"Todd, get back in your seat," I said sharply. I looked at my watch. Twelve twenty-five. I was still banking on getting that interview with McCutcheson before racing to Broad Ripple for the three-thirty appointment. I told myself I could still do it, even if I had to stop at the shelter, as long as whatever the police wanted to talk to Eli about could be wrapped up by one o'clock.

Todd detected I was in no mood to fool around and got in the seat, but he had troubling buckling in. His pudgy little fingers kept pulling on the strap, but it wouldn't meet the buckle, and he began squealing.

I sighed. "Stephanie, would you please help him?" I asked.

When Steph was back in her seat, I pulled into traffic. The commotion started up again. Melissa, no longer interested in my pizza preferences, now wanted a look at my cell phone, and could she use it to call her mother, please? Justin and Dustin were still whining over their spilled Cheerios. A couple of others were crying just to be crying— they did it often enough. Stephanie asked the only intelligent questions of the bunch and the only ones I was willing to answer—who was that on the phone and were we going to school now?

"Yes, honey, we're headed for school," I said loudly, hoping to reassure everyone. "That was a friend on the phone. He's in a little trouble, and after I drop you off I'm going to see if I can help."

"The black man at the shelter?"

Sometimes the kid's too sharp for her own good. "Yes, it was," I said truthfully. I wouldn't lie to her, although now I feared this little drama would play itself out after Joan got home from work, before she left tonight for her mother's house. If Stephanie could just forget about this incident for today, I'd be worry-free for possibly a whole week, by which time I hoped to have whatever story there might be wrapped up.

We pulled into the St. Rita parking lot at exactly twelve-thirty. I parked the van illegally in the fire lane next to the yellow brick school building and unloaded the kids. Herding them like sheep, I directed them into the building and down the hall safely to their rooms. I kissed Steph goodbye and reminded her that Mommy would be home when she got home from school. Knowing I had the three-thirty interview in Broad Ripple, Joan had arranged her schedule so she would be home early. She needed to pack for her trip anyway.

Driving like I couldn't be arrested, I made it to the shelter in under ten minutes. The manager was waiting outside. He hurried me up the stairs, and I burst into a meeting room to find two detectives in plain clothes sitting at a scarred mahogany desk with Queen Anne legs. The room was a converted bedroom, with floral wallpaper in various stages of becoming unattached from the wall. I recognized one of the detectives, Sergeant Jerry Smallwood, an older, particularly nasty investigator I'd met on a couple of occasions when I'd worked for the *Standard* full time. The other detective was a woman about my age, mid-thirties, with police-short black hair and hypnotic hazel eyes. Her chin was strong and squarish, but not unfeminine, and when she smiled she had dimples in her cheeks. She introduced herself as Detective Claire Hurst.

"So, Bertetto," Smallwood said instead of hello, "you're the magic man Mr. Smith has been waiting for?"

"I'm the one, Sergeant," I replied civilly. Eventually things would break down and I'd call him "Smallwood," but I was determined to take the high road initially.

"Well, perhaps now that you're here we can get on with our questions, which were very simple and which Mr. Smith shouldn't have had any trouble answering, with or without you. Now, Mr. Smith," he said, gesturing toward Eli, who sat on an orange suede couch that had seen better days, if orange suede couches ever had better days, "please tell us how you know Calvin Cahill and where you were on May fifteenth, the day Mr. Cahill disappeared."

Eli, sitting upright with his knees locked together and hands in his lap, looked like he was trying to make himself unnoticeable. His eyes met mine in a plea for help. I sat down next to him on the couch.

"First," I asked Smallwood, "why do you think he knows anything at all about Cahill?"

The sergeant gave me a squinty-eyed glare. "Because the nurse at Johnson Memorial Hospital gave us a call earlier today and said she just realized what this man had been saying when the ambulance brought him in. 'Cahill wore red.' "

"*If* he was saying Cahill wore red, which is doubtful considering he was incoherent when he arrived at the hospital, what makes you think that it was *Calvin* Cahill he was talking about?"

"We don't," Detective Hurst admitted, cutting in before Smallwood could respond. "But with Representative Cahill missing, we have to take the chance he knows something about the disappearance."

"And if he weren't talking about Calvin Cahill, would you be here, Bertetto?" Smallwood interjected. "Have you suddenly become interested in helping out folks at the homeless shelter?"

"For your information," I said in my best indignant tone, "this gentleman almost stumbled into the path of my van on the highway, and I've been interested in his welfare ever since."

"Yeah, and if he'd said, 'Kay Hilgore bled,' like the nurse originally thought, you'd be just as interested, wouldn't you?"

"You may be shallow and unfeeling, Smallwood, but don't drag me down to your level."

He huffed, but Detective Hurst interrupted again before he could say more. "If Mr. Smith would just answer the question, I'm sure this could be resolved easily," she said.

"I don't know hardly anything," Eli said.

I had an idea. I turned to Eli. "Elijah, why don't you tell them how you learned what you did about Cahill?"

There was reluctance in his eyes. "You're sure?" he asked.

I gave him a reassuring nod. "It's okay," I said. "Tell them exactly what you told me."

"The angels said it," Eli answered quietly.

Smallwood looked at Hurst. "Angels?" he said.

"That's what I heard," she replied.

"It's what he said," I answered. "He doesn't hear them all the time, though. Do you, Eli?"

"No, I don't see them very often, either."

73

"Oh, sometimes you see them?" asked Smallwood, and not very nicely.

Even better, I thought.

"Glimpses of them," Eli said. He stared past Smallwood, appearing lost in thought.

Smallwood and Hurst huddled. "But Cahill *was* wearing red when he disappeared," I heard Smallwood say.

Hurst nodded.

"Coincidence? Lucky guess?"

Hurst shrugged. "Where were you on May fifteenth?" she asked Elijah. "It was a Friday. Do you remember?"

There was a spot on the peeling wallpaper behind Smallwood where Eli continued to focus. After a short pause, he shook his head. "Wasn't in Indiana yet, I don't think. Came here from Peoria."

That was more than I'd gotten out of him during the last meeting. He was ill at ease in this situation, but his mind seemed sharper than I'd seen it to this point. His concentration had improved at the very least. Having regular meals and a bed for sleeping were obviously helping. I wanted to ask him questions myself, but not with these note-takers around. I could tell Smallwood had heard enough and would soon wrap it up, so I sat quietly.

"How did you get here?" Smallwood asked.

"Hitched a ride with a trucker."

"Do you know his name? Who he drove for?"

Eli nodded. "His name was Paul. His truck was painted orange but it said 'Yellow' on the side."

"Yellow Freight," Smallwood said. "We ought to be able to track that. See if he's telling the truth and figure out when he got here." He said the last two lines to Hurst as if Eli wasn't sitting there.

Hurst watched Eli for a reaction. He had none that I saw.

"Did the angel say anything else about Mr. Cahill?" she asked. "Is there additional information you could give us? He *is* missing, and if you know anything it would be a help. His family is worried."

Eli, still staring at the wallpaper, now had his head tilted as he had when I'd asked him on my last visit if the angels were saying anything. In a moment he turned to Hurst. "Nothing about Cahill," he said. Then he gave me a look which was meant to convey a message, but which I didn't understand.

Smallwood and Hurst huddled again. "We don't have any more questions for you, Mr. Smith," said Smallwood. "We want to check out your story, and then we may want to talk to you again. We don't want you to leave the area."

Eli looked at me. He was nervous. I mouthed the words, "Just say 'fine.' "

"Fine," Eli said.

Smallwood's eyes sent daggers my way. I stood up and offered to shake his hand. "Always good to butt heads with you, Sergeant," I said. He shook my hand reluctantly.

I was much nicer to Hurst. "However, it's been a pleasure to meet you, Detective Hurst," I said.

We shook hands. Her grip was firm, but friendly. She smiled with amusement in her eyes. "The same," she said.

I watched her leave. She had a nice walk.

Eli remained on the couch, his black skin a stark contrast to the bright orange cushions. His shoulders sagged.

"It's okay, champ," I said. "Round one went to you. And there may not be a round two."

He attempted a smile. "Thanks for coming," he said, his voice flat and worn out. "You helped, you really did."

"You seem to be doing better, Eli." I went over and sat next to him again. "Being here at the shelter must be helping." I hesitated before I brought up the next part. "But you're still hearing angels?" I asked.

He gave me a faint grin. "It's not such a bad thing to be able to hear angels, you know." Our eyes met.

His eyes had an amazing clarity. Looking into them I saw so much depth and pain and truth that it was hard not to break away. For the first time, I knew he was completely coherent.

And I was astonished because he knew what he was saying and he truly believed it. "You really do hear voices?" I said.

"I am blessed to be able to hear them."

"Do you also see the angels, like you told the detectives?"

He nodded. "Sometimes. Not often. When they let me see them."

"What about now?" I looked around the room as if I might catch a glimpse if I moved quickly enough.

"No, but they were whispering earlier."

"Could you tell what they were saying?"

"Yes." He paused and looked at the floor. I wondered what that meant.

"What was it?" I asked. He didn't say anything. "You don't have to tell me," I said, covering my skepticism and giving him an out if he needed one. Maybe he wished he hadn't told me about the angels. I checked my watch. I could still fit in McCutcheson before going to Broad Ripple to interview the chef. With Eli having successfully managed his questioning, he needed some time alone to unwind. I stood. "If you're okay, Eli, I probably should go ahead and leave. You just relax. But call me if the police come back or if you need anything."

"I can tell you what they were saying."

I waited. He stood to meet me.

"They're worried about you, the angels," he said. He shook his head in concern. "They say that before this is over, someone you know will die."

His eyes wore that clarity again, that truth. I shivered. "What?" I asked. "Who?"

He shook his head. "They don't know. Circumstances keep changing. But Nick, they say it could be you."

CHAPTER EIGHT

Someone you know will die.

I didn't like those words, even if they came from an unproven source. The best way I know to deal with fear is to go to the gym. Making myself stronger, feeling more comfortable about my abilities, helps me cope better with fear. I decided to go that night after Joan left. I hadn't been to the gym in a couple of days. Plus, being around Mark Zoringer and the other athletes would make me feel safer, at least for a little while.

Putting Eli out of my mind for now, I moved on to my next stop.

Frank McCutcheson, the state representative for all of Franklin, was also the proprietor of McCutcheson's Plant Farm, a business that had been in his family since the thirties. Located just south of the town limits, the farm had been supplying home gardeners and do-it-yourself landscapers for so long they barely needed to advertise. I think they have a billboard along U.S. 31, the main road in and out of Franklin, but I'm not sure anymore. It had been there so long, unchanged, that I now regarded it as I do power lines or telephone poles, a part of the scenery I take for granted. I wouldn't notice the billboard unless it disappeared. I think.

The Bertetto garden, or what was left of it since Stephanie had been born and had created other uses for our meager spare time, grew McCutcheson vegetables. We set out a small tract of tomatoes, peppers, and green beans. I visited the plant farm a couple of times a year, but that was about it. Nonetheless, I hoped McCutcheson would remember me as a customer.

"Thing are picking up, aren't they?" I said as I strolled up to him, standing at the front of the store, greeting customers as they entered the huge pole barn which formed the front portion of the store. The pungent odor in the air was a combination of fertilizer and insecticides, the canisters of which were stocked in aisles flanking the cash registers near him.

"Always do after Mother's Day," he said. There were a fair number of customers wandering around. He had three clerks working the registers, and they were busy. "We're past the last frost date, you know." When I didn't move on, he asked, "Can I help you with something, son? Have you checked out our annuals yet? We've got a lot of new varieties this year."

"I'm Nick Bertetto," I said. "I live in Franklin up on the north end. Judith Blackard, the Ways and Means secretary, suggested I talk to you. I'm profiling Cahill for a newspaper article, and she thought you might be able to provide some information."

McCutcheson's eyes narrowed and he dropped the "friendly farmer" rhetoric. "Judith Blackard, huh? Why would she send you here? She knows we have our differences."

The smile on his ruddy face was gone. McCutcheson was a short, wiry man with auburn hair that stuck straight up from his head. Cut close, it looked like little bristles had taken over his entire scalp. He ran his hand over it often, a gesture I took to be a nervous habit.

"I assume it's because you're both on the committee and

you're both from the same party. Didn't you get along?" I pulled a notebook and pen out of my pocket.

He did the hand thing over his bristles again. "What paper did you say you were with?"

"I'm a freelancer, but on this piece I'm working for the *Standard*."

"Well, at least you're a little more liberal than the *Star*," he said, referring to our main competition, Indy's other daily, a bastion of conservative thinking. "What could I possibly tell you about Cal that I would want to show up in print?"

I'd taken the time to study the fact sheet Judith had given me. Cahill, at least from the propaganda, was fairly even-handed on most issues, seeing both sides. He was pro-economic development, particularly when it came to southern Indiana. He claimed to recognize how poor the areas were and how they needed jobs, even if it meant bringing in big industry and stirring up the environmentalists. Known to be anti-gambling, Cahill was nonetheless sympathetic to a neighboring town he did not represent, Cartersville City, whose citizens wanted to put a riverboat casino on the Wabash. It was the one area where he and McCutcheson were most at odds. From living in Franklin, I knew McCutcheson was very much pro-gambling. Officially, at least, Cahill had not made up his mind on whether he would let the legislation out of committee.

"I'm looking into the issues where he had significant opposition, to give a balanced view of him," I said. "I mean, his bill getting funding for shelters for abused women passed the legislature overwhelmingly. Not much dissonance to report there. But on the gambling issue, I know many people are pushing him to get the bill to the floor of the House, you included."

McCutcheson thought a moment. "Consider the people of Cartersville City. A lot of them want a casino boat. They've seen what it's done for places like Rising Sun and Lawrenceburg—invigorated the area, provided lots of jobs and tax money, things they desperately need. Have you seen their 'green army'? Those people have been here nearly every day wearing their neon green shirts encouraging us to get the legislation out of committee, and then get it passed by the House. How many other bills do you see getting that kind of response from the people they affect, either pro or con? I respect that, and I think Calvin Cahill should respect that."

"What about his general opposition to gambling?"

"This legislature should be all about jobs and economic stimulus. It's what we need right now. Cahill even advertises that he's pro-economic development. His personal views shouldn't be a part of the decision."

Good quotes, and now that I had him warmed up, I wanted him to let down his guard.

"Tell me what he's like to work with. I want to know how he is on the inside, how he thinks."

McCutcheson motioned me away from the entrance to a small alcove where he sat on a stool. He lowered his voice. "Put your pen down and I'll tell you what he's like. But everything I say is for background, not for attribution."

He'd been interviewed before.

"You sure you wouldn't rather . . ."

"No." He sounded definite on that. He ran his fingers over his scalp again.

"Okay, no attribution," I said. I put the pen and notebook on the counter and crossed my arms. "What's he like?"

"He's no saint, despite his image," McCutcheson said.

81

"He doesn't give a damn about anything that doesn't directly affect him. You mentioned the shelters. I know this'll sound cold, but I'm willing to bet there was something in it for him. Hell, his town got one of the shelters. Cahill may have a good sense of public relations, but image is all there is to him. Nothing on the inside." He thumped his chest. "No heart, no soul."

"That's a pretty sweeping generalization," I said. "Can you give me an example?"

"Hundreds," he replied with a grin, "but we haven't got that much time. Here's one I like. Several years ago, back when we had a budget surplus, the vote came up on moving part of the state surplus into funding for the police and firemen pension plan. Where did he stand? Did he stand on the ideological argument the conservatives always use, or did he take the more moderate stance that government employees should be guaranteed an adequate retirement? Neither. He spent most of the debate time posturing, trying his best to look even-handed and getting a lot of publicity, when he knew all along he would vote with the conservatives against it. Which he did."

I started to say something, but McCutcheson was on a roll and talked right over me.

"Let me tell you how things work in the Indiana legislature," he said. "There are a few non-substantive bills that virtually everyone agrees on, like protecting state troopers on the highway. You mentioned another one, shelters for abused women. The votes are nearly unanimous. Most of the issues, though, have votes which divide strictly along on ideology—taxation, business regulations, government controls, education, health care, the like. Everyone knows which way the vote's gonna come down. But Cahill gets attention by looking undecided. He picks a new issue each year and pretends to see both sides. As the Chairman of the Ways and Means Committee, that attracts a lot of attention. He does a great job of manipulating you reporters. Anyone with brains, though, ought to know which way he's gonna vote in the end."

"What motivates him?"

"Some people would say prestige. He likes seeing his name in the paper and receiving accolades. But I think it's power." McCutcheson crossed one leg over the other. "Cahill loves to flash a big insincere smile at you when he meets you the first time. He'll flatter you with all kinds of questions about yourself. What he's really trying to do is assess how to get you to do want he wants. I've never met another guy who tries so hard to manipulate people." He ran his hand through the bristles again.

"Why do you think he disappeared?"

"I don't know. He's only been gone four days. It could be a plan to get attention, although that doesn't feel quite right to me. He wouldn't want to be out of the spotlight for too long. If he doesn't show up in another day or two, then I'd think it's something else."

"Do you think he's dead?" I asked.

"Nobody wants to say it, do they?" he mused. "Everybody's tiptoeing around it, but yeah, I think something's happened to him. And since we've already agreed I can't be quoted, I'll tell you this up front: I'd like to shake the hand of the person who did it."

Wow, I thought, an honest-to-goodness suspect.

"And no," he said, "I wouldn't be shaking my own hand. If he's dead, I didn't do it."

There was really only one question to ask after that, an awkward, obvious one. I asked it anyway. "I suppose you have an alibi for the day he disappeared."

"Of sorts. I was at a benefit luncheon for Goodwill Industries that afternoon. I did go to the Federal Club for a meeting later, but I didn't arrive until after one-thirty. The police have already talked to me, as they did just about everybody who was at the Federal Club that day."

He was a cool customer, all right, staring at me with ice blue eyes that defied me to prove he had lied. A moment of silence passed between us.

"You sure I can't interest you in those annuals?" he asked.

I smiled. "My wife always picks out those kinds of things. I'll send her over."

"Don't forget. The best selection is now." He put out his hand.

"I won't," I said, completing the handshake. "I don't forget many things."

"See that you don't," he said pointedly, "especially that this conversation has been off the record."

I nodded, picked up my notebook and pen, and turned to leave. Then I turned back around. "By the way, does the statement, 'Cahill wore red,' mean anything to you?"

For just a moment, the ice cracked in his frozen baby blues. "No," he said, his façade snapping back in place, "not a thing."

I knew the truth was something else altogether.

What I was going to do with it, I didn't know, but it gave me a spring in my step when I hit the exit.

CHAPTER NINE

Needing to eat another protein-packed meal while I was on the road toward Broad Ripple for the interview, I'd brought along a meal replacement bar. Most people don't understand that bodybuilding is ninety percent nutrition, and that eating the right things at the right time is as important, if not more so, than which exercises you do. I unwrapped the bar and took a bite, then started the van and sped off once again.

Broad Ripple is an interesting part of Indianapolis. It's one of the older areas of the city, located along the White River canal, and picturesque, with an eclectic mix of people, shops, and attitude. The artsy crowd has always hung out in Broad Ripple, but now they mix with young, upwardly mobile professionals. Joan and I loved dining and shopping there, especially when we're looking for something different. If any part of town was going to have a world-class vegetarian chef, it would be Broad Ripple.

I had just pulled onto the street in front of the restaurant when the cell phone went off again. Twice in one day is a record. Instead of struggling to find the singing device while driving, I parked in the first spot I could find along the street and answered the phone.

"The police are on to your little secret about the homeless guy," Ryan Lockridge said. No greeting, again.

"Yeah, I know. I went through a session with Smallwood earlier. How did you find out?"

"Indianapolis Police Headquarters is a very leaky place, if you know where to find the faucet."

"How much do they know?" I asked. I looked at my watch. Two minutes before the interview.

"It's not so much what they know, it's how much they believe."

"And that would be . . ."

"Very little, at least on Smallwood's part. But Smallwood has a partner who is a little more on the ball."

"That would be Detective Hurst."

"That would be correct, the luscious Detective Hurst," Ryan said. "Always coming on to me . . ."

"I bet," I said, gathering up my notebook and a list of questions to ask the chef. I glanced at my watch again. One minute.

"Let me finish. Anyway, she is apparently reserving judgment at this time. Tell me what you know."

"Well, Eli told them he heard the stuff about Cahill from the angels, and then he told them that sometimes he *sees* angels, and that was when Smallwood began to think Eli was a little loony. But Eli said something I hadn't known, that he believes he was in Peoria when Cahill disappeared. He gave the name of a trucker for Yellow Freight Lines who picked him up hitchhiking and brought him to Indy. The police are going to check his alibi. If it fits, we may not have to worry about the police."

"Or at least Smallwood," Ryan said. "Do you believe the hitchhiking story?"

"Listen, Ryan, I really have to go. I have to do an interview at three-thirty."

"Punctuality as a virtue is vastly overrated. Do you believe the hitchhiking story?"

"I guess."

"Then how does he know anything?"

"I don't know yet, Ryan. Maybe the angels told him."

"Right. Well, listen, Sherlock, you need to get in touch with Eli right away, and tell him not to talk to the *Star*. If the police know it, and we know it . . ."

"They'll know it soon."

"Right. And then warm up those fingers and type out a story for tonight's final edition because Clarisse wants something right away."

"There's not much to the story," I protested.

"Agreed, but the police have now questioned someone about the disappearance, and that's the first time they've had a suspect. We need something in the paper, and we need it in there before the *Star* beats us to it."

"Look, you know as much as I do at this point. Why don't you write the story? I won't be able to get to it until after this interview, and that will be too late for her." The notebook and papers in one hand, the cell phone in the other, I pushed the van door open and got out, kicking the door shut with my foot.

"Tsk," Ryan said, obviously unconcerned. "Okay, look, here's what I'll do. I'll throw together an article based on what we know, but leaving out what we don't want others to know. Then you'll call me *immediately* after your interview and I'll read it to you. You'll make additions, edit it, and I'll put both our bylines on the article."

Ahead of me was the Tabouleh Café, a single story, wood-framed bungalow that had been turned into a restaurant. Painted an ugly canary yellow with rosy brown trim, it clashed with its neighbor, a small Victorian housing an upscale Italian restaurant. Both eateries were fairly new. Restaurants in Broad Ripple had short lives, reflecting the attention span of their fad-happy patrons. The door to the café was open to let the pleasant breeze in. I walked toward it, still talking to Ryan. "This one's your story; you don't need to put my name on it."

"Sure I do. We're a team."

"I haven't had a chance to talk to Joan yet."

"And that would affect me, how?"

"You're hoping Joan will notice."

"It's unlikely, given that she's leaving tonight and you already have this morning's edition. Can't imagine why she would stop to pick up the late edition, but I figure it's worth a shot. I don't suppose she checks our website, does she? The story'll be on there, too."

"You're a real help, Ryan."

"Call Elijah before you do the interview, Sherlock. Then call me afterwards." He hung up.

I was about five minutes late when I told the hostess, a twenty-something with an earring through her lower lip, that I had an interview with Chef Ramon for *Healthful Living* magazine.

"Oh, he was here just a minute ago and asked if you'd come in yet," she said. "He said to apologize for not being free for another fifteen minutes. May I seat you and get you an appetizer while you're waiting? Perhaps the chef's famous toasted goat cheese ravioli with garlic and onion cream sauce?"

"Sounds tempting," I said, thinking of the fat calories, "but I need to make a phone call." I held up my cell phone. "Let me handle that and I'll be back in fifteen minutes."

"I'll seat you in our outdoor area," she insisted. "No one's out there now, so you'll have some privacy. It's no trouble."

She was obviously under orders from the chef to see to it

I was well taken care of. I followed her to a small patio on the back side of the restaurant which had a garden-like setting. She dispatched a waitress to get me some ravioli anyway and left me to dine alone.

I phoned the shelter and asked the manager to put me through to Eli. This was a conversation I'd known I'd have to have with him eventually, but I'd hoped to put it off longer. After Eli got on and I was assured he had recovered from Smallwood's visit, I got to the point.

"Eli, do you know what I do for a living?"

"You're a freelance writer."

"That's right."

"Says so right here on your business card."

Inwardly, I smiled. I'd forgotten about the card. Of course he knew. "Well, one of the publications that I work for is a newspaper, the *Indianapolis Standard*. This is going to seem awkward, and I want you to understand that I would be interested in your welfare under the same circumstances even if . . ."

"Even if I didn't know anything about Cahill?"

"Yes."

"I believe you."

"You know that I may want to write a story that includes you or information you've given me?"

"Yes. Do you need to do that now?"

"Maybe not completely. I'll try to keep your name out of it as long as I can. But others may not be inclined to do that."

"Others, as in another newspaper?"

"That and the television stations. So if someone from the media other than the *Standard* should call you . . ."

"They already did."

Probably the *Star* reporters. Damn them for being more

efficient than I give them credit for. "What did you tell them?"

"Nothing. I refused to take their call."

"Thank you," I said, releasing a breath I didn't know I'd been holding.

"As long as I know anything, Nick, you'll have an exclusive."

I wanted to ask how he knew to use those words, and if he had decided not to talk to the media because he knew what they were going to ask. But I worried about saying something that might make him think I thought he was too dumb or too smart. I played it safe. "Eli, you're a wonder."

I could hear him chuckle. "Maybe I am, Nick," he said. I started to sign off when Eli said, "Nick, be careful." I said I would and put the cell phone in my pocket.

The waitress returned with the appetizer, four pillow-shaped ravioli sitting on leaves of spinach and covered with a cream sauce. I could smell the onion and garlic. The dish was sprinkled with basil and decorated with a lemon slice and twigs of parsley. My mouth watered. In the spirit of getting a complete picture of the chef and his food, I disregarded the fat calories and sampled the dish, which tasted so good I wondered if Eli's angels hadn't visited the chef and dropped it off. Sure beat the hell out of the protein bar.

As I finished the last ravioli, Chef Ramon appeared with a sample platter of other foods he wanted me to taste. He was younger than I expected, maybe thirty years old. His face revealed his Latin American heritage, and he spoke with a slight accent I thought might be affected. But he was a great interview, funny and knowledgeable, and I was at the café much longer than I should have been. I thanked him for the talk and the food, then left.

Sitting in the van, I called Ryan right away. As I expected, he'd done a great job on the article, mentioning that the police had a potential lead and had questioned an informant, but that nothing had been substantiated yet. He left out Eli's name and details that could be used to track him down. I had very little to add or edit. All that was left was to hope Joan would not see the finished article or the byline, at least until I could talk to her.

I had asked Joan to start dinner before I got home. I'd selected spaghetti because it could be thrown together easily since I kept containers of homemade sauce in the freezer. Joan had sauce thawing in the microwave, water heating on the stove, and was making a salad when I arrived. On a breadboard, ready to slice, was a loaf of rustic Italian, a wonderful "artisan bread" one of the grocery stores in the area had begun carrying.

It was a reassuring scene, but Joan was spring-loaded. I barely said hello and she went off. "Are you working on the Cahill story?" she demanded.

I kept my voice steady and calm. "Yes, I am. I had lunch today with Ryan and got the assignment. You knew I was meeting with him and Clarisse, although Clarisse didn't show."

Joan didn't look at me. She cut carrots into the salad and fired off another statement. "Well, you must have been pretty sure of the assignment before lunch because I got a phone call this afternoon from Aunt Hildy. She had talked to Judith, who said that you had been there this morning asking questions."

Aunt Hildy was Joan's dad's oldest sister. Judith was her daughter. I could have kicked myself for not thinking a phone call would be immediate.

"I talked to Judith, because I had hoped to get some in-

91

formation that might convince Clarisse to hire me."

"So what are you doing on this story?"

I reminded myself that in therapy we don't always move forward in a straight line. Sometimes we jag back on ourselves. What counts is that there is forward movement, and we had that yesterday when Joan agreed I should have the luncheon meeting. I took a deep breath. "What you and I talked about yesterday, basically. I'm going to scratch out a timeline of Cahill's career after supper and fax it to the *Standard*. Tomorrow I have to finish up a profile on Cahill."

She was still breathing hard. I decided not to bring up Eli. The connection was still factually tenuous. Plus, I could tell she wasn't ready to hear the possibilities.

Joan looked up from the salad. We stared at each other. She put the knife down and crossed her arms over her chest. Finally she said, "Well, I guess that's okay. It doesn't sound dangerous."

I took another deep breath. "Good."

Someone you know will die. I heard the words in my head, in Eli's voice, just as he had said them to me earlier. A chill went down my back. But then I thought, better that she should be in Jasper, then, than here. I worried for a moment about Stephanie. Could I protect her myself? I resolved that I would just have to. And I wasn't sure how good at prophecy Eli's angels were anyway. I pushed that thought from my mind.

"Where's Stephanie?" I asked.

"She's in her bedroom, playing."

Joan began to look embarrassed. "Nick, there is something I didn't handle very well, and I'm afraid you'll have to live with it."

"What's that?"

"Well, Aunt Hildy kept asking if there was anything she could do to help out here while I was gone. I said no, that you were perfectly fine taking care of Stephanie by yourself, but you know how Hildy is. She knew that you would need time for work and kept insisting it was no trouble at all for her to come over—she could fix the meals and babysit so you could get your writing done. I protested, but it's so hard to tell her 'no.' By the time our conversation was over, she'd maneuvered me into saying it was okay. She's going to come over in the morning. I'm sorry."

I gulped. Aunt Hildy. She thought the world of Joan and Stephanie, but gave me the cold shoulder as though I were not good enough for Joan. My only redeeming quality, as I read it, was that I had fathered Stephanie and fortunately hadn't contributed much from my gene pool. The prospect of spending the week with Aunt Hildy was unsettling, and I knew she had one major motive in inviting herself over. She wanted to keep tabs on me. Worse still, she would report everything back to Joan.

"Couldn't you have called me?" I asked, getting testy in spite of my better instincts. "I've fended off Hildy before. And if I really needed help, I would have called my dad, and he'd have come over from Clinton."

Joan's back stiffened. "It's not like I asked her to be here, Nick," she said.

She pushed a diced egg off the cutting board and into the salad, placing the board down with a slight smack. She proceeded to toss the salad a bit. I could see her counting to ten.

She left the salad and moved around behind me to give me a hug, which felt good. "Nick, I'm sorry. Maybe I should have been tougher with her, but it's difficult for me. Hildy pushed her way in. She loves Stephanie and always wants to help. This will make her feel wanted. Let's look at the positive side. You'll have live-in help for the next week."

I wasn't sure Aunt Hildy had a positive side, at least when it came to me. "She and I don't get along. Not that I haven't tried to get in her good graces."

"Be charming, Nick—you've gotten interviews from people who are openly hostile; you know you can do it. Perhaps a few days together will finally put an end to Aunt Hildy's resistance to you. Maybe you'll get to know each other better."

Joan isn't given to lying, so I truly believe she didn't ask Aunt Hildy to come, but neither did she seem too upset over the prospect of having a spy in the house. It didn't matter now. I couldn't stop Aunt Hildy from coming, not without looking bad to Joan. Or Judith, which could jeopardize any flow of information there.

I registered a token complaint. "She serves sauerkraut with everything," I said. "I won't eat it."

Ignoring my comment, Joan kissed me on the lips. "Thanks for doing this," she said softly. "I know it won't be easy."

What could I say? I returned the kiss. "I'll miss you," I said.

At dinner, Stephanie excitedly told me about a play they were working on at preschool. Joan had already heard about it when Stephanie got home.

"I get to be the Fairy Princess," she said. "I lead the other fairies. We find things that start with 'a,' 'b,' 'c,' and 'd.' Then we count things and dance. Mommy said she'll come see it."

"I can get off work for it," Joan said to me. "It's not

for another two weeks."

"Mrs. Smock gave us a letter."

"Is it in your backpack?" I asked.

She shook her head. "Mommy put it on the refrigerator."

"You may be excused from the table to go get it, if you want," I said.

Stephanie got down from the booster seat and ran to the kitchen. She brought back a half sheet of paper and handed it to me.

I read it. "The only help they need is with costumes. That leaves me out, since I don't sew."

Joan smiled. "I'm not much better."

"Melissa's in it, too," Steph said. "She gets to find the alligator. That starts with 'a.' Todd is in it. I forget what he finds. Justin and Dustin can't be in it. They're too little."

We heard about the play and fairy princesses all during dinner, which was all right with me. Joan seemed apprehensive about the trip to southern Indiana, but she smiled at Steph's enthusiasm. It made the time go by somewhat easier.

Stephanie worked on her fairy princess dance in the living room. Joan and I worked on getting her suitcase packed in the bedroom.

Packing reminded me of our days together before Stephanie and before the kidnapping, and what we would do when one of us had to go out of town on business. The one not going would putter around the bedroom, checking the suitcase for completeness, making sure nothing was forgotten. Then, when everything was packed and the suitcase zipped, we'd throw back the bed covers and make passionate, noisy love, clinging to each other until the last minute before leaving. Even with Stephanie in the next room, I found myself longing to start something. While I fantasized about kissing Joan all over and pulling our bodies close together, the topic of Eli and the missing Calvin Cahill seemed very far away.

But not far enough.

"Nick, I know you wanted that assignment on Cahill, and I know you got it and it's something you have to do," Joan said, breaking me out of my daydream, "but just, please, go slow. I don't know if I'm ready."

I went over and put my arms around her. "Ryan is the main reporter on the story. It's his, not mine. I'm not sure you have anything to be concerned about."

Someone you know will die. I tried to ignore it.

She held me close. "Okay," she said. It wasn't convincing.

She zipped up the suitcase and I carried it for her, nearly colliding into her back when she stopped suddenly at the front door. She peered out into the night with a concerned look on her face. I reached over and flipped on the outside light. Her car, parked in the driveway next to the crabapple tree, lay in shadows. The naked tree limbs, stripped of their leaves by a fungus, blew in the wind, making the shadows shift restlessly.

"Walk me out?" Joan asked.

"Sure," I said. "I had planned to. Let me go first."

When the suitcase was in the trunk and Joan settled into the driver's seat, I leaned over and kissed her again. "Drive carefully," I said. "Call me when you get in. Give your parents my love."

"I will." She gave Stephanie, who'd come out with us, a big hug and a kiss. She made her promise to be good for Aunt Hildy and Daddy. "Take care of yourself, and don't get into trouble," Joan said to me.

"I won't. I love you, Joanie."

She reached out the window and squeezed my hand. Then she drove off, waving as she left.

Stephanie turned. "Aunt Hildy's coming?"

"Yep. In the morning."

"I don't like sauerkraut."

"We'll talk about that tomorrow. Right now, how would you like to go play at Todd's house? Daddy needs to go to the gym."

CHAPTER TEN

The tiny parking lot of the Franklin Iron Works was full and cars lined Jefferson Street, so I circled the side streets looking for a space to park. I found a spot one block away under a huge maple on tree-lined Madison Avenue and walked back to the gym carrying my weight belt, lifting gloves, and a bottle of water.

The Franklin Iron Works was a small, mostly free-weight gym, located in a whitewashed brick building on East Jeff. I entered and stopped to let my eyes adjust to the brightness. To the left of the entrance were owner Mark Zoringer's makeshift office and a cardio area with two stairsteppers, an exercise bike, a treadmill, and just enough space to stretch out. On the other side of the entrance were the weights and benches. I printed my name on the sign-in log.

Mark was across the room, spotting a tall, wiry high school kid on the bench. With two fingers under the long iron bar, Mark provided minimal assistance as the 225-pound weight went up and down multiple times. Mark urged the kid on and he responded, grinding out more repetitions with just a little extra assistance from Mark. Together they returned the bar to its rest. I gave a small wave with my hand and Mark nodded. He and the kid exchanged a high five and Mark came over.

"Hey," Mark said in his low rumbling voice. He wasn't big on conversation. Slightly taller than I am and eighty pounds of muscle heavier, Mark's body spoke for him. He wore a black ragtop with an open neck and cut-off sleeves, letting the thick trapezius muscles bunch out above the shoulders and his cantaloupe-sized biceps jut out from the shirt. I always found myself a little in awe of his mass.

"Hey," I responded.

Mark looked at the weight belt and recognized why I was carrying it. "Leg day," he said and smiled. He knew I hated working legs.

"Love those stiff leg deadlifts you've got me doing." His latest program for developing the hamstring muscles was agonizing.

The smile never left his face. "Good for you. Blow up those legs like you used dynamite on 'em."

"Whatever you say, Mark."

He tapped the side of his head. "Attitude. You'll never pack on muscle unless you believe you can do it." He gave me the once-over. "You're sticking to that diet I gave you, right?"

"Yes, sir," I said, adding "mostly" under my breath. My taste buds had not forgotten the exquisite goat cheese ravioli earlier in the day.

"Good." He looked back at the high school kid, who was ready for another set on the bench. "Gotta go," he said. "You need a spot, get my attention."

I changed in the men's locker room and stretched in the cardio area. Looking around, I counted seven men and three women at various levels of fitness. Because Mark was a state-level competitor, he tended to attract other serious bodybuilders to his gym. Two of the men were built like him. Unfortunately, they were exercising legs also, which meant I'd have to work in with them. There were times when I questioned why I was here.

Two years ago I had jumped into weightlifting wholeheartedly. Mark Zoringer, the man who had rescued Joan when she'd been kidnapped, had taken me under his wing to help me get stronger and more confident. There was no question my self-esteem had taken a hit during Joan's ordeal—needing someone else to save my wife had made me feel powerless. With Mark's help I'd made good progress, but now I was at a watershed. I'd reached my limits while maintaining what I considered a normal lifestyle; to put on more muscle would require adopting a bodybuilder's mindset. That meant spending a lot more time in the gym and eating a high-protein bodybuilding diet of six meals a day, not to mention supplements. While I wasn't quite over my desire to be stronger and better able to "protect" Joan, it was becoming less important as I put the incident behind me. Still, I liked the feeling of power I got from weightlifting, even if I looked more like a swimmer than a bodybuilder. I think Mark sensed that my commitment was wavering.

Swallowing my insecurities, I started my workout, taking turns with the bodybuilders. They proved to be friendly, encouraging me as I did leg extensions, presses, deadlifts, and calf exercises with them. After legs, I finished with two different kinds of crunches for my abs which I suspected I'd never see, given my current liberal attitude toward consuming fat calories. "Forget the six-pack," Ryan Lockridge told me once, "go for the two-liter." Gotta love that guy.

Stretching after the workout, my mind went back to the strange case of Elijah Smith and Calvin Cahill.

What did I really know? Not much. Cahill disappeared on May 15. Some people didn't like him, including Representative Frank McCutcheson. If McCutcheson was to be believed, he was a shallow guy. His signature fashion was a pocket handkerchief, the color of which varied, but for which red appeared to carry some kind of significance. A homeless man named Elijah Smith knew that Cahill wore red and thought it was important, although he didn't know why. In fact, he didn't even know where he'd heard it or who Cahill was. All he would say was the "angels" told him. Why the cover-up?

Ryan had doubts about Eli's believability. I disagreed. Even if it looked as if Eli had an alibi for when Cahill disappeared, it only meant he had nothing to do with what *happened* to Cahill. It didn't mean he couldn't have overheard the information after he arrived in Indy. As for the angels, I was convinced that Eli believed in them, but I wasn't convinced that angels were the source for "Cahill wore red." Those angels had human voices, in my opinion.

But if I didn't believe, what did that say about me? Was I not thinking straight? If I didn't believe Eli's angels were supernatural, then why was I concerned about the last thing he'd told me? After all, I'd been in the room. There were no voices. So, shouldn't my fear be unwarranted? Then why had I felt compelled to go the gym?

"Almost finished?" Mark asked, startling me. I'd been so absorbed I hadn't spotted him coming from behind, even though Mark was too big to sneak up on people.

"Yeah," I said. I glanced at the clock on the wall. "Oh, man, I didn't realize how late it was. I need to pick up Stephanie from a friend's house. Joan's mother is having an operation, so she's gone down to Jasper."

"How are things with Joan?"

"Better, I think." Because of Mark's involvement in our lives, he knew what was going on. "Going down to help her mom will be good for her. She'll be focused on someone else's needs. Maybe she'll get a new perspective."

"If you need anything while she's gone, let Marie and me know."

"Thanks."

I changed and left the gym quickly, mindful of the time and anxious to get Stephanie before it looked like I was imposing too much on Tom. Lost in that train of thought, I didn't notice how the leafy maples on Madison shaded the streetlights and blocked the porch lights of the nearby houses. I didn't hear soft footsteps coming up behind me. I too easily talked myself into dismissing Eli's warning and was careless.

Something that felt like a towel was thrown over my head, and all I could smell was an overpowering dose of cologne. I managed to choke out a call for help before a hard fist hit me in the stomach. I doubled over. Then a heavy forearm came down on the back of my head, sending me face-first onto the cold, hard sidewalk.

CHAPTER ELEVEN

I managed to slide the towel off my head and tried to push off the concrete, but a shoe lodged itself on my neck and held me down. I grunted. The shoe pressed harder. My nose and right cheek hurt from hitting the sidewalk but neither felt broken. I couldn't see my attacker clearly. The shoe on my neck was so large, I had to believe it was connected to a male foot. From the feel of the rubber-like sole, I guessed it was a tennis shoe. Focusing was difficult with my head swimming. In the background I heard feet running in my direction. Rescuers or reinforcements? I had to do something fast.

Sweeping back with my hand to grab the foot, I managed to ease the pressure on my neck. As the attacker struggled with me, I heard a thud like metal against flesh, then a yelp of pain. The foot came off my throat and out of my grasp. Once again I heard running footsteps, this time faster and heading away. A car started. Tires squealed.

I rolled over to see an overweight woman leaning over me holding a tire iron.

"Hello, Aunt Hildy," I said.

"You have a knack for trouble," she said in a slight German accent. The round face came into focus. Hildy had steel gray eyes. She used black eyeliner around them, which made them stand out against her pasty white skin. Cherry red lipstick was slopped across her mouth.

"Did you get the license plate number?" I croaked.

"There was no plate. I can provide a description of the car and the man who attacked you, but he wore a ski mask. Not much to go on."

I sat up and rubbed my neck. "What are you doing here anyway?" I grumbled. "Not that I'm not glad to see you."

"I knew the minute Joan left you would get into something dangerous. So I said to myself, 'Hildy, what can you do to look out for poor Stephanie? She will need you tonight just as much as she will tomorrow.' So I went by your house in time to see Joan leave, and then I followed you here. Judith said you were writing a story about the disappearance of Mr. Cahill, her boss. I hope for Judith's sake that is not what this is about. Is it, or are you mixed up in something else?"

Hildy extended her hand to pull me up. I took hold of it, thankfully. "I'm not mixed up in anything," I said. Hildy gave a yank and I rose with ease. "I was here working out. That's all. Someone was just trying to rob me, I'm sure."

She reached to my back pocket and patted my wallet. "If this was what he was after, he would have grabbed it long before. I gave him plenty of time before I got out of my car."

"Thanks for letting him have a sporting chance," I said, touching my forehead. I found blood.

Hildy cupped my chin in her hand and moved my face around, trying to find some light so she could see better. She squinted as she examined me. "You have a big bruise on your cheek and a cut above your eyebrow that need attention. I will take you to the ER."

"I don't need to go to the ER," I said, all the while knowing I really did. I picked up the towel and held it against the cut.

Mark Zoringer and the high school kid he'd been

training came running up. "Are you okay?" the kid asked. "I saw you were being attacked and ran back to the gym to get help, but by the time we got out here the guy was driving off. I called the police."

Great. Now the police were coming. "Thanks for being concerned," I said. "I'm okay. It was just a robbery attempt." In the distance I heard a siren.

"You are very good to want to help my nephew," Hildy said to the high schooler. "Thank you for being a good citizen." She hugged him.

Amusement flitted in Mark's eyes. "Is this your aunt?" he asked.

"Yes, she is," I said, resisting the temptation to add "by marriage." After all, she had rescued me. "This is Aunt Hildy."

I introduced them. Hildy let go of the kid and shook his hand, then Mark's. The siren sounded closer. Within seconds, it had rounded the corner and pulled up.

Officer Ken Roth got out of the car and cocked a thick eyebrow at me. "Haven't you had enough excitement lately, Nick? Now you have to get mugged?"

"Can't stay away from it, Ken," I said. I introduced him to the group and told him what had happened. Since Mark hadn't seen anything, Roth let him go back to the gym. Next he took the kid's statement and let him go. While Roth talked to Hildy, I made sure the young man knew I appreciated his going to get help.

Hildy was quite candid. She insisted the attack couldn't have been a robbery attempt, and she provided a description—white male, about six foot two, muscular build, wearing a black t-shirt and jeans. The ski mask he wore was also black. Even his car, a Chevrolet Tracker, was black, although Hildy said it was filthy and had quite a few dings.

"He was wearing a lot of some kind of cologne," I added to Hildy's description, "or maybe it was just all over the towel." I held out the rag I'd been holding on my cut. Hildy sniffed it.

"Calvin Klein's Obsession," she said. "I think he was wearing it."

I didn't ask her how she knew what the scent was and neither did Ken. He continued to make notes. I downplayed Hildy's idea that the incident wasn't robbery, though I was inclined to agree with her. My best guess was that I was being sent a message. What the message was and who had sent it, I wasn't sure, but I knew I didn't want to spill anything to the police if there was a chance it was related to Cahill. And I especially didn't want Hildegard the Spy to know.

"All right," Roth said to Hildy, closing his notebook and taking the tattered towel as evidence, "not much else to get here. I'm glad you're taking him to the ER. He needs to get that cut looked at." He turned to me. "Nick, stay out of trouble. If you're into something the police should know about and you're not telling me, I will personally kick your ass."

I made noises like he was way off base and went to the van. Hildy said she would follow me to the ER, but I told her we needed to pick up Stephanie first. On the way over to Tom Colby's house, I thought of a nearby immediate care center where I could get treated faster than at the ER. Also, I wanted Hildy to take Stephanie home and get her to bed instead of going with me.

"You look like hell," Tom said when he opened the door.

"Thanks. I don't feel half that good." I told him my version of what had happened. Just as I finished, Stephanie and Todd came to the door. Stephanie began to cry when she saw me, and as I bent down and tried to reassure her, she patted my face.

"Are you okay, Daddy? Does it hurt?" she asked. Her quivering voice broke my heart.

"Yes, honey, I'm fine. Really. It looks worse than it is." I gave her a hug. "Listen, Aunt Hildy is here. She came in this evening instead of tomorrow. I'm going to have her take you home so I can go see a doctor. Everything'll be okay." I thanked Tom for watching Stephanie and carried her out to Hildy. Steph was a little leery, but gave Hildy an obligatory hug. She got into the back seat, buckled up, and the green Impala took off. I got into my van and headed for the immediate care center.

Only two people were ahead of me at the center, neither of whom appeared to need much fixing up. One was a twenty-something man who had cut his thumb deeply, and the other was a woman in her sixties who told everyone, including me, how she was certain she'd taken the wrong medicine. She juggled five prescriptions as she prattled.

I checked the time and thought about Joan. She should have rolled into Jasper by now and be settled in with her mom and dad. She had probably called home to let me know she got in okay. What if Hildy had been there to answer the phone? What had she told Joan? Or, if Hildy hadn't been home, would Joan have panicked that I didn't answer? Hopefully not. With any luck, she'd just left a message and not thought more about it.

Or maybe Hildy had initiated a contact, a good spy sending in an encrypted report. That would do wonders for Joan's frame of mind, I thought.

My turn came and I was sent into a freezing examining room. I had become so adept at calling my run-in a failed robbery attempt that even I was starting to believe it. The doctor who treated me, a semi-retired physician who said he enjoyed medicine too much to give it up completely, put in stitches to stop it from bleeding. He said it might scar. I was told to see my regular physician after a week to have it checked. The swelling around my nose and eyes would go down, he added, but it would still be purplish for a few days.

Hildy was waiting for me at the door when I got home. Before I could say anything, she shook her head.

"This is not the kind of thing that happens in Franklin," she told me. "Had it happened in Indianapolis, I might believe it was random. But I know differently, and I will be watching you. Whatever you are doing to have caused this, I will find out."

The phone rang and I dashed into the kitchen to pick it up, wondering if it was Joan. Instead a male voice, sounding deep and gravelly, said, "Leave Cahill alone." I heard a click on the other end and the line went dead.

I smiled at Hildy as I replaced the phone. "Wrong number," I said.

CHAPTER TWELVE

Two things went through my head. One, how much had Judith told Hildy about Cahill's disappearance? It was the only thing I was working on that could even remotely be considered dangerous, yet Hildy acted as though there were something else I was hiding. Perhaps Judith realized that she had to downplay my assignment if she wanted to avoid her mom's scrutiny as well.

Second, was Eli's warning real? Being attacked had rattled me. Had it not been for Hildy's appearance, would I be dead? Was that what Eli meant when he said things kept changing, and that the angels didn't know who would die? I wanted to go see Eli right at that moment to ask if his "angels" were really that clairvoyant. Maybe he would know who'd attacked me. I felt a little foolish thinking I would learn anything, but I still wanted to go over to the shelter. Since it was late, it would have to wait until morning. Probably a good idea to sleep on it anyway.

The day had been a long one, though it wasn't quite eleven o'clock. I didn't think I'd get to sleep anytime soon, but the prospect of making small talk with Hildy and enduring her suspicious glances made me excuse myself and head to the bedroom.

The picture on the dresser of Joan and me, taken for the St. Rita church directory, drew my attention. I was in a charcoal gray suit and she was in a turquoise dress, and we had both smiled heartily for the camera, trying to appear as though everything were fine. We were still doing that. Would it help or hurt Joan if I told her the truth about tonight's attack? I hoped I wasn't jeopardizing what progress we'd made, but I was not inclined to tell her the whole story. It wouldn't do anything for her frame of mind when she needed to concentrate on her parents.

But laying off the story wasn't the right thing for me to do, either. I needed to see this through. Damn, I hated feeling trapped by a decision that would be wrong, no matter what I did. Was this another opportunity, like the case in Clinton, to show Joan she wasn't in danger just because I investigated a story? I wished I knew.

And then there was Hildy, a wild card. Her interference wouldn't help. I'd gotten lucky tonight—Joan called before Hildy had returned and had left a message that she'd arrived safely and would call tomorrow. What would Hildy say when they talked?

As I drifted off to sleep, only one thing seemed clear to me: that my activities over the last two days had obviously made someone very unhappy. Who?

"Had to be Frank McCutcheson," I concluded to my morning reflection in the mirror. I said it through gritted teeth as I carefully worked around my blackened left eye, trying to put in my contact lens. The flesh surrounding the right eye was skinned and tender, but not bruised. Finally I decided glasses would be better.

My face looked ugly, but the rest of me had come through reasonably well. I could still feel the punch to my abs, and the trapezius muscles at the base of my neck ached from being stepped on. I took two Advil for the pain and slipped the small bottle of pain relievers in my jeans pocket as I dressed.

"The only people I've talked to were Judith, McCutcheson, Eli, and Ryan," I said aloud while pulling a white polo shirt over my head. For reasons I couldn't define, I trusted Eli, although I wasn't sure how he knew what he knew. Ryan was above reproach. While Judith wasn't my favorite person, I hardly considered her a potential murderer. I needed to ask her if she could remember other recent days Cahill had worn a red silk handkerchief in his pocket. A larger sample size would be critical for Ryan and me to determine if the red handkerchief really was important. If so, what did it mean? Why had Cahill worn red on Friday?

That left McCutcheson. Of course, it could have been someone who got the information secondhand, but I doubted it. I reminded myself that McCutcheson had reacted when I asked him if "Cahill wore red" meant anything to him.

Okay, so the connection was weak. Sometimes you have to go with your instinct, and mine was very big on McCutcheson. "He has to be involved somehow," I said aloud.

"Quit talking to yourself and get down to breakfast," Hildy said, knocking on the door to my room. "I cannot keep these eggs warm forever, you know."

Well, it was nice of her to make eggs. "I'm coming."

When I got to the kitchen, Stephanie was sitting at the counter. She was dressed in blue shorts and a pink t-shirt, and was picking at her breakfast. The scrambled eggs had been cooked so long they had the consistency of dryer lint. Also on the plate were two side dishes, potatoes with onions and green pepper, and, of course, sauerkraut. It looked like Stephanie had put ketchup on the potatoes and eaten around the peppers, but the eggs and sauerkraut were untouched. Her milk glass was drained.

"Daddy, can't I have Froot Loops?" Steph asked.

I looked at Hildy, trying to gauge how much I should alienate her this early in her stay. She was frowning, with one hand on her hip and the other hand holding a rubber spatula, ready to put Sahara-desert scrambled eggs on a plate. She wore a hot pink, flowered housedress and a clashing plaid apron.

"Stephanie, it was really nice of Aunt Hildy to cook you breakfast. Why don't you give the eggs a try?"

"Can I have more milk?"

"What do you say?"

"Please?"

I poured her half a glass.

She took a tentative bite of the eggs and a minuscule amount of the sauerkraut, reached for the milk glass, and washed them down without tasting them. "Now can I have Froot Loops?"

"Okay," I said.

Hildy sniffed. "What children eat these days."

"The cereal has more sugar than it should, I know, but at least she eats breakfast," I said.

I got the Froot Loops for Steph. She played around with the cereal, ate some of it, and then excused herself. She must not have been very hungry.

Hildy prepared my plate and put it on the table. I sat and contemplated the eggs, potatoes, and sauerkraut, eventually reaching for the ketchup. "I like ketchup on my potatoes, too," I said. "Have you eaten?"

"At six o'clock, when I got up," she replied. Hildy kept strict hours. It was eight o'clock now.

"I'll clean up here when I'm finished," I said. "You can go on and do whatever you need to."

"What time does Stephanie need to leave for preschool?"

"Twelve-thirty," I said. "I was going to take her to the park to play with her friends earlier, at ten o'clock. A group of us meet there."

"I will take her," Hildy said. "I'm sure you will need the time to work on your story." She dropped the morning's *Indianapolis Standard* next to me. "Now I will take a shower." She left and I glanced at the paper, folded back to page three where my name was visible on the story that had made yesterday's late edition, now repeated for all to see. "Police question homeless man in Cahill disappearance, by Ryan Lockridge and Nick Bertetto," it read. I wasn't going to defend myself to Hildy. After all, Joan knew I was working on the story. Maybe she wasn't aware of the turn my involvement had taken, but she knew.

As I fixed my coffee, I glanced through the article, determining that nothing new had been added since last night. I wondered if the article had appeared in the Jasper paper. Or maybe Hildy was in the office faxing it to Joan right now, under cover of the noise from the shower.

Of Hildy's breakfast, the potatoes were good, the eggs edible (with a little help from the ketchup), and the sauerkraut just right for the garbage disposal, which whirred in delight as I cleaned up the dishes. I poured a second cup of coffee and finished the paper.

There was no sense trying to justify anything to Hildy, so I contemplated my next move. Confronting McCutcheson, while tempting, was not a good idea. Not yet. The best thing to do was to puzzle out his connection to the Cahill disappearance first. I wanted badly to see Eli, but thought I'd better wait until a respectable nine o'clock. I went upstairs to my home office instead.

The office was my refuge, a converted bedroom with one

window that looked out onto the street. An upholstered chair in hunter green sat to the right of the door. The green matched the painted lower half of the walls and coordinated with the striped wallpaper, which went from a chair-rail-height border to the ceiling. I had tried for something a little sophisticated and ended up with something a little pretentious. Such are my designer skills. The desk, opposite the window so I could work without contemplating the view, was a mess of papers, books, a computer screen with speakers, and a fax-scan-printer. No wet footprints from Hildy. I sat down at the chair, a rollabout model on a sheet of hard plastic, and called the *Standard*. Ryan was at work.

"You again," he said. I could hear him chewing: probably a bagel.

"Me again, or what's left of me after last night's beating," I said. "I received a warning."

Suddenly Ryan was a little more receptive. I could picture him straightening up and reaching for a pen. Then I heard a swallowing noise and he asked, "What happened?"

I went through the episode, reluctantly admitting that Aunt Hildy had saved me. When he asked who Aunt Hildy was, the answer took another two minutes. He hummed appreciatively when I concluded with the phoned-in message to leave Cahill alone.

"Cool," he said.

"Easy for you to say."

"I'm sure you'll recover. You do all that weightlifting; it's got to be good for something. Better you took the hit than me."

"Thanks for the outpouring of sympathy."

He ignored me. The chewing sound started again. "Now we just have to figure out who's getting jumpy," he said.

"I've been thinking about that. Seems to me it's got to

be McCutcheson." I went through my rationale. "Or at least he has to be involved somehow. I'm sure there's a connection."

"Well, we know they both sit on the Ways and Means Committee. Since you know Judith, you should ask her if there are any issues beyond the obvious gambling bill straining their relationship. Surely she would know the dirt," Ryan said.

"If she'll tell me."

"You won't know until you try. Have you checked the legislature's website yet, to see if they serve on any other committees together?"

"No, I just got up."

"Log on and see what you can get. The Republican caucus lists committee assignments. You also might try checking their homepages to see if their voting records are online. Some representatives put out reports to their constituents that advertise how they vote. It's a long shot, but there might be something you can glean from that."

"Now that I've been assigned all the grunt work, what are you going to do?"

"Have another cup of coffee for starters. Then I thought I'd do a little checking of my own. I have sources, you know. If Judith won't give you the dirt on McCutcheson and Cahill, maybe I can find out. If they're jazzed over a hot issue, maybe their animosity went to the next level."

"Or maybe they're not so different after all," I said. "Just because McCutcheson told me they hated each other doesn't mean they do."

"Good point."

"Another thing we need to do is check on Cahill's marriage. Judith mentioned how 'devoted' they are to each other. Made me wonder."

"You'd better check that. You know how nervous I get when I hear the 'm' word. In fact, I'm sweating right now and I didn't even use it in a sentence."

"You're sweating because of the jalapeno cream cheese you've smothered on your bagel. No one you date would consider marrying you."

"How do you know it's a bagel?"

"The angels told me." I hung up.

Stephanie pushed the office door open and came in.

"This is where my daddy works," Stephanie said to some imaginary friend. I remembered her fairy princess role in the play. "He got hurt last night, but he'll be okay."

"Are you talking to the other princesses?"

"Uh-huh." She climbed up on my lap. I moved the keyboard out of the way so I could hug her.

"Aunt Hildy's gonna take me to the park. Daddy, will you come, too?"

"No, honey, Daddy has to work and since Aunt Hildy will be with us until Mommy gets home, she offered to take you. I thought you'd have more fun with your friends than being trapped here with me."

She looked up at me and tenderly touched the bruised skin around my eye. "Do you *have* to work?" she asked.

"Yes, this is a very important story. Uncle Ryan is helping me on it."

"Can I come with you when you go see Uncle Ryan?"

"We'll see when the time comes," I said, giving her a squeeze. I checked the time. "You have about an hour before Aunt Hildy takes you to the park. If you want to bring a game in here, you can play it quietly while I work. Or you may watch TV for a little while."

She decided to bring in an electronic spelling game and stay with me, which made it difficult to concentrate. I'd no sooner start to write something when Stephanie would push a button and the talkative thing would spell a word. So I decided to look online for the information Ryan and I had talked about.

The one thing I really couldn't do was fault Steph. I think she was trying to be protective after last night. And it was cute hearing her spell. Before long, though, Hildy came in and enticed Steph to play Chutes and Ladders. I watched her go with both reluctance and relief.

According to the Web, the only overlap between McCutcheson and Cahill was the Ways and Means Committee. Unless there was some other connection outside of their jobs, any animosity we were interested in had to be through that committee.

Next I checked McCutcheson's homepage. There was a brief biography and links to his latest newsletter, which I read. It looked vaguely familiar; I must've received it in the mail, given it the once-over, and tossed it. Now I studied it, but nothing jumped out at me. He trumpeted a school safety bill he'd co-authored that became law, but largely the newsletter put his liberal spin on Republican triumphs.

My search was interrupted briefly by Stephanie and Hildy leaving for the park. I gave Stephanie a big kiss and told her to behave for Aunt Hildy. After they were on their way, I went back to the Internet.

Cahill's homepage was as unenlightening as McCutcheson's. Cahill had his pet projects, none of which appeared to intersect with anything McCutcheson was doing. I couldn't find either McCutcheson's or Cahill's voting record.

I disconnected from the Internet and leaned back in the chair. Maybe Ryan would have better luck with his sources. Since they both served on the Ways and Means Committee, they probably saw each other a lot. Probably disagreed a lot. Liberals and conservatives tend to do that. Probably considered it normal.

I could put my ear to the ground and check on the Cahill marriage next, but my thoughts turned to Eli instead. It was time to find out how he knew things he shouldn't be able to know. I jumped in the van and drove over to the shelter.

The manager answered when I rang the doorbell. "What happened to your eye?" he asked.

"I was mugged last night. It'll go away. Is Eli here?"

Instead of taking me upstairs, he led me into the entryway and looked unsure of what to say. I took that to be a bad sign.

"He hasn't left, has he?"

"Oh, no, nothing like that," he said. His hand went nervously to the frayed collar of his blue oxford shirt. He fingered the top button. "It's just that he was in such a good mood earlier at breakfast. Now he's up in his room, acting afraid, and he won't tell us what's wrong. I've tried to get him to do some work, and his roommates are in there now trying to talk to him. It may not be a good time to visit."

"Maybe he'll talk to me," I said. "It might be something I know about. Have the police been back since yesterday, or has he had any more calls from the press?"

"No. No visitors or phone calls, and really, he's a model guest. It's just the change happened so quickly."

"I'd really like to see him."

He looked at me for a moment. "I guess it wouldn't hurt."

I followed the manager up the darkly-lit walnut staircase to the second floor, the sound of our footsteps plodding out an unintended military cadence. Eli's room was the first door on the right, and I could hear nothing as we stood outside. The manager led the way in.

The room was large; its long, narrow shape must have been created by knocking down walls between smaller rooms. The main furniture was two bunk beds and two single beds. Eli was curled up on one of the singles, leaning against the wall in a semi-sitting position. He had acquired a Jeff Gordon NASCAR t-shirt. If the jeans were his old ones, they'd been washed. Eli's eyes were wet, but he was not crying. His two roommates, one a skinny white man with sallow cheeks and the other a tall, balding black man, sat on their respective bunk beds across from Eli's, studying him.

Eli stared at me when I entered. "Cahill is dead," he said. "The angels keep saying, 'Cahill is dead!' "

CHAPTER THIRTEEN

Everyone looked at me as though it was my turn to say something. "You're sure that's what they're saying?" I asked.

Eli blinked, then nodded solemnly.

I turned to the manager. "Could I talk to Eli privately?"

"Sure. Why don't you use the meeting room?"

"Is that where we talked to the police?"

"Yes," he said.

I made a motion to Eli, who just sat there. It took a bit of coaxing to get him moving.

In the conference room, Eli went straight for the orange suede couch. I took a seat at the conference table, turning the metal folding chair toward Eli.

"When did the angels first tell you Cahill was dead?" I asked.

"An hour ago. They were singing a really sad song. Then I realized they were singing about Cahill being dead."

"Can you tell me how the song went?"

Eli thought a moment and then shook his head. "It was so beautiful that you had to listen to it, and so sad you didn't think you could bear to."

"But the angels didn't tell *you* that Cahill was dead? They didn't talk to you directly?"

"No, but I know I was supposed to hear the song. They were singing it so I could hear it."

"Can you still hear it?"

"No."

Eli stood and touched my face near the eye that had blackened. "Are you being careful? You know what the angels said, 'Someone you know will die.' "

I crossed my arms over my chest. Memories of a previous case, of Anna Veloche insisting she was receiving visions of the Virgin Mary, haunted me. My hand went instinctively to the medal around my neck. "Eli, you know what you are asking me to believe is very difficult."

"You say it's hard to believe me. Is there not evidence on your face?"

I leaned forward. "What do you know, Eli? Why was I attacked? Who attacked me?"

"I don't know anything, only what the angels whisper."

"People tell each other all the time to 'take care,' but just because they don't and something happens, doesn't mean what they've said is prophetic."

Eli sighed. "This is not the same thing."

"I guess. We'll see."

Eli pulled up a chair next to me. We stared at each other.

"If Cahill is dead, do you know where the body is?" I asked.

"No, but I will soon." His eyes brightened a bit.

"The angels are going to tell you at a later date?"

"No, they sang about the body being brought to me."

I frowned. "Why on earth would the body be brought to you?"

"I don't know. That's just what I heard."

"When will it happen?"

"I don't know."

"What else did you hear?"

Eli shifted his position so he could look at the peeling wallpaper behind me. Either he was avoiding eye contact or he was looking for angels.

"Eli?"

"What?"

"What else did they tell you?"

He paused. "Nothing, really."

"Does that mean, nothing at all, or nothing that you're going to tell me?"

"This room could use new wallpaper."

"Yes, it could. Does that mean you're not going to tell me?"

"Just because I've heard something doesn't mean it applies to you or that you need to know it. Didn't I tell you when I heard that someone you know will die? When it concerns you, I will speak up."

I gripped the seat of my chair. "I don't know what to make of you, Eli."

"You will." He got up. "I'd better start to do my work."

I took out my wallet and pulled out a ten-dollar bill and a phone card. Despite having a cell phone, I keep a phone card just in case. It's the Boy Scout in me.

"Please take these," I said, handing them to him. "It may seem like charity, and I don't want you to be offended, but I want you to have them. When you feel like telling me what you know, please call."

"I will take them because you asked me to. Thank you."

"Eli, what do the angels look like?"

He smiled and I noticed the oddest thing—I could swear his teeth had whitened considerably over the last two days. "The next time you come to visit me, I will tell you."

"Promise?"

"Yes. And don't make my silence out to be something it is not. You are a good person. I just have my reasons."

Reasons that had little to do with angels, I was willing to

bet. But I shook his hand and left.

By lunchtime I had knocked off the Cahill profile Clarisse Babcock had asked me to do for tomorrow's paper, based on my Net research and what Judith had told me, when the phone rang. It was Ryan. My portable phone was hooked to my belt, so I was able to simultaneously answer the phone and microwave leftover pasta e fagioli soup.

"Good news," he said.

"You're going to start using deodorant again?"

"I'll ignore that. The gambling bill is bigger than we originally thought."

"Meaning?" I sipped a spoonful of soup. It tasted good but wasn't quite hot enough. I stuck it back in the microwave and set the timer.

"There are a few other important items in the bill that aren't getting as much attention as the Cartersville City casino, but are still of major significance. For example, the bill has a provision allowing casinos to operate 24/7, which isn't permitted now. Also, the new law would allow the two horse racing tracks in Indiana to install pull-tab gambling machines, similar to slot machines, in their operations."

"Isn't it just more gambling?"

"Depends on your point of view. To the anti-gambling forces, every little crack that enables more gambling is bad. They can't stop what's already here, so they'll try to stop whatever addition they can. Every piece of the bill is worth fighting over.

"The legislators, however, are anxious to bring in more revenue, the budget crunch being what it is. The gambling industry is using that to push for their pet projects. The 'anti' forces are lobbying Cahill to stop it in committee. Even though he's generally against gambling, he hasn't said one way or the other what he'll do."

The microwave beeped, and I pulled the soup out.

"What are you eating?" Ryan asked.

"Pasta e fagioli. It's a soup."

"Sounds Italian. Have you fixed it for me before?"

"It is Italian, but you wouldn't like it because it has beans in it."

Sometimes Ryan has the palate of a ten-year-old.

"Disgusting," he said. "Almost as nasty as those protein shakes you drink. Are you having one of those, too?"

"Yes, but that's not why you called. So, is McCutcheson involved at all? Why is he big on gambling anyway? His district doesn't include Cartersville City or either of the horse tracks."

"McCutcheson has a son who is the human resource manager for the race track in Anderson. Since he has a connection to the gambling industry, he abstains on all the votes. But it doesn't mean, as a member of the Ways and Means Committee, he wouldn't 'help' legislation get through committee that would give everyone more gambling opportunities. Now let's consider Cahill, who also has a son, who is a reformed gambling addict working against all forms of legalized gambling in Indiana. As Chairman of the Ways and Means Committee, Cahill sets the agenda, which pretty much dictates which bills get hearings. Do you see the potential for conflict here?"

I took a sip of my "nasty" chocolate protein shake. "But doesn't Cahill, since he's also connected through his son, have to abstain?"

"This doesn't have to do with voting, it has to do with setting the agenda. He can see to it the bill never sees the light of day. But there is another complication."

"I can't wait to hear it."

"Good. Cahill and his son don't get along. So Cahill really doesn't care one way or another. In fact, he may let it slip through just to poke a stick at sonny. That may be why dear old daddy had a secret agreement to let the gambling expansion bill get out of committee in trade for support for increased gasoline taxes, one of daddy's pet revenue enhancers. But when daddy discovered he had enough votes and didn't need the extra support, he reneged on the deal, causing quite a problem for McCutcheson, who brokered it."

"One could believe the pro-gambling forces wouldn't be very happy about that."

"Yes, and those forces have ties to some rather unsavory organizations who don't like setbacks of this nature. Just for the record, Cahill still has not fully buried the bill. He keeps hinting he may let it out of committee."

"I suppose we could dig a little deeper into that issue."

"Precisely, Sherlock. Thank you for volunteering."

"Me? You're the one with all the contacts."

"If you run into a brick wall, let me know and I'll try to knock a little mortar loose. Otherwise, good luck."

"What are you going to do?"

"Well, since I have a real job with the paper and my editor has a lot of other projects she wants me to work on, I thought I'd earn my regular paycheck. Stay in touch!"

He hung up.

I looked at my watch and thought about Joan's mother. She was scheduled to have the catheterization before eleven. By now, I thought, she'd be out and the doctors would have made some decision as to what to do. Joan should call soon.

The soup was still warm so I sprinkled low-fat mozzarella cheese over it. The phone rang again. A female voice was on the other line.

"Hi, Nick, this is Judith. Have you heard anything yet about Aunt Janine?"

"No, Joan hasn't called yet. She should, though, any time. I'll let you know what I find out."

"That would be great. Is my mom there?"

"No, she took Stephanie to the park. Do you want me to have her call you?"

"Please."

She gave me a number where she could be reached, and I started to sign off when she said, "One more thing. Are you still interested in knowing some of the dates when Cal wore red handkerchiefs in his pocket?"

"Yes, I am."

She read the list. It went back about seven months. I read back the dates to make sure they were correct.

"Thanks," I said. "I'm amazed you were able to remember these, they go back so far."

"Well, it took me awhile, but then I remembered that he tends to wear that color on days he has lunch at the Federal Club. I looked back at the calendar for days he'd had a meeting scheduled there."

"So all these were days he had lunch there?"

"That's right." I could hear someone typing on a computer—probably Judith, it sounded so close.

"This is really helpful," I said. "Judith, one quick question. What's happening right now on the Ways and Means Committee, with Cahill gone? Are any hearings being conducted?"

"We've suspended things for a couple of days. Everyone is worried about Cal, and it's difficult to concentrate. But we'll only hold off for so long. By tomorrow or Friday we should be back in session."

"Who takes over as acting chairman?"

"Frank McCutcheson."

I paused. "Seriously?"

"Yes."

We exchanged final pleasantries and hung up. While I ate the soup and drank my shake, I checked a calendar against the list Judith had given me.

The data didn't fit an exact pattern, but on average Cahill wore the red handkerchief and had lunch at the Federal Club every three weeks. Curious.

I called Ryan.

"This is Ryan Lockridge," he said in a nasally voice. "I'm either on the phone or away from my desk right now. If you'd like to leave a message, that's what the upcoming tone is for. If this is Nick Bertetto, you can . . ."

"Knock it off, Ryan, I know it's you. Do you have a membership at the Federal Club?"

"Sure, that's the latest perk we have here at the *Standard*. All us low-paid reporters get ten-thousand-dollar memberships to the Federal Club so we can go bankrupt trying to buy the right clothes to fit in. Why do you ask?"

"We need to have lunch at the Federal Club."

"Yeah, well I think we may be out of luck there."

"If I tell you why, you might try a little harder to pull some strings. I got a call from Judith. She gave me a bunch of dates she believed Cahill wore a red handkerchief, and then said he tended to do that on days he had lunch at the Federal Club."

Ryan thought it over, then said, "I know who to ask to get us in. Jayne Warner. Besides being hot for my body, she's a lawyer and a lobbyist for gaming organizations. Maybe she can help us out on the gambling aspect."

"Got something on that, too. Guess who takes over as

acting chairman if Cahill doesn't come back?"

"Who?"

"McCutcheson."

"I'll give Jayne a call and get back to you." He hung up.

I had just finished eating when Stephanie and Aunt Hildy returned from the park. Stephanie rushed to me.

"Daddy, Aunt Hildy took me to Steak 'n Shake for lunch! I got an orange freeze." She wiggled onto my lap.

"Did you have something to eat, too?"

"A grilled cheese," she said. "But I didn't eat it all."

A beaming Aunt Hildy stood in front of us. I could tell she was thrilled that she had done something Stephanie really liked.

"Thank you," I told her.

"It was nothing," Hildy said. "She wanted McDonald's, but I said I thought she would like this better. I was glad she enjoyed the orange freeze. I'm surprised she had never had one before."

"Judith called. She wants you to call her back."

"I am sure she wants to find out about Janine. I will call her when we hear from Joan."

"By the way, I haven't properly thanked you for being there last night," I said. "I'm lucky you were there when I was attacked."

Her eyes held a mischievous twinkle. "It was nothing."

The home phone rang and I grabbed it. It was Joan.

"Mom's okay," Joan said. "She has blockages in four arteries, but the doctor says none of them will require surgery. They're going to put stents in each one to open them, two tomorrow and two early next week. They're going to keep her in the hospital overnight so they can start first thing in the morning."

"Will she have a recovery period or anything?"

"Not really. Putting in stents isn't invasive surgery. They want to give her a little time between the procedures, but she'll be back to normal in just a day or so."

"That's great news," I said. "Your dad handling this okay?"

"He's doing much better, now that he knows Mom won't have to have surgery. Is Stephanie there?"

"Yes, hang on." I put Stephanie on the phone. I was a little worried what she might say about my black eye and stitches, but it was probably no big deal since Hildy would no doubt give Joan that info, if she hadn't already.

As it turned out, Stephanie was so excited about eating out with Aunt Hildy and having an orange freeze, the subject never came up. When she was finished, Stephanie handed the phone back to me.

"I'm glad to hear that Aunt Hildy is there. When did she get in?"

"She came in last night."

"Can I talk to her, please?"

I handed the phone to Hildy. Anticipating a confrontation and not wanting Stephanie there, I suggested she go upstairs to get ready for preschool.

Hildy inquired about her sister-in-law first. No problem there. Then she told a bold, straight-faced lie. "Everything is fine here," she said. "Nick and I had a nice talk last night. Today he is working while I take care of Stephanie. Just now he was thanking me for helping him out."

And in a moment she handed the phone back to me.

"Well, I'm glad to see that you and Hildy are getting along," Joan said.

"Yes," I replied, looking straight at Hildy, "she certainly has been a lifesaver."

129

"I'll call you tomorrow after Mom's procedure, let you know she's okay."

"Thanks," I said. I paused to see what else she might say. All I could hear was her breathing. I closed my eyes. "Love you," I added.

"You, too," she said.

I placed the phone back in the receiver and turned to Hildy. "You didn't tell her," I said, stunned.

CHAPTER FOURTEEN

"No, I did not," Hildy replied. "She has enough to worry about right now, don't you think?"

"I do, but I thought you were here to . . ."

"Be a spy? No. I am here to keep an eye on you, but I can do that well enough by myself. Though I admit when it was suggested that I do this . . ."

"It wasn't your idea? That's not what Joan told me."

Hildy's eyes opened wide. "Slip of the tongue," she said. "It may have been my idea. I can't remember now who suggested it. Doesn't matter. I am here now, and you are being watched."

"I don't need watching. Joan knows what I've been hired to do."

"If you are so honest, why didn't you tell her about the attack?"

"Same reason you didn't."

"I do not understand why you insist on doing such dangerous work, putting Joan and Stephanie through this, but I can see it is important to you. I cannot stop you, but I can try to make you see it is wrong. Until you realize it, I will protect Stephanie. You, however, are now on your own."

She crossed her arms. I did the same to counter her. "I don't need your protection, and Stephanie I can protect on my own. But I do appreciate your help."

"Fine."

I left the room to find Steph and make sure she was getting ready for preschool.

After Steph had been picked up, I finished the profile for *Healthful Living*. The magazine had asked me to recommend three local photographers, and they'd hired Ann Broden, my favorite of the three, a freelancer I'd worked with on travel articles about local attractions. I called to brief her on the story, and we talked about possible photos. She talked in incomplete sentences as the concepts formed in her mind faster than she could articulate. At the end, I wasn't exactly sure what she had in mind, but I knew from her excitement the photos would be good. One of the great things about my job was working with other professionals.

At one o'clock the phone rang.

"Free for lunch?" Ryan asked.

"I've already eaten, you know that."

"I meant tomorrow. At the Federal Club."

"You got us in?"

"Jayne Warner got us in. She's the lobbyist for the Indiana Casino Association. We're having lunch with her. Have you had a chance to check on the Cahill marriage yet?"

"No, I haven't gotten to it."

"You might want to get to it now. Warner knows some dirt about the Cahills. Contrary to their image, they're really a dysfunctional family. The son and daughter are from his first marriage. It came apart at the seams seven years ago. Both kids hate his new wife and won't have anything to do with either of them. The daughter lives in Colorado and likes a good Rocky Mountain high, if you know what I mean. I told you about the son, the reformed gambler. He now goes by his mother's maiden name of Weber. Well, turns out he may be working against *legalized* gambling, but he's playing footsie with illegal gambling. Rumor has it he's in financial trouble with a local bookie. I'm working on getting the bookie's name. In the meantime, you need to get in touch with either the ex-wife, Virginia Weber, or Cheryl, the current wife. I'd like to hear what they have to say about Cahill and the kids."

Hmmm. So would I. "Got any addresses?"

He gave them to me. Cheryl Cahill lived in Vincennes, three hours from Franklin. Virginia Weber lived in Noblesville, north of Indianapolis. Weber was closer. Ryan also had phone numbers.

"Okay, I'll get right on it," I said.

A personal interview is always the best, but getting over to Vincennes, doing the interview, and then back again would take nearly a full working day. Noblesville is closer, but still time-consuming. I decided to try interviewing Weber over the phone. I couldn't believe my good fortune when a woman answered. I identified myself and started in with my questions.

"Ms. Weber, I'm doing a background story on your ex-husband Calvin Cahill, and I wondered if you could give me just a few minutes of your time."

"Another reporter!" she yelled at me. "I've already slammed the door or hung up on six of them today."

"Please don't hang up, Ms. Weber. I'm sorry you feel like you're being hounded. We're all chasing the same story, is all. If you bear with me, I promise only to take a few moments of your time. Please."

"There's nothing to tell. We were married, had two kids, raised them together for a while, and then we divorced," she said. "That about sums it up."

"I know this is difficult for you."

"Difficult in what way? Cal hasn't been a part of my life for a long time. That's why I don't have anything to say that could help you with your story."

"You were married to him for eighteen years according to the records. Some of those times were surely happy ones. I'd like to hear about the good as well as the bad."

There was a pause on her end. "Look," she finally said. "I really can't talk about this."

"Why?"

"It's . . . it's not in my best interest."

"Ms. Weber, you make it sound as if there's something mysterious there."

"If you want to know the truth about Calvin Cahill, try talking to his current wife. By now she should be well aware of the good and the bad."

"Just like you knew?"

"What I'm going to tell you is for your own good, and it's off the record. Calvin Cahill is not what he appears. When he does something bad, it's for his own selfish pleasure, and when he does something good, it's to make himself feel better about having done something bad. That kind of person you don't want to mess with." Then she hung up.

Not a flattering portrait, I thought, but one which had potential. If the good things Cahill did made him feel better about the bad ones, then I had both sides to chase. One might shed light on the other.

I called Cheryl Cahill next.

A man answered. I asked for Cheryl.

"She can't come to the phone right now. Can I help you?"

"This is Nick Bertetto with the *Indianapolis Standard*. When would be a better time to call?"

There was a sigh on the other end. "There isn't a good

time to call. Her husband is missing and she's having a difficult enough time coping without being hounded by the press."

"With whom am I speaking?"

"This is her brother."

"And your name is?"

Another sigh. "David."

"Do you have a last name, David?"

"Sanders. What is it you want?"

"I'm hoping to get an interview with your sister. I'll make it as easy as I can."

"Well, I'm going to make it as tough as I can. My sister is working with the police to locate Cal, and if you want information you can contact them. Thank you for calling." He hung up.

I know a challenge when I hear one. The Vincennes address went into my notebook. I would have to make time to visit Cheryl Cahill.

In the meantime, an inspired idea came to me on how to get information about the Cahill marriages. I went downstairs to see Hildy.

"Judith hasn't been over to the house in a while, and she could probably use a break from the stress she's feeling at the Statehouse," I said. "Why don't we invite her over for dinner?"

"Are you fishing for information?"

"Aunt Hildy, you are so suspicious. Yes, I happen to be interested in what Judith knows about what's going on, but don't you think it's a lot more pleasant to share a meal and have a nice conversation, if I have to call her anyway? What's a little gossip among family members?"

"You may think you are a sly one, Nick, but Judith is not taken in by you, just as I am not."

"Does that mean you don't want me to invite her to dinner?"

"Of course not. I hope that she will come. But you are still not fooling anyone."

Hildy volunteered to cook dinner. I went to call Judith. I wouldn't say Judith was flattered by the invitation, but she was certainly agreeable. She said she'd be by around six.

Stephanie came home tired from preschool, so I had her take a nap while I checked over the Cahill profile I'd written earlier and e-mailed it to the paper. Then I turned to other matters. A few clients needed to be reminded they hadn't paid me. I handled that and prepared a bill for a small job I'd been working on. When Stephanie awakened and came in to get me, it was after five o'clock.

"Daddy, are you done?"

"Yes I am, honey. What's Aunt Hildy doing?"

"She's making dinner."

We walked out into the hall. It smelled like a German brewery. Stephanie and I headed for the kitchen. I wondered if Hildy had turned our house into a pub.

"It sure smells good in here," I said, checking into the pots on the stove, trying to figure out what was going on. "What are you making?"

"We are having bratwurst and sauerkraut," she said. "I am steaming the sausages in beer."

"Ahh. Are we having any vegetables with that?"

"Sauerkraut is cabbage. That's a vegetable."

"And a very good one at that. But since we're having a guest over, how about if I also make some pan-fried potatoes? I'll pull some of Joan's homemade applesauce out of the freezer, too."

It took some negotiation, but I managed to get enough on the table that I figured Steph and I could get by eating a minimum of sauerkraut.

Judith arrived at six-fifteen. She reacted to the sight of my black eye, and I sent Stephanie into the bathroom to wash her hands while I explained what happened.

"Sorry I'm late," Judith said, after I finished the story. "Things are crazy at work right now. That Frank McCutcheson acts like he owns the place. He is really pushing to become acting chairman, and his first priority is to get the casino bill ready for a committee vote. He's making me nuts."

"What's he in such a hurry for?" I asked.

"Probably because we don't have all that many days left in the session, and it'll have to pass the Senate, too."

I offered Judith a glass of white wine and she took me up on it.

"I have half a mind to retire right now."

"Now you surely do not mean that," Hildy said, coming in from the kitchen. She went over and kissed her daughter on the cheek. "You are too young to retire. What would you do with yourself?"

"I have enough points to retire. And I could always get another job. Or maybe I'll just find an island somewhere and drink margaritas all day." She laughed.

Judith wore a tailored denim skirt and a pale pink t-shirt. Her lipstick was a pale pink that matched. As she stood next to her mom, who had the same height and same build, I was struck by how much more Judith had made out of nearly identical features. Neither had a model's body, but one knew how to find clothes and makeup that flattered her appearance, and the other didn't.

"They would not let you go," Hildy said. "You are too valuable, especially right now."

"Well, I can dream about it anyway." Judith took a sip of

the wine, leaving a light smear of pink on the glass.

Stephanie came in, her hands damp. "I washed my hands, Daddy," she said, waving them at me.

"I guess it is time to eat, then," Hildy said, ushering us into the dining room.

During dinner, I tried to pry information out of Judith.

"What do you know about Calvin Cahill's marriages?" I asked her.

She looked at me suspiciously. "Is this going to end up in the paper and embarrass me?"

I held up empty hands. "Look, no notebook," I joked. "For now, I'm just trying to understand the dynamics of the Cahill family. I've heard that his kids from his first marriage don't approve of the second."

"That's true," she said. "Why would they? Their mom is educated, well-spoken, and loyal. They were disgusted when Cal left her and married a former stripper. They sort of wrote him off after that."

"Why'd he leave his first wife?"

Judith looked at Stephanie. She was concentrating on eating the applesauce while keeping the potatoes from touching it. Judith leaned toward me. "It was all about sex, of course," she whispered.

"Sex?"

"Calvin Cahill has sexual . . ." she paused, looking for the right word, ". . . issues."

"Define 'issues.' "

"Keep in mind that when I say this, it's based on hearsay. He apparently requires certain special . . . stimuli in order to perform."

"Do we have to talk about this here?" whispered Hildy, looking across the table.

Stephanie, like all kids, had radar. When she wasn't supposed to be listening, she was, or at least trying. She stared at Hildy, Judith, and me, all conspiratorially leaning toward each other.

"Perhaps we should save this for later," I said. I was confident Stephanie hadn't heard us, but I thought it best to stop right there.

"There's not much more to tell," Judith said, pushing on. "He made choices that have hurt him. Rumor had it there was some kind of gag clause in the divorce agreement. You can see which way his tastes ran with the next marriage. Though I don't know that he's necessarily faithful to her, either."

Judith seemed to want to talk, and I decided to let her go on since she'd moved away from explicitly talking about sex. If she steered toward it again, though, I'd have to cut her off.

"How does she feel about him?" I asked.

"I think she loves him, in a way. She certainly loves all the attention from the press. He made her legitimate with his money and his position. She didn't want to jeopardize that, at least at first. But they've been married seven years, and I don't think her feelings are quite the same anymore."

"Do you know that, or just think that?"

"Think. I don't have proof. But she's been visiting her brother in Carmel frequently during the last year. It makes me suspicious; Vincennes is not the most exciting place to live, especially for a person of her former occupation who likes the big city."

"I talked to her brother earlier today. He was in Vincennes."

"Only to gather up the last of her stuff. She's moved to his house on a semi-permanent basis, to be closer to the investigation."

"Really?" I said. Carmel was much closer than Vincennes. There was a possibility I could interview her in person. If I could get past her brother.

"As I understand it, she's there now," Judith said.

Judith talked more about House politics, but nothing relevant to Cahill or his divided family. She asked how things were going with my investigation, and I gave her a brief summary. I added that I had a luncheon meeting the next day at the Federal Club.

"That's such a storied place," Judith said. "I've been there a fair amount, as a guest of Cal's or one of the other legislators. Many of them stay there through the week while the General Assembly is in session."

"So I've heard."

"I often think of what goes on there after the legislature adjourns," she said, "the things the public doesn't know about, like secret deals and illegal lobbying." She let it hang there, and I took it that it was meant for me to think about.

After the dishes had been cleared from the table, I sent Steph, Hildy, and Judith out to the family room after dinner, saying that I would load the dishwasher. Judith announced that she really needed to get home, so we said goodbye to her. I had no sooner finished packaging the leftovers and tucking the remaining sauerkraut into a container way at the back of the refrigerator, when the phone rang.

"This is Claire Hurst with the Indianapolis Police Department. Is this Nick Bertetto?"

"Yes it is. Is something wrong?"

"I wanted you to know that your friend Mr. Smith is not out of the woods yet. We looked into his story about being picked up by a Yellow Freight driver, and it doesn't quite check out. First, while Yellow Freight does in fact have a driver named Paul who drives from Peoria to Indianapolis, he was on the road the night *after* Cahill disappeared. So Smith doesn't have an alibi for May fifteenth."

"But wouldn't it have been difficult for a homeless man to be in Indy on May fifteenth and get back to Peoria to be picked up and brought back to Indy on May sixteenth?"

"That brings us to the second point. The truck driver insists that he never picks up hitchhikers, and he doesn't even remember seeing one that night."

"Couldn't it be a matter of convenience?"

"Meaning, could he get in trouble if he were picking up hitchhikers?"

"Yeah."

"Yellow Freight has a policy against it, but the driver seemed sincere to us. He offered to take a lie detector test in front of his employer."

"Hmmm. Thanks." I started to hang up, but Detective Hurst kept talking.

"It just seems *so* coincidental that there was a Yellow Freight driver named Paul that regularly drives that route," she said.

"It does, doesn't it?"

"The driver, Paul Hadley, might be at Yellow Freight's main terminal in Indianapolis tomorrow morning, around eight o'clock."

Ohhh? "So if I wanted to question him further, he might be there?"

"That's right."

"You think there's something more?"

"Didn't say that. Sergeant Smallwood is satisfied that Mr. Hadley is telling the truth and that Mr. Smith has no alibi for that night. It is closed as far as we are concerned."

"I understand. Thank you, Detective Hurst, er, uh, Claire."

"You're welcome. Goodnight."

I was really starting to like Claire Hurst. Smiling, I picked up the dish towel.

"Who was that?"

I looked up to see Hildy standing at the entrance to the kitchen area.

"The police. They were letting me know they checked up on a lead. Didn't pan out."

"Getting familiar with the police, are we?"

"That I used her first name? C'mon, Hildy, it helps to be on a first-name basis with detectives. When you need information, you want them to think of you as a friend."

She stood silent for a moment, considering. "Who are you going to question?" she asked.

"What?"

"You asked this woman, Claire, if he would be there that you could question him. Who is 'he'?"

" 'He' is the lead that the police officially believe is telling the truth but unofficially aren't sure about. And why am I telling you this?"

"Because I asked?"

I sighed. "In the morning I'm going to take a trip into Indianapolis near the airport, and I have to be there at eight o'clock. At noon I have the lunch at the Federal Club, so I'll probably stay in Indianapolis. Can you pick up the carpool from school if I'm not home in time?"

"Of course. Where are you going?"

"If I told you to the Yellow Freight depot, would it make any difference?"

"Well," she snipped, "have it your way." She turned and left.

Nosy, I thought. But I kind of had to admire that.

CHAPTER FIFTEEN

My radio alarm woke me early the next morning. I rolled on my right side and felt a stab of pain, a reminder of the beating I'd taken two days ago. After stumbling into the bathroom, I checked the mirror. The area around my left eye was a little tender but healing. The right eye still looked purplish and slightly swollen, especially around the two stitches. I could have given Frankenstein a run for his money in the looks department.

My plan was to slip out of the house without waking Hildy, but it was not to be. When I got out of the shower at six-thirty, I could smell bacon. A wonderful smell, mind you, but it meant I would have to face the German Inquisition before leaving.

I put on a white chambray short sleeve shirt that looked dressy in a casual sort of way, jeans, and tennis shoes. When I got downstairs, I discovered a situation worse than I expected. Not only had Hildy cooked bacon, she had made pancakes, too. Fat city. On the plus side, there was no sauerkraut to be found anywhere.

"Stephanie told me she does not like sauerkraut and you don't either, so I did not make any this morning," Hildy said, acting a little hurt. It might have been put on.

Stephanie looked happy, though. She sat at the table with a plate of cut-up pancake in front of her, using her fork to dip an already-drenched piece in the syrup pool that covered the plate. She stuck it in her mouth and ate it blissfully.

"Well," I said to Hildy, "when you grow up with a lot of Italian cooking, sauerkraut seems to be an acquired taste."

"You like pancakes, though?"

"Oh, yes," I said, "probably too much."

"What? You think you are fat? You are too skinny! I look at your face and I see no fullness, only cheeks and jawbone. We will have to put a healthy glow on you!"

Great. Now her mission was to enlarge my bodyfat percentage.

But I ate the pancakes. Where I held the line was at the bacon, eating one strip and offering the rest to Stephanie, who loves bacon. If Hildy was offended, she didn't say.

After brushing my teeth, I gathered together a couple of notepads, pens, my calendar book, and a suit to change into for lunch at the Federal Club.

"The pancakes were great, Hildy. Thanks," I said. I gave Stephanie a kiss and told her to be good for Aunt Hildy. Then I started out the door.

"How do I get in touch with you?" Hildy asked.

"The business card on the refrigerator has my cell phone number on the back. I forgot, here's the schedule for the day: Stephanie needs to be ready for school at twelve-fifteen. Melissa's mom, Jill, is driving the kids in. We drive them home at three. I should be home in time to do it, but if not, you know how to get to St. Rita's. The map under the business card shows where everyone's house is. They're all neighborhood kids." I said goodbye and left.

The drive to Indianapolis was fairly easy. I listened to the traffic updates on WTPI, but there were no slowdowns between Franklin and the Indianapolis Airport area, where Yellow Freight was located. I arrived a full fifteen minutes before eight a.m. Signs posted at the entrance said "Heavy Freight Only" and "No U Turn," and big rigs rolled on both lanes of the drive. I passed the unmanned guard shack and drove fifty yards to the two-story main building, taking one of the few parking spots out front. Immense tractor-trailers were exiting from the terminal to the right.

The two-story main building had an odd shape, with the above-ground portion supported on a foot-high narrower base; the first story did not touch the ground. It stuck out a few yards on either side like a square toadstool. Dominated by huge windows on each floor, the building seemed reminiscent of an air traffic control building from the early days of aviation. I thought about sitting in the parking space until eight o'clock, but the building's windows were so large I felt that everyone was looking down at the unknown van. I picked up a notepad and pen and entered the building.

I had already worked out what I was going to say to the driver. First and foremost, I would be casual about everything. Elijah Smith had almost fallen into the path of my van, I would explain. I had stopped to help him and was now concerned about his welfare. He was homeless and the police believed he might have had something to do with Calvin Cahill's disappearance. His alibi for that night was that he was hitchhiking from Peoria on I-74 and was picked up by a Yellow Freight driver named Paul. I knew the police had talked to him, and I just wanted to talk to him also, because of my concern for Elijah.

The office inside had a small waiting area with turquoise vinyl chairs hooked together by their steel frames like something left over from the customer area of a sixties auto repair shop. At the matching receptionist's desk, I asked for Paul Hadley. The receptionist called the foreman, who, after I explained why I was there, introduced me to a man in his late fifties with a head of hair so full and black it looked suspiciously like a hairpiece. His wrinkled, tanned face had a pug nose and he sported a potbelly that pulled tight against the Western-style denim shirt he wore. I stood about three inches taller than he and looked down at him as we talked.

"Yeah, the police asked me about it already," Hadley said, after I went through my rehearsed spiel and the foreman left. "If you've talked to them, you know what happened."

"I just have a few questions, if you don't mind." He didn't say anything, so I went on. "Do you travel the route between Indy and Peoria much?"

"A fair amount," he said. "A couple-three times a week."

"Have you been doing that for a while?"

"Since I cut back to working part-time, about a year. My own business keeps me pretty busy. I run a few short routes in the evening every week to help them out. They're short manpower."

"What other business are you in?"

"Produce delivery. I'm buying into it. We deliver to restaurants and supermarkets. When I worked full time here I got tired of the long drives." He leaned in close to me. "I'm using this job to pay down my business loans."

I nodded. "About the Peoria route. You've probably been running it long enough that it's second nature to you."

He regarded me with a bit of suspicion, as if I was trying to lead him somewhere. Which, of course, I was.

"I suppose you could say that."

"Would you say that one trip is pretty much like another one? That it would be difficult later to remember the exact details of any one night on that road?"

"Nope, 'cause I do remember driving it May fifteenth. It rained like the devil almost the whole night. The only time it slowed down, I pulled into a truck stop."

"Where was that?"

"Covington. It's the half-way point back to Indy."

"How long did you stop?"

"Just long enough to get something to eat."

I tried to envision his stop. "Was it raining hard again when you left?"

"Hard enough I had the windshield wipers going. About ten miles out of Covington the rain picked up again."

"And you didn't have a hitchhiker with you?"

"Nope," he said emphatically. "I don't pick up no hitchhikers. It ain't a good practice."

"Okay, okay," I said, easing off. "I just had to ask."

"Look, is this gonna to take much longer? I got to get to my business."

"I think I'm done. Did it rain all the way back to Indy?"

There was no hesitation on his part. "All the way. Honestly, it felt like one of the fastest trips I ever made. After the stop for food, everything went smooth and I was in Indy before I knew it. But the logbook shows I drove it in about the time I regularly do. Rain must've hypnotized me."

"Is there any way someone might have slipped into your trailer while you were at the truck stop?"

"I weren't there that long. The doors of the trailer were locked. They would've had to get in the cab with me, and I would've noticed that."

I shook his hand. "Thanks for answering my questions. I guess my friend Elijah must be mistaken."

"Must be. Hope it works out okay, though."

"Thanks."

We walked outside in one of those awkward situations where we'd already said goodbye, but we were going in the same direction. He didn't make an effort to say another parting word after we left the building, and I didn't either. I followed the bright green Hadley Wholesale Produce Wagon out of the parking lot and onto High School Road, but at the first light we turned opposite directions. I got on I-465, the loop around Indianapolis, heading north.

Paul Hadley sounded honest, I thought, but there was something about the last part of the trip, his thinking it went fast, that bothered me. He might have been tired or concentrating on the rain, not really paying attention—could Elijah have been hiding in that truck? I didn't know too much about truck cabs, whether there were places a person could remain hidden. But Eli either knew the guy's name or made a lucky guess there was a "Paul" on the route. How would he have known if they hadn't talked? I needed to question Eli again now that I'd talked to the truck driver.

I had looked up the address for David Sanders, Cheryl Cahill's brother, which was fortunately in the phone book. Having learned from Judith that she was staying with him in Carmel, I was pleased I could check up on her without having to make a long drive to Vincennes.

At Keystone Avenue I exited the interstate and turned north, past the gold leaf Carmel city limits sign reminding me I was now among the elite. I'd heard that the Carmel cops targeted older vehicles with out-of-the-area plates, so I drove very carefully to the Sanders place on quiet Windermere Street, well removed from any thoroughfares. The houses were large and had windows on the front and rear exposures only, a seventies energy conservation trait. Maple trees shaded everything and gave the place a bucolic atmosphere. The only sound was the occasional barking of dogs. There were a few cars on the street. I parked two houses away from Sanders' address, a tri-level with ivory siding and colonial blue trim, and settled in to watch.

Among other things, I wanted to know if Mrs. Cahill's brother was there.

After the first half hour I got tired of waiting. I could never make it as a detective—too impatient. I looked up Sanders' phone number in my notes and dialed it on my cell phone. Voice mail picked up after four rings.

I hung up. There were two possibilities. One was that no one was home; the second was that someone was at home but not in an answering mood. I decided to see which it was.

Picking up my notebook, I got out of the van and walked up the long, ascending sidewalk to the Sanders house. I rang the doorbell. Inside, I could hear a dog scamper to the front door. It began to bark.

For a long time nothing happened except the little yip-yip dog continued its barking frenzy. When the barking started to wane, I rang the bell again to get the dog going. We played this game several times. I didn't know if I was driving anyone inside crazy, but I knew for certain that I was having fun manipulating the dog. Finally I could hear someone yelling. The dog got quiet, and shortly the door opened.

The woman standing inside was blonde, shapely, and wearing a short sundress that accentuated every bit of her attractiveness. No question I could envision her as a stripper. At first glance I thought she was in her mid-thirties, about my age, but a closer look at the lines on her face made me guess early forties, a good two decades younger than Calvin's sixty-three. She wore a large diamond engagement ring and a diamond encrusted wedding band. I wondered how much they meant to her, after what Judith had said.

"What do you want?" she asked, and not nicely. She

stared at my right eye, causing me to remember the stitches.

"I'm sorry to bother you, Mrs. Cahill. I know I look like a derelict," I said, "but I'm not, just a guy who had an accident a couple of days ago. My name is Nick Bertetto, and I'm with the *Indianapolis Standard*. I've tried calling you but haven't been able to get through. Do you have a couple of minutes to help me with a story about your husband?"

"How did you find me?" she asked.

"I'm a good reporter," I answered.

She looked like she was going to shut the door, so I started talking. "I know this is a difficult time for you, but the *Standard* is doing everything we can to provide information that may help locate Representative Cahill. If there's anything that's missing in our stories, anything we haven't covered yet, we want to get it in the paper in hopes the police will get new leads." Not to mention it sells papers. I gave her my best look of concern.

She ran her hand through her shoulder-length hair, brushing it away from her face. It was then I noticed that she had a little too much makeup in one spot on her cheek. While I didn't mean to stare, I wondered if it was covering a bruise.

"It'll just take a few minutes, I promise," I said.

She gave me the raised eyebrow once-over, appraising me like a piece of meat. "I guess I could take a couple of minutes," she said. "Come in."

Perhaps she had a thing for roughed-up investigative reporters. "If it's not too much trouble."

"It won't be as long as you're gone before my brother gets back. He's very protective of me."

I nodded. "Yes, I've spoken with him."

She gave a vague smile. "You obviously weren't put off . . ." She opened the door.

"No, ma'am." I stepped in.

"Call me Cheryl."

She guided me from the parquet entryway to the white-carpeted living room. I hoped I hadn't tracked anything in.

"What is it I can help you with?" she asked when I was seated on the couch and she in a rocking chair across the dark coffee table from me.

"Are you aware that the police have questioned a homeless man in connection with your husband's disappearance?"

She showed no signs of surprise, but then, it had been in the papers.

"From what I know, I don't see the connection, but the police are checking into it," she said. She pulled her shoulders back and the sundress drew tight around her breasts. I couldn't help noticing, but I tried to pretend I hadn't.

"I don't see the connection, either, but apparently he knew something about how your husband had been dressed before he disappeared."

She nodded and shifted the rocking chair a little to give me a better look at her profile.

I still wasn't buying. "I've talked to your husband's secretary about the one detail the homeless man seemed aware of. Ms. Blackard tells me your husband had quite a collection of colorful pocket handkerchiefs."

She made a face at Judith's name. "That bitch," she muttered to herself.

I jumped on it. "You and she didn't get along?"

"You're not making a note about what I just said, are you?" she asked, alarmed.

I wanted to, but doing so would probably end the conversation, and I was after a whole lot more than that. "Not if you don't want me to."

"I don't."

"Do you mind, though, if I ask why you two didn't get along? Off the record, of course."

Cheryl Cahill leaned back, looking at me like I was a spot on the white plush carpet. That'll stop the "come hither" stuff, I thought.

"It's just that mentioning handkerchiefs set me off," she said, her voice taking on an ever-so-faint nasty tone. "Judith Blackard was one of those old-school secretaries who handled personal as well as business matters for their bosses. Before Cal and I were married, she handled a lot of things she shouldn't have, especially when you're on the taxpayers' dime, like making his haircut appointments—something Cal should have done whether he was married or not. Anyway, I've managed to straighten it all out with her. Forget I said anything about it."

"Sure." Like hell I would. "I'd still like to ask about the handkerchiefs, though. Did he have any favorites, something like a lucky color maybe, that he wore on particular occasions?"

She narrowed her eyes. "No, why?"

I was fairly certain she was lying. "Something the homeless man had said made me wonder. Probably has nothing to do with anything." I paused, but she didn't pick up on her cue to say something revealing. Disappointed, I moved onto another topic, the one Ryan wanted me to check on. "How long have you and Mr. Cahill been married?"

"About seven years."

"Do you have any children?"

"Cal does, from a previous marriage."

"Do you know how I could get in touch with them? Does everyone get along?" I threw the two questions together as though they were related, as though I expected to get in touch with them only if everyone were amicable. Really, I was more interested in her response to the latter question.

Cheryl's ears perked up. "Do you hear someone pulling in the driveway?" she asked.

Great. The brother.

"That's probably my brother. He won't be very happy to see you."

So few people are. "Well, we were almost done here." I knew I'd have to make it quick. "Did you say the family gets along well?"

"I didn't say."

"Oh. Do they?"

She looked toward the door as if hoping the brother would come in. "Cal's children have made it clear they want little to do with us."

"That probably bothers Mr. Cahill."

"He wishes things were otherwise."

"And you?"

"I wish a lot of things were otherwise. You're cute, but pushy, you know that?"

"I've heard the pushy part more than once."

A booming voice echoed in the house. "Cheryl?"

"In here, David."

I stood up. David appeared, looking nothing like I thought he would. From his ill demeanor and threats, I'd pictured him as an ogre—tall, heavyset, and ugly with dark features. Instead he looked like a surfer. His hair was a blond dye job gone bad, and his tanned face held blue eyes, level with mine, that radiated suspicion.

"I didn't know we had company," he said.

"David, this is a reporter with the *Indianapolis Standard*, Nick Bertetto."

I held out my hand. He shook it, too firmly. I knew what it meant but I wasn't intimidated. I'd been beaten up by better than him.

"A reporter from the *Standard* called yesterday at your house in Vincennes," he told Cheryl. Then he turned to me. "Was it you?"

I nodded. "Yes it was."

He put clenched fists on his hips. "Thought I told you my sister wasn't doing any interviews."

"Yes, you said that, but I wanted to ask *her*. And she let me in."

"I did, David," Cheryl affirmed. "It's okay. We're almost done."

I knew I'd only get a couple of more questions in. David continued to glare. I focused my attention on Cheryl and was reminded again how youthful she looked. "How did you and Mr. Cahill meet?" I asked.

She frowned. "We met at a social function."

"Which social function?"

"I don't know. I can't remember."

"How long ago?"

"About eight years."

"And you've been married . . ."

"About seven."

"In that time, has he ever disappeared like this?"

"Of course not."

"What did you do before you married Mr. Cahill?"

David physically interrupted by stepping between Cheryl and me and clamping a hand around my forearm to usher me out. "Time limit's up," he said. "The interview's over."

I stepped out of his hold. "She hasn't answered the question yet."

"Look, pal, I'm getting tired of you."

I decided he wasn't the type to respond to gentility. "It's mutual. I'm here because I have a job to do. And your sister let me in. So let me finish and I'll leave peacefully."

Cheryl Cahill looked from me to David and back again. "I think I've answered enough questions," she said. "I need to lie down." She turned and left.

David's eyes lit up in triumph. He grinned at me. "Let me show you out." He walked me toward the front door.

His protective nature got me thinking of the makeup on Cheryl Cahill's face, that it might be covering a bruise. I took a shot. "I'm not Cahill, David. You don't need to protect your sister from me like you do from him."

His jaw dropped. "Who told you that?"

"I know what kind of man Cahill is." Another bluff.

He stared at me, and I could almost hear the gears grinding in his brain. Slowly he came to the conclusion I was guessing. "And what kind is that?" he asked.

I opened the door. "The kind who could disappear on your sister," I said. I closed the door behind me before he could say another word.

CHAPTER SIXTEEN

I swiftly left Windermere Street. The van's clock showed it was just past ten a.m., so I had lots of time before the noon luncheon with Ryan and the lobbyist for the Indiana Casino Association. I took Keystone south to I-465, went over to Meridian, and then drove south, keeping my eyes open for a coffee house. After I got back into the city, I found a Hubbard & Cravens. Before entering, though, I sat in the parking lot and dialed Ryan Lockridge on my cell phone. I got his answering machine.

"Ryan, it's Nick. I just finished talking to Cheryl Cahill. There's something stirring in the back of my head that makes me think our missing representative may have been abusive. Heard any rumors? And what do you know about David Sanders, Cheryl's brother? If you get this message before lunch, give me a call. Otherwise I'll see you at the Federal Club."

I disconnected and went into Hubbard & Cravens for a tall decaf. Knowing I would have a large lunch, I didn't order the sesame seed bagel I would like to have had. I doctored the coffee to my tastes, then I sat down at a table to decide what to do next.

Cheryl Cahill needed to be protected from her husband. At least her brother felt so. And it was possible I'd seen a bruise. Or not. But there are other kinds of abuses, too. Could be verbal, could be psychological. Maybe Calvin liked a bit of kinky sex. Judith had certainly implied that.

The question was, where could I find out?

Supposedly the lobbyist we were to meet had some inside information on Cahill. She might know something. Also, I could try Virginia Weber again. Maybe this time she would talk. I pulled out a notepad and labeled the page, "Things to find out." Cahill's bad habits went at the top.

Second on the list was to have a meaningful talk with Eli about being picked up by the truck driver. Was the man I met this morning the "Paul" Eli had hitched a ride with? Had Eli invented the whole thing or was Paul lying? I didn't want to accuse either one, but they couldn't both be right. I confessed to being a little creeped out by the news that Paul had seemed to think the time had gone very fast, although his logbook had showed he didn't set any speed records. I wasn't sure what that was all about. It was, however, residing in the same part of my brain as Eli's angels—strange and mysterious at this point.

A third entry, brought to mind by the stares of the *barista* when he got my decaf, was, who was behind my getting beaten up? My eye was still tender and I knew it looked ugly. Who wanted me off the seemingly cold trail of Cahill's disappearance? There were several possibilities, and I really wanted to believe it was McCutcheson, but no suspect was any more likely than another.

I leaned back in the chair and breathed in the coffee aroma. It always smelled good. I had started drinking coffee at an early age, around ten, a very Old World kind of thing my parents let me do. At first Mom and Dad made it half milk/half coffee with a lot of sugar thrown in so I'd get used to the taste. By high school I was drinking it with just a touch of milk and sugar. Today I can drink it black, but I really like it better lightened and sweetened a bit, dark roast coffee especially.

My brain wanted to continue to work on the Cahill story but I'd reached an impasse, at least until after lunch. I turned a sheet over in my notebook and made a different list, this time on possible assignments. Got to keep the pipeline flowing when you're a freelancer.

A couple of magazine editors owed me answers on stories I'd proposed to them. Both had bought my work before, and I knew them well enough to make phone calls. Supposedly some editors are bugged when freelancers call, but if you've got a good track record I don't think that's a problem. I've gotten work before, not because stories I'd proposed were accepted, but because an editor was thinking about a story when I called and decided to assign it to me.

Of course, the way to really make money is to find different angles for the same basic story so that the research you've done can be used over and over again in different markets. Thus, the interview with the vegetarian chef, which I'd done for *Healthful Living*, could be turned into a nice feature for *Indianapolis Life*, a city magazine. It was just a matter of refocusing and repackaging the piece to show that a cutting-edge chef was making a successful go of it in Indianapolis.

I bought a refill on the coffee and returned to the van so I could make the calls in private. It took forty-five minutes, but in the end I had a "go" from one of the editors who owed me a response and a "maybe" from *Indianapolis Life* if I'd do the piece on spec (which I'd probably do). I left a couple of additional voice mail messages and wrote a proposal which I could type later. Then I took a trip into the Hubbard & Cravens restroom with my suit so I could change for lunch.

The Federal Club is located on Monument Circle, the

center of Indianapolis, a roundabout where north-south Meridian Street meets east-west Market Street. It's also only two blocks from the Statehouse. I took Meridian south. Traffic flow wasn't bad since the lights are pretty well synchronized. I was right on target, time-wise. When I reached the Circle, I found a garage adjacent to the Federal Club, parked, and walked back to the entrance.

The Federal Club is a venerable institution on the southwest quadrant of the circle. Dating back to 1911, the building has a neo-Classic look, with four pillars that span the three-story distance from the ground to the roof. They flanked the darkly tinted glass doors of the entryway. I used the revolving door. In my youth all the downtown department stores had revolving doors, and I've always thought it was fun to quick-step through them. Plus, I could avoid the snooty doorman who opened the other entry and welcomed members by name.

Rich, dark paneling is ubiquitous at the Federal Club, as is low lighting from chandeliers, each containing hundreds of dim bulbs and sparkling crystals which reflect the glow. Arched, painted ceilings add to the feeling of antiquity that permeate the air like dust in a museum storeroom. I crossed the mosaic floor and boarded an elevator with five well-dressed individuals who looked like bankers. Checking my appearance in the brass elevator doors, I noticed my seven-year-old suit, which made me feel shabby. But all my elevator companions saw was my damaged face. Ryan had better be up here, I thought. I didn't want to have to stand around and wait.

At the third floor, the elevator door opened to a narrow waiting area presided over by a hostess at a podium. Dressed in a business suit herself, she smiled professionally at the six of us.

"Six today, Mr. Strauss?" she asked the elder of the bankers.

"Just five. The gentleman is with another party." He nodded at me.

I nodded back. "I'm meeting Jayne Warner for lunch," I told the hostess.

"She's already here. I'll seat you in a moment."

While waiting for her to return, I scanned the dining room. Facing south, it had six large windows set into walls covered in paisley wallpaper; it looked like something from a funeral home. Each window had burgundy velvet drapes tied back, revealing inner sheers that diffused the light. There were elegant circular booths by the windows, with smaller booths and tables scattered around the rest of the room. Ryan waved from a booth for four, but the hostess was returning so I let her officially seat me. Ryan made the introduction to Jayne Warner.

"Thank you for seeing us," I said.

"You're welcome," she replied. We shook hands. Jayne was in her mid-thirties, like Ryan and me, but radiated a sophistication I would be hard-pressed to duplicate. She seemed very at ease with the surroundings and the circumstances. Her short black hair came down to her jaw line, with locks tucked behind her ear on one side. She had a large smile with straight white teeth; her glasses were wide ovals in a bronze wire frame. Her eyes were honey brown.

"Ryan has been filling me in on your investigation," she said quietly. "Most interesting."

I looked over at Ryan, so obviously smitten with her that his tongue was practically hanging out of his mouth. I wondered what all he had told her. Probably more than he would have told anyone else, but I was certain his professionalism had stopped him from blabbing everything. Surely.

"You understand why we wanted to come, then?" I asked.

"Of course. But I'm not sure I can really help you beyond getting you in."

"If you could show us around later, that would help. For now, anything you could tell us about Calvin Cahill would be appreciated, and where you see him fitting in on the new gambling legislation."

A waiter came and asked if we were ready to order. I hadn't had a chance to study the limited menu, but went ahead and ordered what Ryan ordered, a beef medallions dish that was one of the specials. Jayne asked for a chicken Caesar salad. The two of them already had drinks, Ryan a beer and Jayne a goblet of white wine. Although I almost never drink alcohol at lunch, I ordered a glass of red wine to be sociable.

When the waiter left, Jayne held Ryan and me in her gaze. "Keep in mind that none of this is for your story. If you decide at some point you want to use it, you'll need to get my permission."

Ryan's head bobbed up and down quickly in agreement. Any moment, I thought, his eyes will turn into little hearts like a lovesick cartoon character's.

"Likewise," I said, "we want you to hold any information we share in the strictest confidence."

Jayne agreed, and took a sip of her wine. "When I first took this position as a lobbyist for the firm, I was warned that Calvin Cahill is sexist," she said, setting her glass down so softly that the wine barely moved when it touched the white tablecloth. "He is definitely that. It's not really disrespect for any woman's abilities, I think, so much as he simply sees all women as possible conquests. It's an ego thing. He's got power and position and he's willing to use them to get what he wants. To be honest, getting propositioned by him gets old very quickly."

"Why hasn't anyone filed a harassment suit?"

"For one thing, he's really good at it. The propositions are so subtle that harassment would be a difficult thing to prove. I'm a lawyer and I'd have a hard time convincing a jury. Another thing is that you can work around that aspect of him. He's professional enough to know when to back off."

The waiter dropped off my wine. I thanked him and waited for him to leave before I asked her another question. "He's on his second marriage. Do you think infidelity is the reason?"

She gave a slight shrug. "It's probably a contributing factor."

Ryan's brain must've engaged sometime during our conversation, because he asked the next question. "Do you run into that problem with other representatives or senators?"

"Not so much. A little with the older ones, who, like Cahill, obviously got used to being bribed with sex when they did that sort of thing decades ago."

I sat up. "What?"

"You didn't know that?" Ryan said.

"What I've heard," Jayne said to me, "and I'm pretty sure it's true, is that back in the sixties and early seventies when the state legislature was still mostly a man's world, some of the 'gifts' given to certain key lawmakers were encounters with prostitutes."

"I guess I knew it," I said, "but I didn't think it was as widespread as you describe."

Jayne laughed. "After working with some of these

guys, I'm willing to bet it was an effective form of lobbying."

"Let me ask you this," I said. "Does 'Cahill wore red' mean anything to you?"

She gave a blank look. "No," she said, "should it?"

"Not necessarily," Ryan said, interrupting me. "It's something a suspect said about Cahill."

"I suppose red could be some kind of signal, but no, it doesn't mean anything to me."

Lunch arrived, and we began to eat.

"Explain to me how you read Cahill and McCutcheson on the proposed legislation to expand gambling," I said after a few bites.

"McCutcheson is for it; Cahill is on the fence. It's pretty simple," Jayne replied.

"What makes Cahill on the fence?"

"On the positive side, the district that neighbors his is the place where a new casino would go. The spillover effect onto his district would be substantial. However, he's personally against gambling. There's also his son, who works against all forms of gambling, but since they don't get along, it's questionable whether it has any effect on his thinking."

I sipped the Merlot. It was quite good, as was the beef. "Why hasn't he let the bill out of committee?"

"There's limited time to get any bills out of committee, and since he's unsure about this one, it's easy to let it slide. Plus, I think there's more than a touch of ego involved. Cahill loves to flaunt his power, especially to people like McCutcheson. The bill had a lot of backers, and Cahill seemed to enjoy throwing his weight around."

"Are you working on a way to get to him?" Ryan asked.

"Of course."

"Do you work for all the casinos in Indiana?" My question.

"In a sense. I'm a registered lobbyist for the Casino Association, and all the riverboats and horse tracks are members, so I do work for all of them. But they all have their own lobbyists. Often we work in concert, but not always, and not this time."

Ryan seemed surprised. "Why not this time?"

She sipped a bit of her wine and ate a bite of salad before she continued. The way we'd been questioning her, she hadn't had much of a chance to eat.

"With a recession underway, revenues are down for everyone," she answered. "Another casino boat may divide up the pie more. More people may gamble overall, but some existing boats, especially those in other parts of southern Indiana, may see a decrease as regulars try out the new place. Plus, the state is looking to increase gaming taxes, a provision which is in the bill as it now stands. They did the same thing last session when dockside gambling was approved. If the casino boat operator is afraid he'll end up with lower revenue and higher taxes, he won't be in favor of this legislation."

"What about the horse tracks?"

"The horse tracks are not really popular with casino boats, but they're often on the same side because they appeal to different crowds. The new legislation, though, calls for adding pull-tab gambling machines to the horse tracks. Now the tracks start to compete with the casino boats. Again, some operators are really concerned. The 'give-'em-an-inch' syndrome. What we have here is a complex issue for the Casino Association. Our position is generally pro-gambling, but not all our members like this particular legislation."

We chatted a while longer, Ryan and I listening to Jayne talk about the legislature. We asked a few questions about how she got into the business. Apparently, as a lawyer in one of the more prestigious firms in Indianapolis, she'd become friendly with enough legislators that the jump to lobbyist was a natural. She'd chosen the Casino Association job because it came at the right time for her.

About the time she asked about my background, I noticed McCutcheson come in the dining room. He sat near us at a booth for six. Dressed in gray slacks, a white button-down shirt, a red tie, and a blue blazer, he looked appropriate enough for the Federal Club but not quite in the same class as the others at his table, clothed in expensive, conservative business suits. I kept an eye on him as I filled her in.

When I had finished, something interesting happened. Instead of the waitress bringing McCutcheson his drink, the bartender came over with it. Though he was wearing a loose, white tuxedo shirt, the bartender clearly had size. He leaned in toward McCutcheson and said something. McCutcheson looked visibly upset. The bartender walked away. A minute later I saw the bartender disappear out the door. McCutcheson noticed it but tried to appear as though he hadn't been watching. He said something to the rest of his table and started walking toward the door.

Impulsively, I excused myself to the restroom and followed McCutcheson out, but at a distance.

CHAPTER SEVENTEEN

McCutcheson went past the restroom door and down the hall. He turned a corner and for a moment I couldn't see him. I heard a door open. I picked up the pace and reached the corner just in time to see a stairway door close. I didn't want to lose him on the stairs, but neither did I want him to see me following. I waited ten seconds and then opened the door as quietly as I could.

The staircase was an original part of the building and looked old. The lights were adequate but not bright. The steps had been painted brown, the walls off-white with a bluish hue. This was not an area the club spent money on.

I heard footsteps on the stairs above me and then another door opening. Once the door closed and I could hear no other sounds, I bounded up. The footsteps couldn't have been more than one flight above, so I opened the door on the next floor and looked around. McCutcheson wasn't there, but a restroom was. I hurried over to it. There was a transom above the door, an indication of the building's age, and it was propped open. I could hear voices. They weren't loud, but I could make out the conversation. One of the voices had a down-home cadence that I was pretty sure was McCutcheson's. The other, I assumed, was the bartender's.

"I don't want any more of your services. You know that. I've already made that clear," said McCutcheson.

"I'm not here about that. You called me about the leak. I'm in the process of plugging it." The voice was deep.

"I didn't call about any leak."

"Yes, you did. Once Tuesday, and then yesterday. You may have used a voice synthesizer, but only you knew to contact me."

"I'm telling you, it wasn't me. I don't own a voice synthesizer and I don't want anything more to do with you."

I heard a scuffling inside, and I got the impression the bartender was manhandling the much smaller McCutcheson.

"Look, I don't want to hurt you, I just want answers," the bartender said. "How did the reporter find out about Cahill? No one else knows."

"Hell, everybody knows. It's just that you've got everyone blackmailed, so no one will tell."

"I'm not asking everyone else. I'm asking you. I know it was you who called. No one knows about *me*. I've been careful."

"But why would I call you and let you know, if I was the one who tipped the reporter?"

"Maybe you let it slip, then thought better of it, and you wanted me to take care of the problem. Whatever. But the second phone call annoyed me. This has got to stop, understand? No more leaks."

"I swear, no one has or ever will find out from me. I'm not the one who called. I was as surprised when the reporter approached me as I am now to have you threatening me. Let go."

There was more scuffling, and then I heard someone approaching the restroom door from the inside. I looked both ways for somewhere to hide. There was a soda machine a few feet down the hall on the left. I had no time to wonder if I could fit in the cove with it, I just had to run down there and try. As I flattened myself against the machine and

167

squeezed in the hole, I heard the door open. No one passed me, so I assumed they had gone the other direction. I waited a full minute, then stuck my head out. No one was there.

Inching back out, I leaned against the machine. My heart rate had just returned to normal when the restroom door opened again and Frank McCutcheson stepped out.

His blue sport coat was ruffled a bit and sweat was on his forehead. He was in the process of straightening his tie when he saw me. He marched over. "What did you hear?"

"Hear?" I asked.

At that moment, the bartender came back around the corner. He spotted us talking. "You," he said.

"Me?"

He breezed across the carpet and gripped me by the shoulders. His hands were strong. Taller than I was by a good four inches, he leaned his tanned face toward me. The pale brown eyes had menace in them.

"What are you doing here?" he asked.

"Going to the restroom," I said. "The one downstairs was crowded, so I came up here."

At that moment the smell of his cologne hit me and I froze. Calvin Klein's Obsession. Just like the guy who'd attacked me. Hildy had described the man as white, six foot two, muscular build. The guy fit the description.

Before he could say or do anything, I heard another voice in the hall. "There you are," said Ryan. McCutcheson, the bartender, and I all looked at him. I was never so glad to see Ryan in my life.

"Jayne is waiting downstairs to give us the tour," he said, coming over to us. "Did you get lost going to the restroom?"

Instantly the bartender let go of me.

"He did," the bartender said, trying to make light of a difficult situation. "I was just showing him the way." I took a step back and could see the bartender fully now. In addition to the white tuxedo shirt, he had on a black cummerbund, black pants, and shoes. Laying a heavy arm over my shoulder, he pulled me in tightly to his side and propelled me along to the restroom. "It's here, sir. Are you sure you can find your way back? I'll be happy to wait for you."

"No, that's okay, thanks," I said. I was getting the message. "I'll just go in now," I added. Which I did. And I used the urinal immediately.

When I came back out, Ryan was the only one there.

"Is Jayne really down there?" I asked.

"Yes," he said. "What was that all about?"

I looked around. "Tell you later," I whispered.

Downstairs, Jayne apologized for not being able to give us a tour, but she said she had to get back to work.

"You have to leave?" Ryan asked.

She smiled. "I'm sorry, but I really do have to get back. I'll take you to the Membership Director's office. I'm sure someone there can show you around."

Behind her back, Ryan mouthed to me, "Nice going, Nick. If you hadn't taken so long . . ." He scowled.

We followed Jayne to the elevator and she took us down to the second floor, then led us down a long hall. A wooden door with a wide expanse of glass lay ahead of us. "Director of Membership" was lettered on the glass.

Ryan reached the door ahead of Jayne and held it open for her. I followed.

A woman at the receptionist's desk stared into a computer screen, typing. Behind her stood another woman wearing a well-tailored business suit, gray pinstripe, with a blue oxford blouse. Though she struck me as being a recent marketing MBA grad in her early thirties, she might have been younger. She looked up when we entered, and Jayne introduced her to us as Amy Gatwick.

"We're reporters for the *Indianapolis Standard*," Ryan said, "and we're doing research into the Calvin Cahill disappearance. We know he was here just before he vanished. Jayne was kind enough to take us to lunch so we could get a feel for the Club. If you don't mind showing us around, we'd appreciate it. We'd especially like to see the room where he made his speech and then the pool and locker room. We understand he told friends he was headed to the pool after his speech, but disappeared after that."

Amy's receptionist called up something on her computer. "Mr. Cahill's speech was in the Great Lakes Room, and that's occupied for another fifteen minutes," she said.

Amy thanked her and said to us, "Jayne mentioned that she would stop by with you, so I reserved a little time. We need to get going, though. Perhaps I could show you the pool first."

Jayne said goodbye, and soon Amy was leading us down a narrow, second-floor hallway with muted yellow plaid wallpaper. We passed several bulletin boards devoted to athletic activities, and up ahead I could see a door marked "gymnasium." I glimpsed a basketball court through a window before Amy pushed on a stairwell door and took us down to the first floor via a set of concrete steps painted brown, similar to the ones I'd used following McCutcheson earlier.

"I hope you don't mind using the stairs," she said, her voice echoing in the stairwell. "Generally only the staff uses them to keep from being seen by guests. I hate waiting for the elevators though, especially around lunchtime."

On the first floor we came out into a hallway that looked

almost identical to the second floor.

"Where does the staircase go, leading up?" I asked.

"On the second floor, where we just came from, we were close to the athletic center—the gymnasium, weight and exercise rooms, squash courts, tennis courts, you know. On the third floor, the staircase lets out near the kitchen. Above that are the banquet floors and the hotel room floors."

Judith had mentioned the other day that some of the legislators stayed at the Federal Club. "How many hotel rooms are there?"

"Fifty-two. Members can rent them. In fact, some of the state legislators from out of town stay here during the session. We also have reciprocal privileges with other clubs and their members can use them, too."

"Are they occupied most of the time?" Ryan asked.

She nodded. "With so many major events going on in town and with our location, we have very little vacancy. The club amenities make them especially attractive. We're an exclusive alternative to hotels."

"Does Cahill stay here?"

"Occasionally," she replied. "He's from Vincennes."

"You said we were near the athletic center on the second floor. Are there locker rooms there, too?" I asked.

"Yes, and it's a larger area. When the pool was added twenty-five years ago, the Club couldn't put it on the second floor with the rest of the athletic facilities. So they added smaller locker rooms to serve the pool."

She pointed to the entrance to the men's locker room beneath a lighted red "Pool" sign that jutted into the hall.

"You can go on in from there," she said. "I'll use the ladies' entrance down the hall. The pool door is marked from the inside. I'll meet you on the pool deck."

I didn't think the men's locker room looked all that

small. To the right were two alcoves with about twenty lockers each, arranged in a U around a wooden bench. To the left were two sinks, two urinals, and two toilet stalls, all very clean and modern. The walls on the left were tiled white to the ceiling, except for a row of black tiles about shoulder height. A shower area was at the far end of the room.

"No one could hide effectively in here," I said to Ryan. "Either he went through and was in the pool area, or he never got here."

When we entered the pool area we saw two women and two men swimming laps. The pool was fifty meters long with five lanes. I could smell the ever-present chlorine and feel the humidity stick the clothes to my body.

Amy was waiting for us by the hot tub, a separate unit near the shallow end of the pool.

"Do you know if Mr. Cahill swims here often?" I asked Amy.

"The police asked that question. I heard the pool manager say it's usually twice a week."

"Are there regular swimmers at that time? Did any of them see him?" I asked, although I already knew the answer. The police had talked to everyone who had been in the pool that day. No one had seen him in the area, and there had been no time at which at least one person wasn't in the pool. The police had cleared everyone.

Amy confirmed it. I looked at my watch. We still had time before we could get into the Great Lakes Room, where Cahill had given his speech. She saw me look at my watch.

"If you don't have any questions here, perhaps I could show you around until the Great Lakes Room is free," she suggested.

Ryan and I agreed. She led us to the elevators this time.

"We'll start at the top and work our way down," she said.

We started at the seventh floor. She showed us a couple of the beautiful banquet rooms—the smallish Hunting Room, with its deep green carpeting and trophy wall mountings, and the larger Racing Room, with black and white floor tile and vintage race car wallpaper. Both had great views of the city. From the Hunting Room, I could see down to a small roof that jutted out over the east side of the building.

"What's under the roof down there?" I asked.

"The athletic center on the second floor."

I was too far up to see where the tower we were in met the roof, but if the third floor was like this one, there would be windows that looked out onto that roof. I wondered if they opened.

Amy was moving ahead to the upper floor kitchen which serviced the banquet rooms. She referred to it as "back of the house."

"That's what we call the areas members don't see, like the kitchens or stairwells or security room."

"Where's the security room?"

"It's on the third floor. We have small cameras mounted at each exit. That way one guard can observe who's coming and going."

"Do you videotape it?"

"Yes."

"Have the police seen the videos from the day Cahill disappeared?"

"Nearly everyone has seen the videos. The staff was asked to watch them, too, to see if we noticed anything out of the ordinary. No one did. The police kept the videos."

That answered one question. If I wanted to see them, I'd

have to negotiate with the police. Maybe Detective Claire Hurst would be willing.

Ryan spoke up. "If you don't mind, I'd like to see one of your hotel rooms."

She shrugged. "It's just a hotel room, really."

"Still, I'd like to look at one."

She said okay and took us "back of the house" to the sixth floor. Both the fifth and sixth floors were mostly hotel rooms.

It took a minute or two to locate a maid and get her to open one of the rooms. While Ryan and I stood there, I examined the door. It looked vaguely familiar, but I couldn't place where I'd seen it.

"This is a fairly typical room," Amy said, when we'd been let in. "They're all arranged a little differently, but they have the same things."

From what I could see, that meant a queen-sized bed, a television, nightstand with clock, two comfortable chairs, a table, and a desk. The desk was solid wood and much nicer than you would find in the average hotel, but still ordinary.

Ryan wandered around the room, examining everything. I was beginning to see where Ryan was going with this. The rooms were an ideal place for Cahill to disappear into.

"Thanks," Ryan said, as we left the room.

The Great Lakes Room, which was on the fourth floor, was relatively small. We reached it as the last of the occupants was leaving and the kitchen staff was coming in to clean up. The room was narrow. A lectern stood at one end, and twelve tables seating eight each were arranged over the rest of the floor. The tables were covered in white tablecloths and the remains of a chicken dish were congealing on plates, waiting to be removed. The room was blue and featured a large mural of a Great Lakes map from the early days of pioneer settlement. There was one other way out of the room—a single wooden door across the back. Ryan noticed it at the same time I did.

"Where does that door lead?" he asked.

"Out to the hall," Amy replied. "It serves mainly as an emergency exit. The staff occasionally use it if an event calls for serving during a program, but largely it goes unused."

"Do we know if Cahill used it?" he asked.

"As far as we know, he didn't. Witnesses say he shook hands out there," she paused and indicated the anteroom outside the double doors, "before he left. No one remembers him coming back into this room."

I looked around the room again. I could picture Cahill giving his speech here, but that was all I got out of it.

On the third floor Amy showed us the kitchen. I wanted to see the security room.

"I'm sorry, but that's one place I can't show you," she said. "Please understand, not even members can get a look at it. The Board, of course, has access, and we've given the police permission to enter it, but the fewer people who know how it works, the less chance there is to breach it."

"How about just a peek inside the room?" I asked.

Amy sounded very definite. "Sorry, those are club rules."

Ryan and I thanked her for the tour, and she said she would see us out. As we walked toward the elevator, I spotted the bartender heading toward the back of the house. He hadn't seen me.

"Who's the bartender?" I asked when I was sure he was out of earshot.

"Chance Marston. Why?"

"I think I know him."

"You might be able to catch him if you hurry. He's probably on his way out. He only works through the lunch hour. How do you know him?"

"Well, maybe I don't," I said evasively. "That name doesn't ring a bell. He looks familiar, though. Has he worked here long?"

"At least as long as I have, three years. He's very popular. Some members prefer to eat lunch at the bar and talk to him."

"Maybe I will try to catch up with him," I said. I added a hasty goodbye and hustled off after Marston, leaving Ryan with a bewildered look on his face. I turned around halfway down the hall and motioned to Ryan that I'd call him.

If Marston was heading for his car, he would be parked in the same garage I'd parked in. I had no intention of catching him, but I planned to tail him for a while. Plugging the leak, indeed. He worked for someone other than the hotel, someone who wanted me gone or at least off the story. With any luck, he'd lead me to whoever that was.

CHAPTER EIGHTEEN

I didn't see Marston in the hall ahead of me. Where the hallway made a T with another hall, I looked both ways. The right corridor ended at a door marked "Garage, First Floor." I opened the door cautiously, in case the bartender had set up an ambush, but no one was there. Relieved, I looked for the visitor section where I'd parked the van. I found it, climbed in, and started the engine. Within in a minute Marston drove by in a black Mustang and pulled up to the gate for employees. Then he drove out of the garage.

I quickly backed out of my space, drove to the attended gate, and paid the clerk. Traffic only goes one way around the Circle, so I hung a right and spotted the Mustang turning west onto Market Street. Maneuvering around a stalled Camaro, I pulled into the right lane, reached the Market Street intersection, and made the same turn. There was a gray Honda Accord between us, and that worked fine for me. The van was tall enough I could see over the Honda and keep track of the Mustang without being directly in Marston's rear view. As long as he wasn't looking for a tail, I figured I would be okay.

There's an art to tailing someone, and at times like these I wished I'd taken the time to learn it. The best advice I'd heard on the subject was to think about what you'd see if someone was tailing you and make sure your subject didn't see any of those things. I kept that in mind but hoped

Marston was thinking about something else as I pursued him.

Two blocks later, where Market Street ends at Capitol Avenue, I almost lost him. The green light was short. While the Mustang and the Honda rushed the yellow and squeaked through, I couldn't make it. I stopped in time to see a policewoman in an unmarked car pointed south on Capitol waiting for the light to turn. She'd have nailed me for sure.

But I got lucky. The Mustang moved into the right turn lane for Washington Street and had to wait for pedestrians. By the time he was able to turn, the light had changed for me, and I pulled into the turn lane two cars behind him. I watched him speed away, only to be trapped at a light two intersections down. In no time I was reasonably well positioned in the same general clump of traffic headed west, one lane over and two cars behind him. We rolled together, crossing the bridge near the zoo. Then I dropped back, putting five cars between us as we continued west on Washington Street and the distance between traffic lights lengthened.

As I followed, I thought about the conversation between Marston and McCutcheson. McCutcheson denied that he'd leaked anything to "the reporter," which I presumed was me. Leaked what? It was something about Cahill, and all I could think of was that Cahill had worn red. That came from Eli. Was he a "leak"? If so, how was he connected to Marston? Or whoever employed Marston?

McCutcheson denied he'd called the bartender. If Frank was telling the truth, then someone else had put Marston on to me. Who?

Then there were the hotel rooms. Why had that one seemed familiar? Ryan and I had both been intrigued. They were easily accessible, but at the same time discreetly handled. Anyone renting a room was either a member of the Federal Club or of a related, high-priced club. The staff would look the other way to protect privacy.

What did that mean? I wasn't sure, but Calvin Cahill could have disappeared into one of those rooms, either of his own free will or without his consent. Using one of the "back of the house" staircases, he could have easily gone from the pool area up to a room without being seen. That is, if he ever made it to the pool. No one had seen him in either the locker room or the pool area.

Plus, a day had passed before anyone started looking for him. According to reports, Cheryl Cahill had called the police with her concerns the next morning, but an investigation didn't get going until later that day. Nearly twenty-four hours went by between the time he told friends he was going for a swim and the time the police showed up at the Federal Club to search for clues. That gave him a wide interval to get out of the building unnoticed—or be taken out unseen. Whatever had happened, it must have been clever because everyone had seen the videos of the exits and nothing was detected. Could they have used the windows on the third floor that overlooked the athletic complex's roof? Did the windows open? Could someone get onto that roof unnoticed? I needed to check that out. Though I was sure the police had done a thorough job, I wanted a look at the videos myself.

Washington Street is the local name for U.S. 40, the old National Road. Downtown the street is well paved and has many upscale shops and restaurants, not to mention one of the Midwest's premiere playhouses, the Indiana Repertory Theatre. But as the street winds its way out, the neighborhoods become an uneven mix, some in need of repair, some revitalized, some venerable. Going west, I bounced over a railroad crossing in need of repair and followed the Mustang into the booming Hispanic district, an older area of town where the most recent immigrants have settled. We drove past the El Segundo grocery store and other businesses with their signs and billboards in Spanish. Dotted among them were remnants of the street's degenerated past—seedy motels and adult bookstores. Chance Marston in his Mustang continued westward to the outskirts of the county with me in steady pursuit. We were headed toward I-465.

At the Federal Club, Jayne Warner had remarked that the handkerchief might have been a signal of some kind. Did McCutcheson know? I was confident he had lied to me. Maybe he'd had Marston attack me to discourage me from finding out. How was the bartender mixed up in the whole thing anyway? I had to believe the answer would come from the Federal Club. It was the one common denominator in every clue I could come up with. Well, except for Eli. I had no idea where Eli fit into the scheme of things.

We passed under I-465, nearing the airport where I'd been earlier in the day. Washington Street runs along the north side of the airport, and the airport's expansion had changed the character of the neighborhoods. Anything too near the boundaries had been purchased and torn down, making way for businesses. The small, family owned motels which had dotted U.S. 40 during the fifties had succumbed to the newer, high-rise motels along the interstates. The older ones attracted less well-to-do traffic—drifters or families who were struggling financially. Strip bars, though modernized with attractive exteriors and amenities like buffet luncheons, remained fixtures of the community. They shared space on West Washington Street with machine shops and fast food restaurants that had sprung up to support the airport and its daytime personnel.

The black Mustang pulled into the parking lot of one of those businesses, Squared Circle Fitness, a small facility occupying a couple of storefronts in a pole barn redesigned to look like a strip mall. There were several empty spots along the front row and he parked in one of them. I passed the parking lot entrance and pulled into the next lot, the N. Heat Showclub. The lot contained no cars on the side nearest the gym, so I parked closer to the showclub where I could put at least a couple of vehicles between me and the Mustang. Marston got out, opened the trunk, pulled out a gym bag, and went inside. If he had noticed me tailing him, he didn't show it. There were no glances, discreet or otherwise, in my direction.

Wanting to let five minutes or so go by before I drove over to get a closer look at the gym, I examined the N. Heat Showclub building. The place was constructed from split-face block painted off-white, with a brown roof. Horizontal lines of red and blue neon lights circled the building. Though the club was separate from the pole barn shops, they both had the same look and were clearly part of the same complex. The lighted sign along Washington Street announced that an amateur wet t-shirt contest was coming up in two weeks. Idly I wondered what sort of women competed in the professional division.

But then I thought, Calvin Cahill had been a part of the legislature at the time sex had been a part of the lobbying equation. Judith said he'd had sexual difficulties. Who better to take care of those difficulties than a prostitute? Jayne had said that kind of stuff didn't go on any longer, but what if it still did? What if the practice had continued, but more underground? McCutcheson said he didn't want any more "services." Were those the kind Marston provided? Maybe he was pimping in addition to mixing up drinks.

Of course, it was all circumstantial. Marston happened to go to a gym that happened to be in the same complex as a strip club. I cautioned myself that just because a woman was a stripper didn't mean she was a prostitute. But that didn't preclude the possibility of one or two strippers who'd be willing to supplement their incomes in whatever way they could find. How far would the bartender go to satisfy someone's thirsts? Like, maybe Calvin Cahill's?

I should call Ryan, I thought. I checked my watch. Two-thirty. In a half hour someone would need to pick up Stephanie and her friends from St. Rita. Hildy had agreed to do it if I wasn't there, but I felt I should call to remind her before I called Ryan. I used the cell phone.

"Hello, this is the Bertetto residence," Hildy said in her booming voice. I had to hold the phone away from my ear.

"Aunt Hildy, this is Nick," I said. I got a burst of static.

"Just a minute, Nick," she said. The squawks continued in short, staccato fashion for a few more seconds, and then I got a crystal clear reception.

"What was that all about?" I asked her.

"I don't know. Sometimes when I hear noises like that on my cell phone I have to move until I am clear of whatever is causing the problem. Did you move to another place?"

"I couldn't," I said. "I'm sitting here in my car."

"Well, then, I don't know. But it is okay now."

"Good. Aunt Hildy, it looks like I won't be able to get back in time to pick up Stephanie and her friends. Can you take care of it?"

"Of course. I was planning to. When do you think you

will be home? Should I plan supper late?"

"No, I shouldn't be more than another ten minutes here. It's just that I'm pretty far away from Franklin."

"Where are you?"

"On the west side of Indianapolis," I replied.

"There will not be a problem. I have the driving instructions you left on the refrigerator."

"Good. Thanks."

"You are welcome."

Four large guys came out of the gym. I slid my cell phone into the little basket between the two front seats and leaned forward to make sure the bartender wasn't in the group. I didn't recognize any of them but figured I'd better call Ryan before anything new developed. I reached for the cell phone, but it wasn't there. Bending over to see where it had gone, I noticed a wire dangling from the underbelly of the dashboard. I felt around, then ducked under the dash to see what it was. The wire was in shadow and I couldn't make it out. I hunted through the glove compartment and came up with a flashlight. When I shined the light on it, I couldn't believe it. In fact, I had to look twice to be sure what I was seeing.

Someone was very interested in me. The wire was a microphone and I was being bugged.

CHAPTER NINETEEN

My first reaction was panic. I felt violated. Not only had someone broken into my car, they were listening to everything I said. I looked around the parking lot, but there was no one in sight. Serpentine waves of ice slithered down my spine and I shivered. Who was keeping tabs on me?

I tried to slow my breathing and think. I didn't have experience with devices like this. How far was its range? My gut instinct was that whoever was listening would have to be relatively close. Maybe they were following me. I swallowed hard and looked around again.

A woman whom God had apparently endowed with the ability to look up "plastic surgery" in the Yellow Pages came out of the N. Heat Showclub and walked across the parking lot toward the pole barn shops. She glanced in my direction but didn't give the van a second look. Her upper half bounced as she went along. She had long, lean legs that looked even longer thanks to tiny, cut-off jean shorts that hugged her crotch. Had I been in a less apprehensive mood, my testosterone would have surged just watching her walk. She arrived at the gym entrance and went through the same door Marston had.

I looked down at the wire again. I could yank it out from under the dash, but I wasn't sure I should. If I did, whoever was bugging me would know I was onto them. Maybe it was better to pretend I didn't know. Ryan might have some advice. Wished I could call him and ask. If I stepped out of the van to make the call though, it might indicate to someone watching that I knew about the tap.

Instead, I drove the van over to the pole barn shops and parked in the second row. Though I wanted to get back to Franklin where I could call from the relative security of my office, I also wanted to know more about Marston and why he was here. Pulling out my notebook, I made a sketch of the building. The shop on the far right had no windows and no sign outside, but the door was labeled "Richardson Enterprises," with lettering below that read, "No Admittance. Gym Entrance Next Door." The middle shop was the gym, "Squared Circle Fitness, Boxing and Tan"—"Squared Circle" in red and blue neon—written on the front of the building. A muscular male torso in boxing stance, his six-pack abs rigidly defined, was painted on the door. The third shop at the far end had several large windows; written in large lettering was "West Washington Street Coin-Operated Laundry." It boasted of Speed Queen washers and dryers. I copied down the addresses for each tenant. While I was at it, I copied down the license plate number for Marston's black Mustang, parked in front of me. I sat there for about five minutes staring at the place, waiting for something to happen. No one came out or went into any of the shops.

Maybe I should make something happen.

I had to slap myself first. Marston was in there. He'd tried to "plug the leak" once before, and now he knew I was on to him. He was in a place where he felt comfortable. I didn't. Oh, I knew my way around a gym, but not a boxing gym, and especially not this one. What would I do if he saw me?

There might not be another chance like this one, though. Was the gym connected to what was going on? Was Marston here to work out or was he a part of something bigger that was housed here? Taking a deep breath, I knew what I had to do. But first I needed to let someone know where I was.

The obvious choice was Ryan. Despite my earlier apprehension about stepping outside the van to make a call, I did. I brought Ryan's number up on the cell and pressed the dial button. In a few seconds, it was ringing. I prayed. Ryan answered the phone.

I cut off his usual smart remark. "I can't talk right now," I said. "But I'm at the Squared Circle gym on West Washington. If I don't call you back within an hour, call my friend Mark Zoringer and get over here. I may be in trouble." And without giving him time to argue me out of it, I hung up. Then I pulled my gym bag out of the back and locked the van.

Most gyms will let you work out for free once or twice to try their facility. I banked that Squared Circle wouldn't be any different. I pushed open the door and entered.

The gym portion of Squared Circle was underwhelming, even by the modest standards of Mark Zoringer's Franklin Iron Works. To the right was a tiny counter where a woman of retirement age presided over check-in. Just beyond her was the machine portion of the gym, with ten different weight-training stations. The gym equipment was from a manufacturer that had gone bankrupt about a decade ago, but it looked to be in good condition. To my right through an open doorway was the free weight section, with two bench press benches, a rack of dumbbells, two adjustable benches, a stairstepper, and an old exercise bike. A wall of mirrors at the back of the room allowed me to see around the corner into the boxing area. In the whole of the Squared Circle gym there were maybe two people working out, one of whom was the buxom stripper from the N. Heat

Showclub. I didn't see Chance Marston at all.

"Come around here to the front, honey," said the woman behind the counter.

When I rounded the side and got a good look at her, I decided she was actually older than I first thought, maybe in her seventies. She was well-wrinkled around her eyes and her chin sagged. But with friendly brown eyes and a head full of auburn-dyed hair, she was doing her best to look a decade younger.

I told her I was working at the airport and was looking for a place to exercise after work.

She glanced at the stitches over my eye. "Do you box?" she asked.

"Not very well," I replied.

"Normally our manager would give you a tour, but he's not here right now," she said in a nasal voice that made me think of Granny in the old "Beverly Hillbillies" TV show. "I see you have your gym stuff. Would you like to work out? I'll give you three free passes."

I said yes and she gave me a spiel about their rates, hours, and tanning packages. "I can't leave the counter to show you around, but you look like you've been to a gym before," she added. "If you have any questions, I'm here."

She told me where the changing rooms were, a new one in the boxing area and a smaller one tucked behind the exercise machines. I chose the closest one and discovered I'd made a bad choice. Though newly painted white, it had a leaky sink faucet, a drop ceiling with water-stained tile, and a short stack of lockers, six high and five across, that looked like they'd been broken into more than once. I decided to keep my wallet with me.

The first thing I did after I changed was look around. Part of me hoped to locate Chance Marston and part of me didn't. He obviously knew who I was, and I wasn't sure how he'd react. On the other hand, I liked the idea of surprise—I might be able to get something out of him since he wouldn't be expecting me.

I scouted the three rooms that composed the gym. I checked the nicer men's locker room in the boxing area but still found it wanting. I walked past the tanning beds and even lingered outside the women's locker room a moment or two to determine that no one was in there. As I turned, I noticed a vending machine that stocked juices at the far side. A short hallway led away from the machine toward the front of the building. I looked over the juice selection while scouting the hall out of the corner of my eye. The short hallway led to the "Richardson Enterprises" entrance that had been marked no admittance, and off the hall was an office. It had several keyholes on the door. I took a step into the hall. I could see two shadows through the frosted glass pane in the door, one seated and one standing. Though I didn't have a good angle, the bulky, standing shadow could have been cast by Marston. I also noticed several dark shapes about the size of file cabinets just inside the door. I wondered what Richardson Enterprises was and what was in that office.

"Sorry, honey, but that's not part of the gym," the receptionist called.

I turned and found her watching me more intently than she had earlier. One of her hands rested on the counter; the other was below and not visible. That made me kind of nervous. "Oh, sorry," I said, keeping my voice casual. "I didn't know."

I took a few steps over to the machine bench press and did a warm-up set. The buxom stripper was seated next to me at the "pec deck," a machine which exercises chest muscles. She brought her forearms—upright, at her side, and pressed against pads that provided resistance—together in a quarter circle of motion in front of her, causing her breasts to swell against the tight t-shirt she was wearing. She did eight repetitions. By the end of her set, my heart was beating fast and I was making a too-conscious effort not to stare. I noticed that the receptionist was still watching, but now she smirked as though she could read my mind. I moved to the free weight room to use the bench press over there.

Okay, I thought, Marston has to be in the guarded Richardson Enterprises office, because he sure wasn't anywhere else in the gym. There was a certain irony in the fact that the door was locked in a major way with all those keyholes, yet had a frosted pane. Curious. During the rest of my workout I kept my eye on the forbidden hallway and the receptionist kept her eye on me.

Afterwards I changed, thanked her for letting me try out the gym, and asked for the free passes she'd mentioned. She gave them to me, but grudgingly, I thought. She made me fill out my name and address for their records. Of course I wasn't about to give her mine so I gave her Ryan's particulars as a joke. Maybe they'd mail him a lot of literature.

When I got out of the parking lot, I turned east toward the interstate. I stopped in a Super K parking lot, got out of the van again, and called Ryan to let him know I was okay. He wanted details. I promised him those would come after I returned to Franklin.

Continuing on West Washington Street, I stayed alert for any vehicles following me. My untrained eyes saw none. I took the turn for I-465 South and kept watch. For a brief five minutes my heart beat faster as a green Jeep Grand Cherokee switched lanes twice when I did, but then it got off at the Harding Street exit. I took I-65 south to Franklin without further excitement.

Off the interstate going east on the way into Franklin is an apartment complex. I pulled in and drove behind one of the buildings where I couldn't be seen from the main street and could view anyone coming into the area, just in case. It was time to get a better look at the bug.

I got under the dashboard and did a more thorough search of the wire that I had found hanging down. It was a lapel mike with a small cord that must have served as an antennae, because it wasn't attached to anything. Wireless. I searched the rest of the car. It was possible the microphone was broadcasting not to a person, but rather to a recorder. It took awhile, but eventually I found a voice-activated microcassette recorder in the rear of the van under an armrest compartment for the back right seat. It was attached with wide, double-sided tape, fastened so securely the tiny machine didn't wobble at all. The inscription on the machine indicated it was a twelve-hour long-play recorder. Not much of the tape had been used. I rewound it and pressed "play," hearing myself making a phone call to Ryan. After a minute or two, I reset the tape to the place it had been and restarted it.

As long as I knew I was being bugged, I could work around it.

By the time I pulled into my driveway, I felt a little more relaxed, about as relaxed as one can get shortly after discovering that he's being bugged.

I was no sooner in the door than Melissa the Motormouth appeared.

"Hi, Mr. Nick," she said. "Thank you for letting me play. We don't have much room in the motel. Mommy and me had to move. My toys are at my old home until Mommy finds a new home. But Daddy says it's another phase Mommy's going through and it will blow over soon and we'll be back in our old home. I hope so 'cause Mommy's sad now and she says she has to find a job. I don't want her to get a job 'cause she says I'll go to a new school while she's at work. It's all day, that's what Mommy says. So I'm glad that I got to come here and play. Can I stay for dinner?"

Stephanie appeared in the doorway with an old burgundy leather purse of my mom's that Dad had given her. "C'mon, Melissa," she said.

"Okay," said Melissa, and the two girls disappeared.

Hildy sat at the bar in the kitchen sipping a cup of tea. She looked upset. "Did you hear that?" she asked. "Jill and Jason Farrigut are breaking up. It is so sad."

"Do you even know them?"

"Well, no, but it is sad when any couple breaks up."

I sat at the bar across from her. "I've been afraid this would happen eventually, the way things have been going between those two. Melissa tells way more than she should." I couldn't believe I was discussing this with Hildy.

"Do you know where they are staying? They are staying at the old Clover Haven Motel on 144. It is a dump. No place for a child."

"Jill's never told me to drop her off there. How do you know that's where they're staying?"

"I did not know at first. Melissa told me to drop her off at the house even though they were not staying there anymore, because her mother did not want anyone to know. Her mother was waiting when I dropped her off, and so I asked her, and one thing led to another. She needed someone to listen to her. You know I am an easy person to talk to."

"And so you invited Melissa over?"

"Surely you do not mind! And I think she should stay for supper, too."

I could feel a Hildy-induced headache coming on. "It's okay for her to stay, as long as it's okay with Jill Farrigut. I just don't think we should be getting too involved in this. Jason is a volatile guy, and I for one don't need any more people looking for me."

"That reminds me. I am to be the pick-up and drop-off person for Stephanie from now on. The parents in the carpool have decided they do not want to take chances with you."

"What?"

"You know, because of the other night. They feel it is too risky for their children to be in the car with you."

"That isn't true! Tom Colby for one would never *not* trust me with his kid."

Hildy shrugged. "It is true."

"We'll see about that!" I said. I marched out of the kitchen and up to the office, got on the phone, and called Tom. Sure enough, he didn't want me driving Todd around.

"It's not that any of us don't trust you, Nick," he said. "But you can't control whoever might want to stop you from investigating. And don't give me the line about you being the victim of an attempted robbery. You can claim that until you're blue in the face, but who wants to take that chance? Until this thing blows over, we think it's best someone other than you be responsible for the kids. The rest of us will cover the carpool. Plus, Hildy's great! As long as she's staying with you and wants to handle your turn, we're glad to have her."

"But Tom . . ."

"But nothing, Nick. You know if the situation were reversed, you'd be thinking of Stephanie's safety and make the same decision."

I started to protest that I wasn't involved in anything dangerous, but that was the game face I was putting on for the outside world. Tom was right, I'd make the same decision for Steph.

"All right. I guess I can't and shouldn't try to talk you out of it. But I'm really going to miss being with the kids."

"Of course you will. So get the investigation finished, and we'll all go back to normal."

I said goodbye and hung up. If Tom, my closest friend among the Throwbacks, wasn't willing to place Todd in my care, there was no sense in calling anyone else. They would all feel the same way.

How had Tom found out? As far as I knew, it hadn't been in the paper. Was Hildy, in her sly way, letting everyone know about the attack and my injuries, or was it the Franklin grapevine? Franklin may be a city, but not a big one. Gossip travels fast.

I started to call Ryan, but then I worried that my office phone might be bugged. I got out the cell phone, hoping it was more secure that the office line.

"I'm being bugged," I told Ryan when he answered.

"Cool," Ryan responded. "I've never been bugged, at least that I know of. Now, you've got to fill me in on what happened in the Federal Club, where this Squared Circle gym is, and what you've been doing the last two hours."

I told him about the conversation I'd heard between the bartender and McCutcheson, how the bartender fit the description Hildy had given of my attacker and the same scent of cologne, and my visit to Squared Circle Fitness, which I was certain was somehow involved in what was going on.

"The circle is getting bigger, not smaller," he said.

"It only seems that way. I think we're getting closer to the truth. We just don't see it yet."

"Maybe not. Where did you find the bug?"

I recapped it for him. "What do I do now?" I asked.

"About the bug?"

"Yes."

"Can you remove it?"

"I think so. The thing's just a wire under the dash. But I've been thinking I should let it stay. If they know I know, they'll probably just try again, and next time I may not be able to detect it. At least if I'm aware, I can be careful not to say anything that might tip someone off. For the moment, the bug goes to a voice-activated tape recorder hidden in a rear compartment of the van. I get this creepy feeling of violation. Whoever did it is confident they can retrieve the tape any time they want."

"Well, they didn't have any problems installing it, did they? As long as you didn't discover it, they probably figured you'd keep to your same routine and they'd have access to it. What are some of the things you do on a regular basis? Maybe we can figure it out."

I sank into my office chair. "I regularly pick up Stephanie from preschool," I said, "at least I did until I got bounced from the carpool. That was three days a week, but I was never there for very long. I don't think they could have installed this thing in that short time."

"What about that gym you go to? Aren't you there for an hour or so?"

"The days I lift weights I am. The days I do cardio only about forty minutes."

"Still plenty of time."

"It'd be pretty obvious, though, in the parking lot."

"If I remember right, you don't always park there."

My blackened eye was a powerful reminder of that. "True. The night I was attacked I parked on a street about a block from the gym. Hildy was watching the car that night, but I don't know for how long."

"You should ask her when she got there. Maybe it is your friend the bartender who wants to know what you know."

"I have his license plate number," I said. "Would you mind running it through your sources? I'd like to see who it's registered to, if not him." While we'd been talking, I'd propped my notebook up against my computer monitor with the page open to Marston's license plate. I gave it to him.

"Okay," Ryan said. "I'll have it checked. But first I want to talk about why you're being bugged. Cahill. Our visit to the Federal Club wasn't great, but I think we both have a sense he could have been killed in one of those hotel rooms, the body smuggled down 'back of the house,' and then carried out."

"I still question how they got him past the security cameras." I leaned back in my chair. "Sounds like the police have looked over the tapes pretty thoroughly. They must've gotten out another way. The roof to the athletic complex may be accessible from the third floor if there are windows and if the windows open. Seems to me a person trying to get a body out of a window on the third floor would be obvious, though."

"Let's not worry about 'how' right now, let's figure out 'who.' "

"I think it would be helpful to get a listing of everyone who stayed at the Federal Club on the dates that Calvin Cahill wore red. See if there are any names that appear frequently."

"All right," said Ryan. "I'll try to get that. But what about your bartender friend? Isn't it possible he's the connection?"

"Well, he does work there. Presumably he knows lots of people, and therefore would be able to find out which rooms were empty at any given time." I paused. "Ryan, guess what other company is in the same complex as the boxing gym he goes to?"

"I give up."

"The N. Heat Showclub."

"N. Heat is a stripper bar."

"Kinda fits in with what we think Marston is doing. I can't help remembering Jayne Warner's story on lobbyists using sex as a lobbying tool years ago. Maybe the practice is still going on. Ever hear of Richardson Enterprises? They're also in the same complex."

"No, haven't heard of them, but I'll run a check. You notice how we've stopped thinking of Cahill as missing and started thinking of him as dead?"

"When a person's missing this long, they frequently are. Did I tell you Eli thinks he's dead, that the angels told him?"

"You neglected to tell me that important fact. I don't suppose he was able to get out of them where the body is?"

"He said the body was being brought to him."

"He's a little too nutty for me. I'm getting fed up with this angel stuff. We need to confront him and get his sources. Have you checked in with him lately?"

"Not since yesterday."

"It'd be worth a shot."

"I'll talk to him if you'll call your friend about the license plate."

"Deal. Will you be around?"

"I'm headed out to the Franklin Iron Works. I worked out at the boxing gym, but I want to find out if Mark has heard of it. Then I'll stop by to see Eli. As long as Hildy's here, I might as well take advantage of it."

"Have fun pumping up, or whatever it is you're going to do there," he said and hung up.

Hildy had finished her tea in the kitchen and was working on dinner. The clock had just chimed four when I interrupted her.

"Smells good," I said. "What are we having?"

"Pork roast," she said. "I found it in the freezer."

"Good."

"Where are you going?"

"To the gym."

She looked down and noticed I wasn't carrying the gym bag. "How long will you be gone?"

"An hour."

"At least it is not dark out."

"I should be safe, Hildy. No one is going to take me by surprise this time. You don't need to follow."

"That is good, because I must remain here with Melissa and Stephanie. See that you are home in an hour."

"Well," I said, hedging, figuring out how to get around the German Inquisition without telling her I was also going to visit Eli. "I might be later than that. Just in case, you might want to wait an extra half hour or so before you call the local police."

"You think you are funny."

"I'm hilarious," I replied on my way out.

At the gym Mark Zoringer was busy training a young man in a wheelchair who was doing rehab exercises, so I walked on a treadmill for a short while until he finished. He noticed me at the front desk and came over. Today Mark

197

was wearing a white tank top at least one size too small. It stuck to his torso like it'd been shrink-wrapped on him.

"How's your face?" he asked, looking at the stitches.

"Getting better. It doesn't hurt like it did. I know it looks worse, though, with the bruise around the eye."

"Yeah, a black eye does that," he replied in his clipped manner. "You taking care?"

"I'm a lot more aware now. Mark, have you heard of a gym called Squared Circle Fitness?"

"Yeah, it's on the westside of Indy. More boxing than weightlifting. They train thugs."

"Are you kidding?"

Mark raised an eyebrow. "Only half. It doesn't have a good reputation. But there aren't many places in the Indianapolis area that train boxers, so you'll find both the legitimate and the knucklebreakers in there."

"I wondered."

"You worry me."

"Well, Squared Circle may be related to something I'm working on."

"Are the police watching over you?"

"No."

Mark looked at me.

"I mean, really, there's no reason to. What happened to me the other night was just attempted robbery."

He did this squinty thing with his eyebrows that clearly indicated he didn't believe me. "Right."

"Okay, maybe there's the possibility that someone tried to send me a message. But I'm on to the guy who did this, and I won't give him another chance."

"Does he work at Squared Circle?"

"He has some connection to it," I said. "Where I know he works is the Federal Club downtown as a bartender.

Name is Chance Marston."

"Never heard of him. Know why he hurt you?"

"Not yet. But I'm working on it."

"Me and a few of the guys have been talking. We think you need a bodyguard. If the police aren't looking out for you, we will."

Part of me liked the idea. Mark was a good friend and handy in a fight, as he'd proven before. But another part reminded me I couldn't become dependent on other people for "protection." That was why I was at the gym, wasn't it? Strength, confidence. I'd never been a very physical person until two years ago, when it seemed I needed to become one. Sooner or later I was going to have to prove to myself I could win my own battles, or at least wage them for myself. Stupid, macho reasoning, I knew, but it felt right. I wondered if someone like Mark ever accepted help.

"Great of you to offer, Mark, but I really don't need a bodyguard. I'm taking precautions."

One corner of his mouth edged up in slight amusement. "You know anything about boxing, Nick?"

"No. Do you?"

"A little." He stood there, silent, watching me. His head nodded slightly as though he were having an argument with himself and making a decision. "Hopefully, enough," he said. Then he went back to training.

Despite the fact that it was still daylight and I was parked this time in the lot adjacent to the building, one of the bodybuilders followed me out. Granted, he went to his car and I went to mine, and he didn't follow me down the street, but still I wondered if something was going on.

CHAPTER TWENTY

Angels were everywhere in the long, narrow room Elijah shared with his two roommates. They looked surprisingly like I had expected them to look, with halos on top of their heads and wings at their backs. Some had the faces of men, rough and ruddy, while others had delicate, fine facial lines and looked like women. They all wore floor-length robes. Four of them sat on the shelf behind Eli's bed, two stood on the desk, and three stared at me from across the room. The tenth one, on Eli's lap, was being pushed and pulled into shape from a light gray lump of clay.

"Eli, these are remarkable," I said, taking one of the foot-tall statues from the shelf. The one in my hand had a narrow nose on an angular face, with eyes that were large and expressive. Her mouth was big enough to balance the eyes, but it was not wide. The corners of her mouth were turned up, making her look pensive. "When did you find time to create all of these?"

"I've always been pretty good with clay," Eli answered, glancing up from his project. "I started on them yesterday. One of the ministers got me the clay. You had asked what angels looked like and I promised you I would tell you the next time you came. Do you like them?"

Today Eli wore a Tony Stewart NASCAR t-shirt, spotted with clay. I wondered if someone at the shelter was a NASCAR fan and if I could expect to see a Bobby LaBonte next time I visited.

"I love them," I said. "Are these angels you have actually seen, or are you making them up?"

"These are the guardian angels of people around here. Sometimes, you know, they let me see them, and since I started this project they've been really good about it."

"Why would they want to be known? I thought they were unseen for a reason."

Eli tilted his head back from his work and looked at me. "I think the people around here have such a strong need to believe that the angels have let me open the door just a crack." He smiled. "But it's just a guess."

I hadn't thought about guardian angels in a long time. Sister Mary Patricia at Holy Family grade school in my hometown of Clinton had been really big on guardian angels, I remembered, but that was then. "We really do have guardian angels?"

"Yes, but not like they're portrayed."

"Meaning?"

Eli held up the clay figure he was working on and appraised it. He returned it to his lap and worked on the arm while we talked. "Well, some people think that they are supposed to keep you from all harm or that you have one assigned to you for life. It doesn't work like that."

"What do you mean?"

"Well, for starters, while angels are more perfect than humans, they aren't all-seeing and all-knowing. So, an angel can be your protector and try to keep you from harm, but just like you, they don't always see what's coming. And they can't save you from your nature. If you want to do wrong, they can try to exert some influence, but they can't stop you from doing evil nor can they stop someone else from doing evil. Plus, angels have intelligence and free will. Like humans, how smart they are varies, and free will gives them the ability to make bad choices, too. It's not a perfect system. But God works with it to produce good."

In truth, I had never thought about angels being imperfect or having intelligence and free will.

"And you say we don't have the same guardian angel during our entire life?"

"Angels aren't alike, and you have different needs at different points in your life. God sends the best available angel. But both you and your guardian angels have to journey to your ultimate destiny by your choices."

"Eli, how do you know these things?"

Eli sighed. "I know some very good angels, Nick, whether you believe in them or not."

If I stayed with Eli too long, I might actually begin to believe in his angels. "My guardian angel, can you see him? What does he look like?"

"What makes you think it's a 'he'?"

"It's not?"

"Angels are spirits; they really don't have form. For us, some of them adopt a form, which is what I see. It's a part of their personality, but it isn't them."

"I want to know what my guardian angel looks like. Can you see it?"

"I've caught a glimpse." Eli put the clay angel aside and looked me in the eyes. "What do you want it to look like, Nick?"

I sat back for a moment. What would I want my guardian angel to look like? "Some extension of me, I suppose, but bigger, better."

"Such as?" he said, and he had a smile on his face. The impression it gave was that he already knew what I would say.

I took a deep breath and exhaled. Then I told him. "For

starters, I would want it to be a 'he,' " I began. "And I would want him to be a warrior angel, fierce and loyal and strong. But not unthinking or uncaring, just someone who always knew right from wrong and always sided with right. Someone who was so smart he didn't overthink a problem and was unafraid to do what needed to be done. And something else . . ."

To my surprise, Eli's eyes were wide, and he looked at me as if he were seeing me for the first time. I closed my mouth. Now I worried my pronouncement would keep a psychiatrist busy for months. I had clearly misjudged the situation.

We both sat quiet for a time. Eli busied himself with the clay angel. Finally I broke the silence. "So, what does my angel look like?" I asked gently.

Eli shook his head. "Let's just say I wouldn't want you to be disappointed. It would make your guardian angel unhappy."

"I'm sorry."

"Don't be. You were honest. That's a good thing." He resumed work on the angel in his hands. "Was there any other reason you stopped by?"

"Just to check on you. Are you doing okay?"

"I'm fine."

"Do you need anything?"

"No."

"Eli, are you still sure that Cahill is dead, and the body will come to you?"

"Yes."

"Do you know when that'll be?"

He shook his head. "Do you want me to call you when it happens?"

That he talked matter-of-factly about a dead body being

brought to him was almost funny. "Actually, I would like you to call me," I said. "Not only for the story, but because I'm concerned about you."

"Okay, I'll call you."

"One last question. Are the angels still saying that someone I know will die?"

"They have not changed their position."

"Is it still possible that it will be me?"

"They are still worried about you, yes."

Eli seemed a little miffed. Since he was giving me short answers, I said my goodbye.

Returning to the van, I discovered Ryan had left a message on my cell phone to call him. I didn't feel like talking to him right then so I waited until I got back to my office. I called him on my cell phone before I even bothered to sit.

"Boy are you impatient," I said.

"Not nearly as impatient as Clarisse," he replied. "The *Star*, it appears, has done a number on us. In today's final edition they cited unnamed sources that say Eli is the police's only suspect in the Cahill disappearance and published not only his name but also the name of the homeless shelter where he's staying. Clarisse wants a story on her desk tonight."

"We don't have anything."

"The *Star* didn't interview Eli. You did."

"But I told him I'd try to keep his name out of the paper."

"It's already out. He can't hold you to that now."

"Yeah, but even then, we don't have anything."

"We have Eli's denial that he's guilty. We know his alibi isn't airtight. That's a story."

"But it makes Eli look guilty, and we don't think he is."

"Then find a way to put doubt in the minds of the

readers. I know you like the guy, but this is business. We've got to get something out, something that puts us back on top of the *Star*. Oh, and Clarisse expects us to have an article every day on Cahill's disappearance until we find out what happened to him."

"Every day?"

"So after you finish your article get busy thinking of an angle for the day after tomorrow."

"I suppose we could do something on Cheryl Cahill if we had more than just a suspicion of abuse."

"Work on it. Get some kind of corroboration for your suspicion. Call the ex-wife."

I frowned and tried to think of some other angle we could use, but nothing came to mind. "Okay, I'll work on it. But we could really use a break in the case."

"So could the police. Maybe something will come up."

"What do you know about the license plate?"

"Nothing yet, but I'm working on it."

"Work harder," I said. I hung up.

Hildy appeared at the door. "It is time for dinner. Are you coming down?"

I looked at my watch. Six-thirty. Now that she mentioned it, my stomach was growling. I hadn't even had a protein bar that afternoon. Although I had a story to crank out, taking a short break to eat with Stephanie would be a good thing. With her mother gone, I should keep things as normal as possible.

"Melissa still here?"

"Yes, and the two girls are hungry. Children should not have to wait this late for dinner."

I followed her back to the kitchen and helped put the meal out.

The pork roast was good, and Hildy served it with peas,

applesauce, and macaroni and cheese that she'd made from scratch. Melissa liked it so much it kept her quiet most of the meal. We talked about what they'd done that day during preschool. Stephanie showed me her drawings. She retrieved them, stick figures of fairy princesses playing with a purple puppy in bright orange sunshine. They'd been attached to the refrigerator with magnetic alphabet letters. I complimented her on her imagination.

Hildy shoved the dishes in the dishwasher, and soon Jill Farrigut was there to pick up Melissa. Hildy charged the front door with a plate of food to offer Jill, and I took the opportunity to slip back upstairs to write.

In an hour and a half I had it done. I had called Eli to let him know what I was writing and to make sure I quoted him correctly. He seemed preoccupied and not all that concerned about what the *Star* had reported or what I was doing. In the end, the article was good enough to satisfy Clarisse Babcock. We both knew there were matters I wasn't addressing, but she said she would back me up for now. Unspoken was the message that my confidence in Eli would have to bear fruit soon or she would expect my reporting to go in a different direction.

After I'd wrapped that up, I went downstairs to check on Stephanie. Hildy was giving her a bath, so I sneaked past them on my way to the garage. I wanted another look at the tape recorder, just to see if it had been tampered with. But there was no change.

When I let myself back in the house, Hildy was standing there.

"What are you doing?" she asked.

"Cleaning out the van," I said.

She looked back into the garage. "Does not look much cleaner than it was."

"I'm not done."

"Stephanie has finished her bath. She wants you to help her get ready for bed."

"Sure," I said. Hildy followed me down the hall.

When Stephanie was ready for bed, we called Joan so she could say goodnight and Hildy and I could get the latest news on her parents.

"Mom's doing great," Joan reported after she'd talked to Stephanie. "Putting in the stents went fine this morning. After the hospital monitored her and made sure there weren't any complications, we were able to bring her home. She'll rest up Friday and over the weekend, and then we'll take her back in Monday for the last of the stents."

We talked about how things were going at home. Again I didn't mention the beating I'd taken; again Hildy spared Joan the information. We talked mostly about Stephanie.

Then Joan said, "If Mom continues to do well, I think I'll come home for the weekend. She really doesn't need any special care, and Dad is doing just fine, now that he's seen how Mom came out of it. I miss being home. So I'll probably leave early on Saturday. I'll come back Monday for the second set of stents."

I had to catch my breath. There's no way I could wrap up the Cahill story by Saturday. "Sure, that would be great," I said. "Your dad's okay with this, though? I mean, he'll be able to handle taking care of your mom by himself?"

"Yes," Joan said. "By tomorrow Mom will pretty much be taking care of herself. Is there a reason you don't want me to come home Saturday?"

"I—I do want you to come home on Saturday," I said. "I'm just glad everything is going so well."

"All right," she said, but I could tell she wasn't convinced. "I'll definitely see you Saturday, then."

"Great. Love you."

"You, too," she answered.

I looked at Hildy as I hung up the phone. "She's coming home Saturday."

Hildy touched my stitches. "You will have a lot of explaining to do."

"I'm not alone," I said.

CHAPTER TWENTY-ONE

The call came at three a.m. The sound of it set my heart racing. Phone calls in the middle of the night are either bad news or wrong numbers, both of which put me on edge. I snatched up the receiver in hopes of catching it before the ringing woke anyone else in the house.

"It's Eli, Nick."

"Eli?" I said fuzzily.

"I've heard from the angels, Nick. The body is being brought to me."

"What?" I said.

"The body—it's coming," he said again.

"The body?"

I was just beginning to put it all together, who I was talking to and what he was saying, when Eli added, "Yes. I'm going out to wait for it." And then he hung up.

"No, Eli, don't do that," I barked into the phone, now fully awake. But there was no response. I stared at the receiver in the red light of the clock numerals. Had I really just had this conversation, or was I dreaming?

I heard Hildy stirring in the room next to me. In seconds she was outside my door. "Who was that on the phone?" she demanded. "Is everything all right?"

Damn. It *was* real. "Go back to bed. Everything's fine," I lied.

I waited until she was gone, then scooted out from under the covers. I pulled on a sweatshirt, jeans, socks, and shoes, and grabbed my wallet and keys. I opened the door, and there stood Hildy.

"If everything is all right, where are you going?" she asked.

Hildy, in the middle of the night, is a fright unto herself. Her blond hair, normally kind of poofy, was rolled up in large pink curlers, and her body was wrapped in a leopard print nightgown. On her feet were fuzzy black slippers with big, man-in-the-moon faces on them. She took up a good section of the doorframe, and I couldn't get by her.

"Okay, it's not all right," I admitted. "One of my sources thinks the body of Calvin Cahill is about to show up, and I've got to get there."

"Is Cahill dead?"

"We'll know when he arrives."

Hildy let me pass her in the hall. "When will you be home?"

"I don't know. Just take care of Stephanie," I said, accelerating into a run as I headed down the stairs. I grabbed a jacket from the closet and made for the door.

"I bet he will be dead," Hildy said, shuffling behind me. "Abusive people like that, they get what they deserve."

Abusive? Where had she heard that? But I didn't have time to find out. I bolted out the door, closing it behind me.

Mercifully the van started without complaint. I drove faster than I should have to the shelter, pulling up in front and jamming the gearshift into Park. The trip had taken ten minutes.

Streetlights shining on stately oaks threw shadows across the front of Good Shepherd's shelter house. The building looked ominous. There were no lights on inside that I could see. Eli was not out front. I dashed across the lawn to the right side of the house and then slowed down, approaching the backyard cautiously. The area was dimly lit, most of the light coming from a security lamppost several houses down. Good Shepherd's shelter had a small backyard, typical of its old-style residential neighborhood. I stood between the shelter and a house of similar size on my right and peered into the near darkness. There was no fence between the two yards. Good Shepherd's had a hedgerow of bushes along the back of the house. Beyond it was an alley, and beyond the alley I could see into the backyards of houses on the next street, also dimly lit. I scanned the area for Eli but didn't see him. Maybe he'd done the smart thing and stayed inside. Before I could turn around, I heard the rumble as a car pulled up in front of the shelter. My van was parked there. Someone with the body? I moved toward the hedgerow looking for a place to hide.

And then I heard something that made me stop. I turned in that direction. A small sport utility vehicle, maybe the size of a Chevrolet Tracker, had its motor running. It was parked on a tiny pad of concrete in the shadow of a one-car garage just beyond the hedgerow. The back of the vehicle was dark—no parking lights, no brake lights, no license plate light. I could see a faint green glow in the front seat, silhouetting the driver. As I moved forward to get a better look, I heard footsteps running from the backyard next door. In the dark someone tackled me. I thudded to the ground beneath him.

He was heavier than I was by maybe forty pounds. Lying on my back, I instinctively pulled my knees up for protection. It worked, but in an unintended way—I nailed him in the crotch with a knee. He flopped on his side. I scrambled to get up, but he grabbed an arm and yanked me down again. He rolled back on top and punched me in the ribs with his right fist. It hurt. I rolled to my left, using the momentum to swing out with my right fist, aiming for his cheek. I felt the sting of my hand connect with bone. It made a good crack. Before I could draw back for another swing, he pinned my arm across my chest. I saw his fist pull back. He had set his sights on something higher than my ribs this time, my face, probably where I'd been hit before. I closed my eyes and braced for impact, but it never came. I felt his body being jerked off mine and I looked up to see Mark Zoringer.

Mark pounded a fist into the guy's stomach. The guy was taller than Mark and grabbed for his head, trying to bring it down as he jerked his knee up. I'd seen that move in professional wrestling matches. Mark grabbed the knee as it came up. He flipped the guy over using the momentum of the leg.

As I jumped up to help, somebody else entered the fight. He caught Mark by surprise, pummeling his right side with quick jabs. Mark grunted in pain. The first attacker turned toward Mark. I took a few steps and launched myself on top of him. He hadn't seen me coming and didn't have time to brace. I knocked him down, taking the air out of him. Then I rolled over onto the second guy's feet, trying to bring him down, too. Hugging his knees, I dug my feet into the ground and pushed against him.

It didn't work. He kneed me in the face, not where the stitches were but close enough that I winced. He stepped out of my hold and continued to land punches to Mark's side. Mark gave up trying to hit back and took three steps away to catch his breath. Instead of following, the second attacker grabbed the first by the shirt, yanked him off the ground, and the two of them raced off for the Tracker. When I finally picked myself up and started in pursuit, it was too late. Tires screamed as the Tracker roared backwards into the alleyway, sputtering when the vehicle lurched forward on the gravel path. Rocks were thrown into the air. I heard them ping against the garage.

Mark stood a few feet away from me, bent over at the waist, breathing hard and rubbing his jaw.

"Are you okay?" I asked.

"Yeah." He straightened and winced. "Son of a bitch, that hurts." He touched the side of his torso that had absorbed all the blows.

"Thanks for being here," I said, "but why are you here?"

"You needed someone watching over your shoulder. Between me and some others at the gym, we've been shadowing you every night."

"Must've been boring. I've been home every night."

"Until now."

In the distance I could hear sirens. Then I heard someone moaning. Mark and I squinted at each other. It was an eerie moment when we realized it wasn't either one of us. The moan sounded again. We dashed off in the direction it had come, the yard behind the neighboring house.

We looked around while our eyes adjusted to the dimmer light. When I smelled whiskey, I went in that direction. A few steps later I stumbled across Eli. Reaching down to help him, my hand touched blood on his shirt. It was cold and sticky. I wiped my hand off on the grass. The whiskey odor was strongest near Eli's head. Something in his hand was gleaming.

"Eli," I whispered. He didn't answer. He just lay there on the ground. I noticed how quiet it was. Even the sirens, which had seemed to be getting closer, had stopped. There was a faint crunch of gravel from the alleyway.

"The police are coming," Mark said.

Suddenly there was light everywhere. Mark and I were

213

bathed in a spotlight, and red and blue lights spun from the top of a police car. In the brightness I saw two bodies beside us, Eli's and another's. The second body, longer and fatter, was dressed in a dark suit with a paisley tie with a red handkerchief stuffed in the breast pocket. Calvin Cahill. There was blood on his clothes. In Eli's hand was a gun. I didn't like where this was headed.

"Police. Put your hands out where we can see them," said a stern male voice over the police system.

For a moment, neither Mark nor I moved. Then, whether it was instinct or we had just seen too many movies, we raised our hands above our waists. "We're unarmed," I said.

"You two men on the ground. We need to see your hands."

"One of them is dead," Mark replied. "The other may be badly wounded."

The policeman on the PA didn't say anything. I heard someone coming up from behind; I slowly turned my head and saw another policeman with his gun out and pointed at us. His car must've been parked on the street in front of the shelter. I looked to the side and saw a third policeman covering from the left in the yard behind the shelter house.

"Slowly kneel on the ground," ordered the voice over the PA, "and then lay face down with your hands over your heads."

Mark and I did as we were told.

The policeman who had come up from behind advanced cautiously toward Eli. He kicked the gun out of Eli's hand and away from Cahill's body. Holding his own gun on Eli with one hand, he knelt and felt for a pulse on Cahill's neck.

"This one's dead," he called.

He nudged Eli with his foot. Eli rolled over. The policeman checked him for a pulse. "This one's breathing, but
he's got blood on him."

Everyone sprang into action. Mark and I were hauled to
our feet, handcuffed, and checked for weapons. The police
bagged everything we had in our pockets, including cell
phones. Two more vehicles arrived on the scene, lights
flashing. One was an ambulance.

The police separated Mark and me. I was jerked to the
yard behind the shelter by one of them, and Mark was taken
by two burly policemen to the alley. The medics jumped
into action and, after checking Eli over, put him on a board.
They took him away in the ambulance. A policeman went
with them.

"I didn't do anything," I said. "I was here trying to prevent something from happening."

"First tell me your name."

"Nick Bertetto."

He paused. "The reporter? Officer Roth's friend?"

"Yes."

"Okay, tell me what happened." He was clean-shaven,
young, and had a fleshy face. I guessed him to be in his
twenties. I spotted a small microphone clipped to the front
of his shirt; it was common procedure nowadays to audio-
tape every interaction the police had while on duty. Even
though the policeman had a notebook, I was being re-
corded.

"I got a call from Elijah Smith," I said. "He's the guy
who's hurt. He's lived here at the shelter since Monday
when he stumbled off the shoulder of U.S. 31 and I almost
hit him. I brought him here because he's indigent. He
called me at three o'clock this morning to say he was going
outside because," and here I paused to think how I wanted

to say this, "well, because he thought someone was coming to give him something. I told him not to do that, but I wasn't sure he'd heard me, so I rushed over. When I arrived, someone attacked me. My friend Mark Zoringer, who followed me here, helped me fight off the first guy, and then a second one jumped in. But I think they just wanted to get away. As soon as they could, they ran for a Tracker that was in the alley and they took off. Then Mark and I looked for Eli and found him right where he was when you arrived."

"Do you know who the dead body is?"

I knew I was saying too much but the adrenaline had hit and I was anxious to establish my innocence. "If I had to guess, I'd say it's Calvin Cahill."

"Why would you say that?"

"It's just a guess."

"But why?"

"I've seen his picture in the paper."

Yet another police car arrived. A plainclothes detective got out and began to look over the scene. Neighbors came out of their houses and began to gather.

At least five Franklin Police officers were there, two sheriff's deputies, and two State Police officers. A news van from one of the Indianapolis television stations had pulled up and was shooting video. More were no doubt on their way. This was clearly the biggest thing to hit Franklin in a while.

But I didn't have time to watch much else. Mark and I were hauled off, still handcuffed, in separate cars and taken to the police station. When we got there, Ken Roth was waiting for us. He did not look happy.

"They called me in because all policemen on duty were tied up on some murder over at Good Shepherd's," Roth told me. "Imagine my surprise when I found out that one of the two murder suspects was you. I told you, Nick, that if you held out on information I would kick your ass. And I intend to do that once we get you cleared of this murder charge. You might be hiding something, but I know you're not a murderer."

"Thanks, Ken," I said.

"You won't thank me when I get done with you. Now as for you, Mark, you're lucky we've all worked out at your place one time or another. You've got a good, clean reputation. We all want to believe what you've told us is true. So, for the moment, we're going to take the handcuffs off both of you and put you in the conference room. Me and another officer will be outside the room. Don't think you can take liberties with us."

Roth walked us to the conference room before he removed the handcuffs. I was grateful to be able to get some circulation going in my arms again. Having them cuffed behind my back had become painful.

Mark looked at me when Roth stepped out and closed the door.

"Are we being overheard?" he asked.

"Probably, but I'm not going to worry about it. We're not guilty and they know it. What did you tell them?"

"Just that I was there to protect you, that I had been worried about your safety since you were attacked the other night."

"Did they ask about Cahill?"

"Who?"

"The dead body."

"I told them I didn't know who it was, which is the truth. Of course, you lied to me about the attack not being related to the story you were working on."

I squirmed. "It wasn't exactly a lie. I haven't been able to figure out the relationship between the two, why I would be attacked for looking into the Cahill disappearance. There are lots of reporters from around the state investigating it, and you don't hear about them being attacked."

He crossed his arms over his chest. "Nick, we've been friends a long time. You owe me more than that."

He didn't say anything for a long time, and I didn't feel like talking.

After an hour, the detective who had shown up last at Good Shepherd came to question us. He was in his early forties with eyebrows that connected, far too bushy for his youthful face. Once again, Mark and I were separated. I got to go first.

"I've read over what you told the officer who brought you in," he said, rubbing his eyes as though he were still trying to get the sleep out of them. "I want you to start at the beginning, from when you first met Elijah Smith, and tell me how you got to this point."

"Am I under arrest?" I asked.

"Not at this time."

"Do you suspect me to be a murderer?"

"No, but if we do develop a case against Elijah Smith, you could be charged as an accomplice."

"You don't have a case against Eli," I said confidently. "Cahill was already dead when the two guys dropped him off. His blood was cold. I know. I accidentally touched it. He was killed somewhere else and brought to Good Shepherd's."

The detective leaned back in his chair. "Doesn't absolve Eli. He knew the body was coming. How did he know that, if he wasn't one of the killers?"

"How he knew, I don't know," I said. "But he's been at the shelter since Monday. You ought to be able to track all his calls."

"There was only one person he called or took calls from: you."

"Oh."

"So let me ask you this again, what happened in the time between when you almost hit Elijah Smith with your van and this morning?"

"If I tell you what I know, will you answer questions for me about what you found back at Good Shepherd's?"

"Not for the record," he said.

"But if it's not for attribution?"

"Talk to me, and then I'll decide."

I told him an edited version. I left in the part about being attacked outside Mark's gym (Ken knew, and Mark would have told him anyway), but left out my pseudo-suspects, Chance Marston and Frank McCutcheson. I didn't really have any proof they'd done anything. I covered my interview with the truck driver who wouldn't provide an alibi for Eli, and the conversation I'd had with Cheryl Cahill and her brother who lacked social skills, but I didn't mention I was being bugged.

The detective took notes. When he finished, I said, "Now it's my turn."

"I don't know if I'll answer you, but ask away," he said, yawning.

"Did you find evidence that Cahill has been dead for some time?"

"Again, it's not for publication, but yes. There were two bullet holes in Cahill's head. Only one from the gun the suspect had. We're confident that was *not* the bullet that killed him."

"How long has he been dead?"

"We won't know until the coroner has had a chance to do his thing."

"If Eli is being framed, which it looks like, why Eli?"

The detective laughed. "Why not? He's homeless, his name appeared in the paper as a suspect IPD had questioned, and he was easy to locate." He pushed his chair out and stood up. "That's enough questions."

"One more," I insisted. "Where is Eli?"

"He's being cared for at Wishard Hospital. It's the only secure hospital in Indianapolis. We sent a policeman along to watch over him."

"But if he's innocent, he doesn't have to stay there, does he?"

"I think we're going to keep him there awhile, as much for his protection as anything else. We'll want to be able to question him further as we learn more."

The detective left and went to question Mark. By seven-thirty, more than four hours after the ordeal began, we were out. The police gave us back our stuff and dropped us off at our cars in front of Good Shepherd's shelter. I assured Mark that I would be all right during the day and sent him home to his wife.

Now that I had my cell phone again, I checked my voice mail and found five messages, three from Hildy and two from Ryan. The call to Ryan would no doubt take longer so I called Hildy first, being careful to stand away from the van so I couldn't be heard by whoever was bugging me.

"Hildy, it's Nick."

"You are all over the news," she said. "I have seen a video replayed over and over again of you being taken away in handcuffs. Are you all right? Are you a felon?"

"No, I'm not a felon. In fact, the police have let me go.

I'll be home in a little bit. Stephanie hasn't seen the video, has she?"

"She is still in bed."

"Well, thank God for that," I said. "I'm sure it would scare her."

"You will be home soon?"

"Fifteen minutes."

"I will make you breakfast."

"You don't have to do that."

"I have been up for hours. I have to do something."

Ryan Lockridge called me almost immediately after I hung up. I hadn't even had time to press the automatic dialer for his number.

"You look good in chains," he said. "I'm having a picture blown up from Channel Thirteen's video this morning. Too bad we didn't have a news reporter there. Oh, wait, you are a news reporter."

"Ha, ha," I replied.

"As our dear editor explained it to me, she would prefer our news reporters *get* the news rather than *make* the news."

"I can file a story," I said, "of sorts."

"Well, you don't have time for that now. You need to call in to work and give your story to the political reporters; they're handling Cahill's death. Then I need you at the Statehouse as fast as you can get here to help me cover a breaking story."

"I need to go home and clean up."

"No, you don't. This one is really big."

"How big?"

"A dead body. Police have blocked off a section of the building that only the legislators have access to. Rumor has it it's another legislator."

"Who?"

"The grapevine doesn't have a name yet, but I'm working on it."

"Where do I meet you?"

"Police have the west and north entrances blocked. They're allowing press into the lobbies on the other two sides. I'm in the middle of the back on the east side."

"I'll be right there," I said. And I had a bad feeling about whose body had been found.

Someone you know will die.

CHAPTER TWENTY-TWO

I made a quick call to Hildy to let her know there'd been a change in plans. She wasn't happy, but I didn't give her a chance to argue with me. Though I looked like hell, I didn't dare go home to change. I didn't want to answer her questions, and I didn't want Stephanie to wake. With Hildy there, Stephanie would be fine, but once she saw me she would need some face time. I couldn't give her that until later.

I called the *Standard* and talked to the reporters working on this morning's story. Eli's name came up and I verified that he had held the gun but, because Eli was unconscious, I doubted he had killed Cahill. I was careful not to reveal what I'd been told in confidence by the police, though it would have helped the story, of course. They seemed satisfied when we hung up.

Because I drive to so many locations and work out of the van, I keep notebooks and pens in there. After collecting the bare essentials, I dug through the glove compartment and came up with a couple of protein bars. They'd have to do for breakfast. Then I scooted into Indy on I-65, hitting rush hour. Traffic wasn't stopped but it was slow. Time dragged until I exited on McCarty Street, wound around to Illinois, and then went north to my favorite Circle Centre garage. I parked and hustled over to the Statehouse.

Ryan had certainly been correct about the crowd. Television vans were parked everywhere, and reporters were all over the place. They held their microphones like trophies and talked to cameras with solemn faces. They interviewed legislators from the General Assembly, who, never wanting to miss the chance to get their faces on TV, had swarmed the Statehouse. They were all reciting tributes to Calvin Cahill. I pushed my way inside, press pass held high, and found another batch of reporters inside. Most of us knew each other, though we were in different media. They swarmed me with questions about the Calvin Cahill dead body scene I had been a part of that morning. There was such a buzz in the lobby that I had to shout, "No comment" several times while carving a path to Ryan.

"I got the information back on Richardson Enterprises," he said, as a couple of cameras shot video of us. "Only a few of their businesses are legitimate. They own a dry cleaners, for example. The rest are strip bars and adult bookstores. Fill me in on what happened to you."

We huddled. Ryan, with his considerable bulk, had carved out a spot near the police line. Beyond it, a little press area had been set up for briefings. We had a good location for whatever came next.

Ryan shook his head when I filled him in. "So, you're doing a great job of keeping a low profile on this one. Have you heard from Joan yet?"

"Not since last night, but she's coming home tomorrow. Her mom is out of the hospital and doing well, and she thinks her father can handle the second round of stents on Monday. It was all going to come out anyway, I guess. If we could prove who killed Cahill before tomorrow afternoon, though, it would be helpful."

"Oh, well, of course, it would," said Ryan. "Do you have any idea how to do that?"

I smiled conspiratorially. "Actually, I do."

Ryan turned and I saw Judith standing behind him.

"I saw you down here," she said. "I heard you found Cal's body, and I wanted to know what happened." Her eyes were tired and reddish; they matched the red scarf she had in the pocket of her navy blue blazer. I wondered if the scarf was a tribute to Cahill.

"I really didn't find the body, Judith. It was more like it had been dropped off," I said.

"The killer was also found?" she asked.

I looked around at the reporters near me. No one appeared to be listening other than Ryan, but I didn't believe that for a moment. "This really isn't the right place," I said.

She clutched my wrist and I was surprised at how cold her hands were. "Please, I won't tell anyone," she said. "I need to know."

I could tell she had been crying. This had to have been hard on someone like her; she'd worked with Cahill so many years. "All right," I whispered, bending down to her ear. "But I really can only tell you a little. The truth is, Cahill was dead long before this morning."

"Really?" she said. "What about the man with the gun?"

"Framed."

"The police believe this?"

"I can't tell you what the police believe, only what I know. Cahill died from a gunshot wound many days ago."

She didn't say anything and I straightened up. But her eyes were wide and she pulled at my wrist again. "Do they know who the killer is?"

"I don't know if they do or not," I said.

She studied my eyes. "Do you?"

"Well . . ." I began.

Ryan interrupted. "You do?"

"I thought I did. I still might. The death today may

225

change that, if it's connected."

She didn't say anything for a moment, just kept searching my eyes. Finally she said, "Okay," and left.

Ryan looked around, impatient. "Nothing's going to happen here for a while," he said. "We need to get upstairs, where all the action's going on." His eyes fixed on a column not too far from us.

Spread out in the main rotunda of the Statehouse are four massive square columns supporting the weight of the floors above them. Each has a door made of dark wood that looks like it came from a European monastery. Several feet above each door is a small circular window, like a porthole. If a person thinks to look that far up, they'll see stacked furniture through the windows, giving the incorrect impression that the rooms behind the doors are used for storage. What most people don't know is that the columns actually contain staircases that run to the top of the building. Ryan's thoughts were ahead of mine.

"You don't really think the door in that column is open, do you?" I asked.

"I wouldn't, except for one thing—Judith just came out of it."

"What was she doing in there?"

"Don't know," Ryan said, "but that's not as important right now as how we can get in there without anyone noticing us. What we need is a distraction."

We got one, albeit unplanned. The governor arrived on the north side of the Statehouse. Even as he waved off the reporters, shaking his head to indicate that he would not answer their questions, they rushed to the police barricade nearest him and thrust their microphones in the air, shouting questions. After the stampede had passed us, Ryan and I quietly opened the door and crept inside, closing it firmly behind us. After climbing four flights, we came to a plainer door at the top. Beyond it lay an area closed to everyone but legislators and their staff.

There was no window in the door; we couldn't be sure if anyone would be out there. Ryan, winded from the climb, let me get past him. I listened, but didn't hear anyone. Carefully I pushed the door open.

The Statehouse is rectangular, long on the north and south sides. The design is symmetrical with a large, ornate skylight in the center of the building and two identical, lesser skylights on the north and south ends. We were in the attic area where the skylights are inlaid. I could hear voices, but they were far away, somewhere in the vicinity of the north skylight.

I slipped out the door and motioned Ryan to follow me.

"I've never been here before but I've heard about this place," I said. "Supposedly there's a long history of secret political deals that have been worked out up here. Most of the gerrymandering was done here until the sixties."

We stepped around cables and girders and ducked our heads to avoid the metal pipes where the ceiling was low. The sounds of talking grew louder as we approached the north end. We could see light ahead. Finally we rounded a corner and stood upright in the huge sunlit area. Above us were large panels of frosted glass that let in sunlight to illuminate the decorative glass panels in the floor below. Those lay ahead of us, the police surrounding them. Only a few police guarded the side nearest us, and they had their backs turned, obstructing our view only a little. No one had bothered with yellow police tape.

I softly took a couple of steps closer. The decorative glass panels were set in an iron framework, each panel about a square foot in size. Those on the perimeter contained blue cornflower designs while the rest were frosted white.

That is, except the glass panels on the opposite side, where the police were looking. Many of those were smeared in red, and they supported a body lying face down. The body of a man who, when he'd been alive, was short and feisty and had red hair.

Frank McCutcheson.

Ryan pushed forward to see around me. I stumbled over a girder. Although I caught my balance and didn't fall, I made enough noise, as my mother would have said, to wake the dead. Almost. Frank McCutcheson didn't move, but everyone else looked at us. The nearest policemen drew guns. For the second time that morning, I raised my hands above my head. "We're unarmed," I said.

We were fortunate that one of the detectives was Claire Hurst. "I know these guys," she said. "They're reporters."

"How did you get up here?" a familiar voice asked. It was Hurst's senior partner, Jerry Smallwood. Him, I was not delighted to see.

"We came up the stairs," I answered.

"Get them out of here," said a fuller, more commanding voice, "and for God's sake secure whatever stairs they used. The last thing we need are more reporters crawling around up here." He was wearing a dark blue suit, wingtip shoes, and a subdued tie, and couldn't have looked more like an FBI agent if he tried. Later I found out he was the top investigator for the State Police.

"I'll take them down," Hurst said.

After we were checked for weapons—I was getting used to being frisked—we followed Detective Hurst to the third floor, using the regular staircase the police had already secured. She led us to a suite of rooms that had been set up as a kind of command post for the investigation.

"Sit down," she said. She waved us toward two sturdy, wooden chairs. Claire dumped Ryan's confiscated cell phone and our notebooks on the desk, then leaned against the edge and faced us.

"You're resourceful, I have to say that," she said, looking at me. "First you're found at the scene where Calvin Cahill reappears, and a few hours later you find your way up here to another murder scene. You want to tell me how you managed to do that?"

"Good fortune?"

"Look, we're not stupid. We know you're not telling us everything. Given the events of this morning, we can make life really uncomfortable for you. Don't make us do that. Tell us what you know."

All three of us sat there, looking at each other. Ryan was going to let me take the lead, I could see that, unless I said something he considered stupid. Claire Hurst stood there trying to look mean, but she had this way of positioning her mouth so that it worked on me like an inviting smile. It was kind of sexy. But I could sense the steel resolve underneath.

It was a tough decision, really. I knew for a fact I wasn't going anywhere until I divulged some of what I had learned. The police could hold us for at least twenty-four hours without charging us for any particular crime, which was what Claire probably meant by making life uncomfortable. I had already missed having breakfast with Stephanie, and if I were locked up I would miss many more. Joan, when she found out, wouldn't be very happy with me. And I couldn't be a very effective reporter, especially at such a critical time. Both Ryan and I had a lot to do; it would demand both of us and then some.

"Okay," I said, "but I want some promises first. Number one, no one in the press gets any information ahead of the *Standard*. Ryan and I have worked too hard to have you take our information, use it, and then share what you get with everyone else. And I won't budge on this."

Claire shook her head. "At the moment, I can't promise you that. There are too many agencies involved. The Franklin Police and IPD each have some claim on the Cahill investigation. We're working together, but IPD can't unilaterally agree to this. Plus, the Capitol Police have control over the investigation here in the Statehouse. They've invited us to participate, since there's a chance the two deaths might be related, but we don't have jurisdiction. And I needn't remind you the Capitol Police are a division of the State Police, so now you've got the state involved. Do you have any idea how tough it will be to get them to agree to anything?"

I thought about that for a few seconds. "What if I make a deal with you, and share the information with you alone?"

"I can't do that," she said.

"No, I suppose you can't," I said. "You probably have to review everything with Smallwood, since he's the senior investigator. That way he can take credit for anything that happens. But he's a good guy. I'm certain he makes sure your contributions are noticed."

She sat there, stone-faced.

"Ryan and I could make sure you know everything we uncover first, and we're ahead of the police on this one. All we want is to be there when you make the arrest. Both of us get what we want, and no one needs to know."

Claire didn't respond right away, but I knew I had her. It might take a little while for her to justify it, but she'd get there. In everyone's life there's a point where they have to weigh end results versus inane rules, and when it happens, most intelligent people side with the end results.

Detective Claire Hurst was intelligent.

"This is the biggest case of my career," she said.

I looked over at Ryan and raised an eyebrow. He knew what to do.

"Let's face it, it's the biggest case in Smallwood's career, too," he said, "and you'll break the case while he's still sucking up to the Staties."

"You know who murdered Cahill and McCutcheson?" she asked, looking into Ryan's eyes first, then mine.

"We know who's involved," I said, leaning forward and making my voice softer, more conspirator-like, "but not who's guilty. Yet. Help us."

She drummed her fingers on the table, still thinking. I gave her space, easing back into the hard chair.

The heavy door to the room swung open and Smallwood entered. He looked at the three of us and immediately made a bad assessment.

"Not getting anywhere with them, huh?" he said.

Perfect.

Claire Hurst glared at him.

"Well, we don't have time for that right now. I need you to take Nick Butt-head-o over to Wishard Hospital. The homeless guy that shot Cahill is awake but won't talk to anyone else. The Franklin Police want him over there. I'll stay here and help with the State."

"Sure," Claire responded. Her voice was tight.

"Leave the other guy here. I'll have one of our patrolmen guard him." Then he disappeared.

Ryan leaned over and snatched his cell phone off the desk. Claire didn't try to stop him. "Don't worry," he said to me. "Our legal department will have me out of here in no time."

Within minutes, Claire Hurst and I were on our way to Wishard.

In Claire's unmarked patrol car, we sealed the deal. I told her we were fairly confident Calvin Cahill was involved with prostitutes, possibly even being bribed by sex, and that the red pocket handkerchief he wore was the signal that set up the sex session. "The Federal Club is involved because it's the place where Cahill used the signal most and where I think he met the prostitutes. But," I added, "I'm not sure Federal Club management knew about it. I believe it was run by one of their employees, Chance Marston, a bartender. Marston was also connected to McCutcheson. I overheard Frank tell Marston that he didn't want Marston's services anymore."

"What was the reason Cahill got killed, and how does it tie to Frank McCutcheson?"

"That I don't know. At least not yet," I answered. "Cahill pulled the rug out from under McCutcheson on a compromise over the new gambling legislation, and that really made McCutcheson mad. It's possible the stakes might be bigger than we know. Certainly a lot of gambling organizations want that legislation to pass.

"Marston may have also been employed by Richardson Enterprises," I added. "Ryan told me he ran a check on them. They have some normal businesses like a dry cleaners, but only a few. Most of their holdings are sex-oriented, like strip bars and adult bookstores."

"They're also involved in gambling," Claire said. "Vice has been looking into them."

We sat there thinking.

After a few moments, I broke the silence. "I have a hard time figuring out why both McCutcheson and Cahill would be killed, though. Either one of them alone makes more sense. McCutcheson knew about Cahill's prostitutes, I think, but unless he knew who had killed Cahill, and was murdered to prevent him from talking, it doesn't figure. But why wouldn't McCutcheson have come forward sooner, if he knew who the murderer was?"

"Good question. Your scenario also doesn't explain why Cahill's dead body didn't show up until this morning."

"Well, I'm working on it."

"That's all you've got?" she asked.

I nodded.

"Christ. I can't believe I made this deal and 'prostitutes' is about all you know. Got any suspicions?"

"I suspect Cahill was an abusive husband. I don't have any proof, just a feeling based on an interview with his widow. And I don't know how that plays into his death, if it does at all."

Claire didn't look happy, but I think it was just an act.

It's a short trip from the Statehouse to Wishard. Claire had taken one-way Michigan Street west and then turned back east on New York Street to catch the hospital. I hoped I hadn't waited too late to get a few answers out of her.

"What's the scoop on Cahill's body? I know Elijah Smith didn't kill him. Someone tried to set Eli up. How long had Cahill been dead?"

"Autopsies don't get done fast, you know that, Nick. Even on a high-profile cadaver."

"But you have some preliminary guesses from the medical examiner, don't you?"

She was quiet a moment, obviously thinking it over. Then she said, "The bullet from Smith's gun was not the

233

only one in Cahill's head. But we don't know yet when Cahill died. He had marks on his head that are consistent with burns his flesh might have received if he were stored in a freezer. Plus, his body temperature was well below ambient. So it's possible he may have been dead since his disappearance."

"What about McCutcheson?"

"What about him?"

"What did he die from?"

"Well, you saw the body. It was a gunshot wound."

"Same type as Cahill's?"

"Not the same gun Smith had in his possession, at least that's what I've been told. I don't know about any other bullets that might be in his body."

We pulled into the Wishard parking lot.

She spoke to a man at Reception, showed him her badge, and we were directed to the elevator. We took a car to the fifth floor. Walking toward a secure area with two broad-backed policemen as guards, Claire again showed her badge and they waved us in. I went ahead and opened the door. Elijah was sitting up in bed. His head, which had been shaved bald a couple of days ago, had stubble growing. His eyes looked bright and alert, and he toyed with a lump of clay in his hands. Beside him was a tray with a half-eaten bagel. Eli smiled at me.

"Nick," he said, "it's good to see you. I thought you'd never get here."

I sat on the edge of his bed. "I wasn't sure I would get here, either. Are you all right?"

"The doctors say I have a concussion, but nothing that will permanently harm me. The policeman here," Eli said, indicating the Franklin policeman who had boarded the ambulance with him earlier that morning, "wants me to tell

234

him what happened in the middle of the night."

"I think you should tell him, Eli. You could choose to have a lawyer present if you want, but either way I think you should tell him. Without you, they may not be able to figure out who killed Calvin Cahill. Without them, you may be in real danger."

Eli didn't respond right away. He held out the chalk-colored clay. "Look what the hospital chaplain got me."

"That's nice. Are you making more angels?"

"Just one more," he said. I could see he was working on the face, but it was turned away from me.

"Eli, when did you get up last night?"

"It was three. I called you when the angels woke me."

Both Claire and the Franklin policeman took notes. Eli saw what they were doing but ignored it.

"The angels got you up, why?" I asked.

"Because the body was on its way."

"Did you hear me tell you not to go out to wait for it?"

"Yeah, I thought I did, just before I set the receiver down. But the angels seemed to think it was important for me to go out there."

"What happened?"

"Well, I put my clothes on and snuck out of the house, because I didn't want to wake anyone."

"Go on."

"And then I couldn't see anything out back, so I started over toward the house next door because I heard a noise."

"What kind of noise?"

"A shuffling sound, like people dragging something."

"Why did you go into the backyard to begin with?"

"I had the feeling that was where the body would be."

"And then?"

"Then someone hit me over the head and poured

whiskey on my face."

"You're sure it was whiskey?"

Eli shrugged. "I've had whiskey before, you know."

"Go on."

"That's all I remember until I heard you call to me. And then there were lights everywhere, and the emergency people took me away."

I turned to the policeman. "Why did the police come, anyway?"

"One of the neighbors reported a strange car parked in their driveway. Then they called back and said two men ran to the car and tore off down the road. We suspected a burglary."

"Eli, did you know you had a gun in your hand?" I asked.

"No. I could feel something metallic and heavy. Someone kicked it out of my hand. I've never held a gun before."

I looked to Claire and the Franklin policeman. "That pretty much sums it up. I've already made a statement on how I got there and what happened when I found Eli."

Both Claire and the other policeman had questions. I was fairly certain they thought he was innocent, and I didn't try to stop him from answering them. Nothing he said would make them think otherwise. He came across as very credible, except for his angels.

Both of them urged Eli to let them keep him at Wishard for the time being. I concurred, telling Eli someone obviously tried to set him up, and that he would be safer here. He agreed.

Before Claire and I left, I asked Eli if I could see the angel he was working on. He looked at the face he was sculpting, then smiled at me and said no. "I'm sorry, Nick, but it's not ready yet. I should have it finished the next time you come to see me, though."

He paused. "It's not a straight line, Nick."

"What's not a straight line?"

"The path to the truth."

"It never is," I said.

Eli smiled. "But you want it to be in solving this case, and it won't be."

"Do you know what the truth is?"

"No. But the angels said you should know."

"At least we know it was McCutcheson the angels were talking about when they said someone I knew would die."

"It's not McCutcheson," Eli said. "You didn't really know him. He was just someone you met. This will be a person you know."

I took in a breath. "It's not over yet? Have the angels said who it will be?"

He shook his head. "Sorry. The circumstances . . ."

". . . keep changing," I finished. "I've heard that before."

"It could still be you," he cautioned. "Please be careful."

"Eli, there are times I want to believe you, and times I don't. In this case, I don't." I turned to leave.

"One more thing," he said. "Would you stop by the shelter and pick up an envelope? It's under the angel on the dresser. There's a photograph in there for you. I've had it since we met. I meant to give it to you, but I kept forgetting. It doesn't mean anything to me but it might to you."

We left. Claire broke the silence first as we passed the receptionist's desk. "What a strange character. What's this about someone you know dying?"

I filled her in on the angels' greatest hits. She shook her head.

"Well, I need to check with Vice. If they have anything that could tie Richardson Enterprises into this, it might help. The head is Gus Richardson. He's a lesser, but still well-known, mob figure in Indianapolis."

Great. The mob. Just what I needed.

Claire dropped me off at the Circle Centre garage.

Before I got in the car, I remembered the bug and pulled out the cell phone to call Ryan. He answered, said he was working under deadline on the McCutcheson article, and hung up before I could say anything else.

Driving home, I decided to give whoever was listening to me a real treat. I put in an Elton John CD and sang along with the music, off-key as always.

Before long, though, it ceased to be funny. I turned off the CD player and drove back to Franklin in peace.

I stopped at the shelter and told the manager what I was looking for. He led me up the stairs to Eli's room. What little stuff Eli had was spread out on the bed in disarray; I would have bet the other homeless men had been through it looking for valuables. My phone card was no doubt gone.

But the little envelope wasn't. It sat under the angel as if it were protected. I slipped it out from underneath and opened it.

The Polaroid photograph had been mangled somewhat from handling, but there was no mistaking the image. It was taken outside a room at the Federal Club. The room was number 632, and written on the back was a time, one-thirty p.m.

CHAPTER TWENTY-THREE

How had Eli gotten hold of this, I wondered. I remembered now that I'd seen it in his back pocket on Monday when he'd fallen into the ditch. What had happened in Room 632 at one-thirty? And on what date? There was no date on the photograph. What came to my mind quickest was May 15, the day that Calvin Cahill disappeared. I put the photograph in my pocket, thanked the manager, and went out to the van.

I pulled the cell phone out and called Ryan while pacing on the sidewalk. Having a bugged vehicle was definitely a nuisance.

"This better be good," Ryan said. "I'm racking my brain right now for the perfect conclusion to the article, and I've got about five minutes till Clarisse comes in here and screams that she can't hold the paper any longer."

"Can't help you there. I've got more questions than I've got conclusions."

"Then what good are you?"

"Eli gave me a photograph of the door to a hotel room. I recognized it immediately as a room at the Federal Club. On the back, it says 'one-thirty p.m.' He doesn't know what it means or how he got it."

"Did the angels give it to him?"

"I didn't ask. He said he meant to give it to me earlier."

"Well, the way things are going, we should check it out."

"My thought exactly. When you get your article done,

will you see what you can find out? I think we should check out who stayed in that room on the days surrounding Cahill's disappearance."

"Why not you?"

"Because my van is bugged, I'm standing outside Good Shepherd's shelter right now, I don't have access to all the phone numbers you do, nor do I have the contacts you have. And I haven't even had a shower yet."

"Since you put it that way."

I hung up.

There was quite a scene when I arrived home. Television trucks with satellite dishes on top were parked all over the neighborhood, and reporters with microphones were camped around my driveway waiting for someone to interview. I saw a brick red Buick LaSabre parked in the driveway, which jolted me more than the reporters did. I used the garage door opener to get the door up before I pulled into the driveway, waving at the reporters and shaking my head as they screamed questions at me. They followed me up the driveway but at least got out of the way as I said, "No comment," and closed the garage door. I charged into the house through the back door.

Stephanie must've heard me pull in, because she rushed me when I came into the kitchen. "*Nonno*'s here," she said. As I hugged her, my dad came in behind her.

"*Nicolo!*" Dad exclaimed, using my Italian name.

"*Papá!* What are you doing here?" Dad lives in Clinton, a couple hours away.

"It isn't every day I turn on the news and see my son being hauled away in handcuffs. So I drove over. You have quite a fan club out there."

"Yeah. I noticed. I wonder how long they've been here."

Hildy appeared behind Dad. "Since before ten o'clock," she said.

"*Perque elle e aqui?*" Dad asked in Italian. 'What is she doing here?'

"Dad, you remember Joan's Aunt Hildy, don't you?" I said lightly, in English. "She volunteered to look after us while Joan is in Jasper caring for her mother."

"Of course I remember Hildy," Dad said. "I've been here awhile and we've had the chance to talk. She was the one who told me you were all right and had been released by the police. My own son doesn't notify me. I have to find it out from someone else. *Chi ha nipotina mio,*" he added. 'Who is looking after my grandchild.'

This was not going to be an easy visit. I set Stephanie down.

"Have you been here long, Dad?"

He shrugged. "About half an hour."

It was nearly two, and all I'd had to eat today was a couple of protein bars while driving to the Statehouse. "I'm in need of a shower and lunch. Give me ten minutes and then perhaps we can go out and get a bite to eat. I'll fill you in on what's going on."

"There is no need for you to go out," Hildy said, interrupting. "I will be happy to make you something."

"It's okay," Dad and I said together.

"Joan called," Hildy said.

I looked at her. "When?"

"After she saw you on the noon news being taken away in a police car."

"Damn," I said.

"I told her everything was okay, that you had been released and were working on an article about the death of Mr. Cahill."

"Was she freaked out?"

"Yes, but I told her it would be best to stick to her plan to stay there until tomorrow, that everything was fine here."

"Is she going to stay?"

"I talked to my brother. He is going to keep her there as long as he can. He will emphasize that she will be of more help to them than she could be to us. I think she will stay, but you should call her."

"Yes, I should," I said.

I called her from the office. The phone rang once and was snatched up with a breathless hello. Definitely Joan. When she was certain it was me on the other end, she began to cry.

"Joan, it's okay. Aunt Hildy told you that," I said. "I'm fine."

"You lied to me, Nick."

"No," I said. "You knew I was working on this story. I just didn't tell you when it became bigger than I expected. I felt it would be best for you to concentrate on helping your mom and dad, which you couldn't do if you knew this was more than just an ordinary assignment. Even Hildy thought so."

"You can't make those decisions for me. I need to know these things."

"Are you ready for them? Every time we finish a session with Dr. Moore, I'm less and less confident about that. I keep feeling like I need to protect you."

"Dr. Moore doesn't know me. She makes me talk about the same things over and over again, as if she doesn't want me to get past them."

"You think that, too?" For once we were in the same place. "Then let's get past them, Joan. Here's the truth. I love you. I also love what I do. I've tried hard to be the kind

242

of reporter you want me to be, one that's more interested in personalities than issues. It doesn't work. That's why I've gravitated back to this. I feel like I'm trapped between loving you and being me, and it's painful."

Joan's breath came quickly and noisily. She wasn't crying but she was emotional. "Do you really love me, Nick? I thought that if you really loved me, I wouldn't be a hundred miles away, watching the television and seeing you handcuffed and taken away in a police car."

"Yes, I love you, Joan. I would give my life for you. But I can't stop being the person I am for you to love me. I can't be anybody else."

There was an awkward pause.

"Let's look at the facts," I said. "You're in Jasper, and you're okay. Hildy and now my dad are here, and Stephanie is safe. This story has nothing to do with her or with you. What I ask you to do is this, stay in Jasper until I finish this story. It's coming to a head, and your coming back to Franklin will not change that. Your mom and dad can use your help. When this is over, we'll talk. We'll see a different counselor, we'll work out what happens next. But your being here won't make things better. For you, it might even make them worse."

We were both quiet. Then Joan said, "Tell me what's happened on this story."

"The man I almost hit on Highway 31 a few days ago turned out to have had information about the Cahill disappearance. Ryan Lockridge and I started looking into it. Last night that same man called me from Good Shepherd's shelter and when I went out there, Cahill's body showed up. The police thought I might have something to do with his death, so they took me to the police station for questioning. I'm okay, and now that Cahill's body has been found, the whole thing should come to a conclusion soon."

"I may still come home tomorrow," she said. "I don't know. I have to think about this."

"Take the time you need."

There was another awkward pause. I asked, "Do you love me, Joan?"

"I think so. At least, I'm more sure than I have been in a while. Be careful, Nick," she said.

We hung up. I let out a sigh of relief. I wasn't crazy about Joan coming home, but I felt more optimistic that we might yet make it.

I went upstairs to shower, passing by a window; the press was still outside. I knew I still looked disreputable, but I decided to get rid of them.

Back downstairs I went, choosing to confront this head on. I walked out the front door and they all went into attack mode, charging at me with their microphones out in front, cameramen trailing behind. They all talked at once.

"Is it true you found Cahill's body?"

"How did Cahill die?"

"Who told you where the body would be?"

I held up my hand to silence them. "I really can't make any statements right now. The police are investigating Mr. Cahill's death, and I'm cooperating with their investigation. Now, I'm not going to say any more, so you may as well leave."

I turned around and headed to the door. They continued to shout questions. It dawned on me that maybe some of them didn't know I was a reporter, so I turned around again. "As many of you know, I'm a freelance reporter for the *Standard*. If you're seeking the latest information, the best place would be to look there under my byline."

There was some grumbling. I closed the front door and hoped for the best.

When I came downstairs later, toweling my wet hair but otherwise ready to go, there were only a couple of reporters out front. Those, I decided, I could dodge.

I inhaled and stretched. It felt good to finally have shaved, showered, and put on clean clothes—a blue polo shirt and khakis.

In the kitchen, peace reigned. I could sense a kind of truce, uneasy but nonetheless effective, between my dad and Hildy. Stephanie sat on *Nonno*'s lap at the kitchen bar. She was helping Hildy cut out cookies and put them on a baking sheet. I recognized the cookies, a licorice-flavored German confection called a springerle, which I couldn't stand but Joan liked. As far as I knew, Stephanie had never had them before. It would be interesting to see if she liked them.

"Ready to go, Dad?"

"Can I come, too?" Stephanie asked.

Much as I would have liked to take Stephanie, Dad and I would be discussing things I didn't want her to hear. I gave her a kiss. "*Nonno* and I are going to be talking about grownup things, very boring. You're better off here with Aunt Hildy."

"*Nipotina*, I think Aunt Hildy needs your help with the cookies," Dad said. "*Nonno* and *Papá* will be back soon."

Stephanie seemed okay with it, and knelt on one of the stools when she climbed off Dad's lap. Before we got in the van, I told Dad we couldn't talk in there because it was bugged. For a minute I thought he would volunteer to drive, but instead he seemed excited at the prospect of riding in a bugged vehicle. So we talked about the weather. I didn't even ask him where he wanted to eat, because it was our tradition to go to Minnie's Diner, a fixture in downtown Franklin. Dad liked the place because Minnie was of Italian descent, and he could get an authentic Italian sausage sandwich there.

When we were seated at a booth and the waitress had dropped off menus, I said, "Joan claims Hildy volunteered to come take care of Stephanie and me while she's in Jasper, but based on what Hildy said, I think Joan asked her to come. Hildy's serving as a spy. I think it's pretty clear Joan suspected that unless she watched me, I'd get involved in something dangerous."

"Which you did."

The words were pointed but accurate. I couldn't very well get mad at him for saying them, so I just looked at him sitting across the table. We butt heads occasionally, but overall I'm thankful he does things like show up when he thinks I need him.

Minnie spotted us and came over, brushing a strand of her hair back into place, tucking it behind the salt-and-pepper braids coiled on top of her head. She was a plump, but beautiful, woman. I guessed her to be about sixty. She flirted with my father as though I wasn't seated there. My father is handsome in the way some Italian men get as they grow older, with a beautiful olive tint to his skin, eyebrows and mustache that are dark and prominent, and a distinguished nose that is noticeable but not dominating. I have it on good authority from relatives that he is pursued by Clinton's large community of widows. As I got to thinking about that, it occurred to me that he might be able to help me out in a way he hadn't intended.

Minnie left, assuring us that she would send a waitress over.

Dad said, "It doesn't sound like Hildy has been a very

good spy if Joan just found out you were in the thick of an investigation."

"No, that's the funny part. Hildy actually *has* been a good spy. She seems to know what I'm doing even when I'm trying to hide it from her. But she's been protecting Joan as much as I have. I don't think she's said a word to her, although she's had a lot of chances."

The waitress interrupted us to take our orders. Dad, predictably, ordered the Italian sausage sandwich. I was running light on protein that day, so I ordered a stuffed chicken parmesan that's absolutely delicious. Both of us had decaf coffee, which the waitress brought immediately.

"Is there anything I can do to help you?" Dad asked. "I thought you would need help with Stephanie, but I don't want to be in the way. I know it will cause problems for you to send Hildy away."

"Actually, there is something I'd like you to do."

Dad leaned forward. "Do you want me to spy on the spy?"

"Well, that too, but what I was thinking of involves some background I haven't been able to get. The first Mrs. Cahill said that her husband's good deeds were only designed to make himself feel better about having done bad deeds. I think there's probably a lot there. Would you be willing to try for an interview with her? Say you're working for the *Standard*; that's mostly true, since you're doing this for me. I didn't get much over the phone, but she might be more receptive if you went in person. She lives in Noblesville. You need to charm her, get everything out of her that you can. I've seen the current Mrs. Cahill, and it looks to me like she may have been abused. I'd like to know if that was a problem in the first marriage."

"I don't know about this. I'm not a reporter, Nick. And I

don't know if I can ask about that kind of thing."

"I'll outline a few questions to get you started. Tell her this is all for background. She won't give the interview any other way. Just be charming, Dad. Once you get her confidence, she'll probably open up."

He looked doubtful.

"C'mon, Dad, women your age look at you like hungry cats look at a piece of prime meat. All those widows and divorcees out there are suffering from a shortage of single men. Don't tell me you haven't noticed. I don't care what wiles you resort to. Get the information."

Dad smiled at me. "Okay," he said. "I'll give it a try."

I outlined what we knew about Virginia Weber and her children, and how there was animosity between the first family and the second wife. "Weber's son Chad, who also goes by Weber, is a reformed gambler who works for one of the anti-gaming organizations. Chad didn't get along with his father. I'd like to know more about the son. I've called him several times but he won't return my calls."

Lunch was served shortly afterwards. Both of us were pretty hungry, and we ate swiftly. Dad tried to get me to have dessert, but I declined. He also insisted he would pay.

We had coffee refills while I caught him up on the investigation and all that had happened. Since it was the middle of the afternoon and Minnie's Diner didn't have many patrons, I was candid.

"What are you going to do next?" Dad asked after I'd finished.

"Two things. First, I don't know what has happened in Room 632 at the Federal Club in the last few weeks, but I need to find out. Second, I have to get to the bottom of how Richardson Enterprises is involved. Everywhere I turn, one clue or another leads back to that business. I'd like to get into that office and talk to someone."

Actually, I'd like to get into the office without anyone being there, but how to do that? The door to Richardson Enterprises had quadruple locks. Probably that meant the building had an outside electronic security system, but not an inside system on the offices.

The funny part of it is, I wasn't bad with locks. Dad's brother, my Uncle Angelo, who was sort of the black sheep of the family until he went legit as a locksmith, had taught me a few tricks with locks and bequeathed me his set of picks. We all knew how he'd obtained his training, but we tended to look the other way once he'd become respectable. Dad didn't know what Angelo had taught me.

But I couldn't do something like that. I mean, besides being illegal, it was definitely dangerous, especially since we were talking about a mob figure.

"You seem to be able to talk your way into a lot of places," Dad said. "I'm sure you'll come up with something. But I want you to promise me you'll be careful. I don't like you messing with the mob. It's dangerous. We may be Italian, but our family has never been a part of that kind of organization."

"I'll be careful. I promise."

By the time we returned home it was after four. Dad and I huddled in the study. I gave him the address and phone number for Virginia Weber and helped him find her on a map of the greater Indianapolis area. Dad called her and requested the interview, suggesting that they conduct it over dinner. I could tell from this end of the conversation that she was reluctant, just as she had been with me. Dad poured on the charm. It bothered me to hear Dad working his magic on someone other than my mother, even though I had asked him to, so I left the room. Hildy and Steph had finished making their cookies, and Steph came looking for us so she could tell *Nonno* all about the fairy princess play at preschool. I let her in the office after Dad finished getting the interview. He assured Stephanie he would come over from Clinton to see her play.

Dad gave Steph a big hug and told her he had some things to do that evening and probably wouldn't be home until after she went to bed, but that he would be here in the morning. Hildy glared at us suspiciously. I told her Dad was going to do an interview for me that I didn't have time for. I don't think she believed me. Dad left.

"Have a cookie, Daddy," Stephanie said, offering me a springerle.

"Boy, that looks good," I said. "Why don't you and I take our cookies into the family room and play a game of Chutes and Ladders?"

I put on the news while we got the board game out. Stephanie didn't touch her cookie. Neither did I. Fortunately the game didn't require a lot of concentration, and I was able to check out the opening of the early evening news while playing.

A perky reporter with Katie Couric hair gave me the latest on Cahill and McCutcheson—that Cahill's body had turned up this morning in Franklin and that McCutcheson had been found murdered in the Statehouse a few hours later. No surprise there. The police wouldn't comment as to whether the two deaths were related. Video footage also showed Eli being taken away in the ambulance. He was mentioned as a possible witness. Stephanie's back was to the television, but I shut it off before they had a chance to show Mark Zoringer and me being taken away in handcuffs. I knew it would distress her if she saw it.

I noticed she still hadn't touched her springerle. I leaned over and whispered, "Don't you like the cookie?"

She shook her head and seemed upset.

"Don't want Aunt Hildy to know?"

"No."

"Let's go upstairs to the office. I know what we can do."

We put the game away unfinished and went upstairs. I closed the door, took her springerle and mine, wrapped them in several tissues, hid them in an envelope, and dumped them in the trash can. I whispered in her ear, "I don't like them either. Aunt Hildy won't find out."

She seemed relieved.

She sat on my lap while I sat at the desk and checked my voice mail. The box was full. Most were from reporters fishing for information or, at the very least, quotes. It bothered me to delete them without giving some response. As a reporter I knew how tough it was to produce any kind of meaningful story when no one talked. This, however, was business, and only the *Standard* was getting my information, preferably with my byline attached.

I had just about worn out the button for deleting messages when the next one got my attention.

"This is Chad Weber, Mr. Bertetto. You called me a couple of days ago about my father, Calvin Cahill. I understand you found him this morning." He coughed as he choked on the words. "I would like to meet with you, today if possible. Please give me a call." And then he left the number.

Part of me wanted to dial the number as fast as I could, but I hesitated. This was quite possibly the worst day of his life, to have his father found dead. Even if they didn't get along, death has such finality. It means there's no chance for reconciliation. And death has a way of bringing to mind all the good memories of the deceased, the ones people too often forget when they're fighting. So why did he choose now to call? He sounded as though he wanted to meet with me, not have a phone conversation. Why?

It was four forty-five, so I didn't have a lot of time to think about it. Stephanie played with dolls while I made the phone call.

Remembering that my phone might be bugged, I picked up the cell phone. I didn't know much about Chad Weber. I decided that if we met, it would be best in a public place. He answered on the first ring. The voice was recognizable.

"Indiana Coalition Against Gambling," he said. I was surprised he was at work, given the circumstances.

"This is Nick Bertetto, Mr. Weber. I'm returning your phone call."

"Yes. You wanted to talk to me about my father. Well, I'm ready to talk. But I'd like to know some things from you, too, like how you found him and what happened to him."

"Have the police been to see you?"

"Yeah. They asked me all kinds of questions and didn't give me much in the way of answers. If you know what's going on, I'm willing to bargain for information. You said something about doing a profile on him."

"It's deeper than that, now, since he's passed away."

"I figured as much. Well, let's meet and we'll talk."

"Where would you like to meet?"

"Are you downtown?" he asked.

"No, but I can be there in half an hour."

"You know where the Abbey is?"

"On Mass Av?"

"Yeah. Let's meet there."

"I'll get there as quickly as I can," I said. I looked at my clothes and told him what I'd be wearing.

"It's okay. I've seen a video of you several times today. I know what you look like."

"Well, please be aware that I've cleaned up since then."

He chuckled. "We'll find each other."

I kissed Stephanie goodbye and told her I had to run to Indianapolis for a meeting. She clearly wasn't happy, and I was sorry that another evening would go by without my being home. Hildy asked what was going on and I told her who I was going to see. Though I wasn't willing to trust her with everything, I'd come to see her more as an ally than an adversary. She didn't make any comments about Chad Weber. She said supper was almost ready. I told her I didn't have time to eat, but that if she had leftovers, I'd heat those up when I got home.

She seemed satisfied, and soon I was on my way downtown with the hope I'd find out how much, if any, the gambling issue was involved in Cahill's death.

CHAPTER TWENTY-FOUR

The Abbey is a coffeehouse that serves a variety of sandwiches and coffee drinks, located where Massachusetts Avenue meets College. Since Mass Av is a diagonal street and College a north-south street, the lot is triangular and so is the building. The building is old, and the booths, tables, and chairs are probably older. The wallpaper is hunter green with maroon diamonds. Painted on the ceiling are clouds, the sun, and the moon. The coffee at the Abbey is dark and strong, and any drink they make with it is excellent.

At five forty-five the Abbey had a few customers but wasn't crowded. A young man of about twenty-five raised his hand. He was seated in a green upholstered chair at a round table that needed to be stripped and refinished. We appraised each other as I approached.

I don't know what he saw when he looked at me, but I saw him as a bundle of nerves dressed in a short-sleeved white oxford-cloth shirt, navy slacks, and a wide blue tie with Looney Tunes characters all over it. Unlike his heavyset father, Chad Weber Cahill was rail thin. He tapped a pen against the table and indicated for me to sit down. His long, narrow face had angular cheekbones and a small mouth that showed slightly-gapped front teeth when he spoke.

"Chad Weber," he said, and extended a hand across the table. The handshake was firm but damp with a touch of perspiration. His eyes were weary, with a depth that spoke of experience.

"Nick Bertetto. Thanks for seeing me. I know this must be a difficult time for you."

"I wasn't close to my father, not even remotely, but I am sad that he's gone."

I nodded. "I'm going to have a cappuccino. Can I get you something?"

"Thanks. I'll have the same."

I went to the counter and spoke to a waiter wearing a nose ring. When I returned with our drinks, I asked Chad, "When did you and your father last talk?"

"Not that long ago, maybe three months," he said. He took a sip of the cappuccino. "It wasn't as father/son, but more as lobbyist/representative. I wanted his help blocking the effort to put in another casino boat and expanding gambling machines to the horse tracks. Are you familiar with the gambling problem in Indiana, Mr. Bertetto?"

"Call me Nick," I said, "and no, I'm not."

"You ever gamble, or place wagers?"

"You mean, like going to a casino?"

He nodded. "Or playing poker with your buddies, or buying lottery tickets . . ."

"Every once in a while, when the jackpots get big, I buy a couple of lottery tickets."

"Are you rich, Nick?"

I nearly choked on my cappuccino. "No, not even close."

"Why don't you play all the time, then, when the jackpots are smaller?"

I snickered. "I know I don't have much of a chance to win, so it's a waste of money. But when the jackpots are big, I think it'd be worth a couple of bucks to get my hat in the ring. You can't win if you don't play," I added, mimicking one of the lottery's commercials.

"You see, you are rich. At least, to a lot of families in Indiana. I bet you live in a nice house, have two cars, at least one fully paid for, with steady income and no prospect that you'll lose that."

"True," I said.

"So to you, the desire to have a few million dollars is not a big draw if the odds are, as you know, stacked against you. It's entertainment money you're spending. You buy only when the amount of money is so big that the dream of winning it is worth a few dollars of fun."

"I can see how you would think that."

"The problem is, there are a lot of families in Indiana, particularly in the southern counties, where they can't see their way to a nice house, to a fancy cruise, to a better life. They're stuck in a rut, maybe not in poverty but close enough that they're lucky if there's money left for clothes after they pay the rent and groceries. To them, gambling represents hope. If they need money for a better life, and they can't see it coming any other way, then gambling can become the ticket. Easy money? Yep, if Lady Luck is going your way. It's easy to get hooked on that hope, especially if that's the only hope you have. People will spend money they don't have on that hope."

"And that's why you wanted your father to bottle up any attempt to expand gambling and never let it out of committee?" I asked.

"I'd like to eliminate the gambling boats altogether, but it'd be tough to put that genie back in the bottle. I settle for slowing down gambling wherever I can."

"Does your anti-gambling stance come out of personal experience?"

Chad looked me in the eyes. "Yes, it does. I'm a gambling addict in recovery. I'll always be in recovery. Every day I can stay away from gambling is a victory for me."

"Are you staying away from it? I'll be honest; I've heard otherwise."

His upper body shifted back like I'd hit him, like it was a shock. Grimacing, he took a big gulp from the cappuccino. "I'm not perfect. God knows, I'm not perfect." He put his forearms on the table and looked me in the eyes again. "But working for ICAG helps me. If I'm out there campaigning against it, I'm much less likely to do it. And I'm finding other reasons to hope for a better life."

"Why did you agree to see me now, with funeral preparations underway? Why not continue to ignore my calls?"

"With my father's death in the news, I thought this would be my chance to get some publicity for the cause. I'm using my fifteen minutes of fame to promote this."

I wrote down that quote. Eventually he cleared his throat and lowered his voice, even though there was no one around. "I was also hoping you might be able to tell me something, since you're the one who found him. Did he say anything about me, or have anything with my name on it in his possession?"

"I'm really sorry, but the reports are true. He was dead when I found him."

"Did you go through his pockets, find anything?"

Now I wish I'd had the chance. "There wasn't time. I'd no sooner stumbled across his body when the police showed up. Haven't they given you his possessions?"

"The police gave them to the bitch. I'm sorry, I mean to his current wife, Cheryl. I'm not a big fan of hers. We don't get along."

"Chad, was your father abusive?"

"To me?"

"To your mom."

"Off the record?"

"I'd like it to be on the record."

He shook his head.

"Okay, off the record."

"I never saw him physically abuse my mom. He intimidated her; I never liked that about him. Right before the divorce, he may have been. I was pretty young at the time. Something happened to motivate Mom to want out, though. She was usually easygoing."

"You've never discussed it?"

"She never wanted to. I think she's tried hard all these years not to drive a wedge between my father and me beyond the anger I already felt toward him. After the divorce, he wanted nothing to do with us, didn't want to put in the effort. As if he'd been putting in time *before* the divorce."

"Had your dad made any promises about holding up the latest gambling legislation?"

"Don't use the word 'dad' to describe him. He wasn't my dad. A dad is someone who's there for you, who at least pretends to care. Biologically he happened to be my father."

"Okay. Did your father make any promises?"

"He seemed inclined to help me, which was something of a surprise. But he said there were things he had to check into."

"Such as?"

"He didn't say."

"Did you see him after that?"

"No, but he called."

"When?"

"The day he disappeared. He called me that morning.

Said that he had something that could help me, but not in the way I'd asked."

"Did that make any sense to you?"

"No. He said he was sending me a photograph. Room 632, and that he would explain it to me when I got it. But I never got it. I was hoping you might know something."

I sat there quietly for a moment. How had Eli gotten hold of that photo? And what should I tell Cahill's son about it? I decided to deflect the question for the moment.

"Have you asked Cheryl if she found it?"

"Yeah. We talked down at the police station this morning. She says there was nothing for me in his possessions, and no photos."

"Do you believe her?"

"I really don't like that woman, but when I asked her if there was something for me and she said 'no,' it seemed honest."

I liked this. A photo of Room 632 at the Federal Club would help Weber derail the new gambling legislation without Cahill involving himself. How? And was it the thing that got him killed? If it did, how did McCutcheson's death fit in?

"Did you know Frank McCutcheson?" I asked.

"Professionally, a bit. We've tried lobbying him on gambling issues. Since his son works in the industry, he's generally pro-gambling. Of course, I have to say that he abstains on related votes, so I respect his integrity. Since we believe he's not going to vote on issues of interest to us, we don't usually take the time to lobby him. Why?"

"He was found dead this morning, as you probably know. I'm trying to find out if the two deaths are connected."

"I can't help you there. I know my father and Frank were combative, liberal versus conservative, but that's all I know."

"I'm sorry I couldn't help you," I told him.

His eyes were downcast. "I didn't really expect that you could, but I thought I should take the chance. Thanks for the cappuccino."

We said our goodbyes and I decided to call Ryan, to see if there was anything I could do on the story since I was in town, even though it was evening. But first I called home to talk to Stephanie. I'd felt guilty abandoning her at suppertime to do this interview, and I knew I hadn't spent enough time with her lately. I didn't want her growing up the way Chad Weber had.

"Hello?" she said when Hildy put her on the phone.

"Hi, Stephanie. It's Daddy. Did you have a good supper? I just wanted to say that I was thinking of you."

"Aunt Hildy made grilled cheese. She said it was just the two of us."

"Was it good?"

"Uh-huh. Daddy, when will you be home?"

"Soon, I hope, honey. I'll know after I talk to Uncle Ryan."

"Is it about your story?"

"Yes."

She didn't say anything.

"In case I'm not able to be home before you go to bed, I wanted to say 'goodnight,' " I said.

"Okay."

"Be good for Aunt Hildy. I love you."

"I love you, Daddy. Bye."

The real shocker came when Hildy got back on the phone. I asked her if everything was going all right, and she said, "Judith resigned."

"What?"

"She called me after you left. She said she was shaken up over Mr. McCutcheson's death, and did not feel she could work there anymore. She did not even give two weeks' notice. She packed everything and left."

"Wow. I'm surprised. When I saw her at the Statehouse today she looked a little dazed, but I had no idea she would quit."

"I do not know what to do."

"Would you like me to come home so you can go over to her house?"

"Let me call her. Are you coming home right now?"

"I was going to check with Ryan first about doing more on the story while I was downtown. But if you need me to come home, I will."

"I will call Judith and then call you. I have your cell phone number."

We hung up, and I phoned Ryan. He said he was headed over to Circle Centre Mall for dinner and suggested I meet him there. I needed to eat something, even if I was only going to head home, so I agreed to meet him at the food court.

Hildy called before I had a chance to start the van. She said that Judith wasn't home and she had left a message. I told her I was meeting Ryan and to call if she needed me.

"What were you doing downtown anyway?" Ryan asked. For a change he looked decent. He had on blue dress slacks that actually had creases down the pant legs and a dress shirt with a checked pattern that had, as yet, no food stains on it.

"I just got through talking to Chad Weber, Cahill's son,

at the Abbey. Seems his father phoned him the morning before he disappeared, claiming to have something that would help Chad derail the new gambling effort. He mentioned Room 632. I didn't tell him we had the photograph he was looking for."

Ryan's eyes were staring straight ahead, and I could tell his mind was quickly running through the data. "This is great," he said. "This is a breakthrough. We now know for sure that Room 632 is connected. The Federal Club wouldn't tell me who stayed there, but I think I know how to get around it. I called someone who knows the maids. She's going to find out who took care of that room and what they know."

"When will you hear anything?"

"Probably not until tomorrow."

"Whatever this secret is about 632, it may have gotten Cahill or McCutcheson killed."

"Or both," Ryan said. He crossed one arm over his chest and rested the other arm on the wrist of the first, his hand on his chin. He looked deep in thought. "Do you think Judith would know anything about it?"

"We could ask, but I don't know where she is. Hildy's trying to get in touch with her. She resigned today."

"Really? Why?"

I filled him in on what Hildy had told me. "I may have to head home if Hildy gets in touch with her," I said. "Hildy wants to go see her, but can't leave Stephanie."

"I'm going to try to push my contact to see if we can get the list of people who stayed in 632 any sooner." He pulled out his cell phone. Several minutes later, he still hadn't managed to get hold of her, but he'd left messages all over the place. "It may have to wait until tomorrow," he said.

We looked over our options at the food court. Ryan

bought Chinese food while I opted for a protein-rich steak sandwich. The noise level at the mall was pretty high; after all it was a Friday night. Single-gender packs of twenty-somethings wandered around eyeing the opposite sex. I imagined them with their faces turned up, sniffing the air for a scent that would justify at least a howl.

Ryan finished his cashew chicken and began to talk out his theory.

"So this is what we know," he began. "Calvin Cahill wasn't going to use his authority to keep the new gambling legislation buried, but he was prepared to pass information to his son that would get the job done behind the scenes. Before he could get some kind of cryptic information about Room 632 to his son, he's murdered. If he wasn't killed at the Federal Club, he was at least abducted there. No one saw Cahill's body leave the club, not even on videotape. Whoever got the body out had to know his way around."

"Like Chance Marston."

"Exactly. Marston, the bartender. We already think he was running some kind of prostitution ring from the club. And it was almost certainly he who gave your eye that lovely yellow-purple color when you started investigating Cahill's disappearance from the red handkerchief angle, which may have been a signal from Cahill."

"And it might have been Frank McCutcheson who tipped Marston off, because the attack came after I confronted McCutcheson," I added.

"But that would imply McCutcheson knew something about Cahill's disappearance, and I'm not convinced yet the connection is that strong. McCutcheson and Cahill might have been at odds, and McCutcheson might even have been very angry over a double-cross on the gambling legislation, but that's hardly a reason to kill him."

"Don't forget Richardson Enterprises. They have an interest in both legitimate and illegitimate gambling. They may have been putting so much pressure on McCutcheson to get the bill out of committee that he felt threatened, and when Cahill first reneged, it pushed him over the edge."

"Maybe Richardson Enterprises is behind the whole thing, and McCutcheson had nothing to do with Cahill's death," Ryan said. "Maybe he just suspected the whole thing."

"Then why tip them off to our investigation?" I asked. "He had something to hide?"

"And another thing. Why was he killed? Why the Statehouse? And how did he end up on top of the decorative skylight?"

"I don't know."

"Then there's Eli's photo of the door to Room 632 with one-thirty p.m. written on the back. If it was meant for Chad Weber, how did Eli get it, and what does it mean?"

"I hate to suggest this to you, seeing how Judith is your wife's cousin, but could she be involved? She knew enough to put you onto the red handkerchief/Federal Club connection. And she suddenly quit after Cahill and McCutcheson were killed. Maybe she's afraid she knows too much."

I shook my head. "The one constant in this whole thing is Richardson Enterprises. Everything ties back to that."

"What about the abuse angle? Don't you also suspect Cahill's wife or her brother?"

"Sort of. I wish we had some certainty that Cahill was abusive. My dad's checking that out."

Ryan raised his eyebrows. "You have Victor looking into that?"

"Don't ask, Ryan. He came over from Clinton this afternoon when he saw the video of me being handcuffed. If he's able to get the information, fine. If not, it'll be okay. I can see how the abuse aspect would get Cahill killed, but how would it relate to McCutcheson? I'm not sure there's a connection."

"So we're back to Richardson Enterprises, basically."

"I'd like to get into that office," I said. "It's got four different locks on the door. They've got to be hiding some really good stuff in there."

"Like you could get in."

My hands were starting to sweat with what I was contemplating. I picked up a napkin and wiped my palms. "Actually, I'm not bad at picking locks," I said. "It's a talent I haven't shown you before. The real problem is getting into Richardson's complex at night. I don't want to set off an alarm breaking into the building."

"I can't believe you're talking breaking and entering!"

"I say that, but you know I don't have the guts to do it." I started thinking about it out loud, though. "Although the gym, the boxing area, and Richardson's office are all connected, only Richardson's office is locked. If we were to hide in the gym past closing time and they secured the building, we'd have plenty of time to pick the locks and search his office."

"We?"

"Well, of course I wouldn't dream of trying this without you." I put the napkin on the table.

"How would you get out?"

"*We* might be able to unlock the door to the building from the inside and leave."

He ignored that I had included him. "What if you can't turn off the alarm from the inside? Sounds pretty risky."

"Why don't we just go over to the gym tonight while it's still open and check it out? It might give us some ideas."

Ryan sat there. Finally he said, "So tonight we would just go in, look around, gather some information. We don't have to do anything dangerous."

"No more dangerous than working out."

"We have to do *that?*" he asked.

"We can't very well saunter in and look around. We have to at least pretend to be prospective customers."

"Now I don't like this."

"C'mon, it's no big deal. I promise, all you have to do is tell the trainer you want to ride the stationary bike to sweat off a few pounds, and he'll leave you alone. You can put it on the lowest setting and you'll be fine."

He wasn't convinced but I pushed him along. "We're only going in to look," I reminded him. I picked up both our trays and dumped them. We headed out of the mall.

I had my stuff in the van. Ryan needed clothes, so we drove separately to his house to pick up shorts, a t-shirt, and a towel. I drove after that. On the way to Squared Circle Fitness we cruised by a Wal-Mart. I bought Ryan a gym bag. By the time we got there, he was really having second thoughts.

"I don't want to do this," he said.

"This isn't exercise," I said. "This is investigative journalism. People have to take risks for good stories. Remember *All the President's Men?*"

"They never had to go to a gym."

"No, they had to do worse. C'mon."

The small parking lot was full, much more crowded than I thought it would be for as late as it was. I would have assumed it was overflow parking from the N. Heat Showclub, but that lot still had some empty spaces.

We entered a few minutes after eight o'clock. The hours listed on the door indicated they closed at nine. I surrendered one of my two remaining free passes to the clerk, a gentleman who looked to be in his mid-sixties. Somewhere in the neighborhood of five foot seven, he had a square face with thin, graying hair and a mustache. His eyes were blue and piercing, like a vulture focused on dead meat. He had a barrel chest and a thick belly. He looked tough but not mean, and I wasn't sure which I preferred, him or the nosy woman who'd checked me in yesterday.

"You're not here for the fight?" he asked.

Fight? I thought. Then I saw a poster with a boxing card printed on it leaning against the counter. "Kid Lightning vs. Kevin 'the Loot' Lutempka" was the main event. It was a welterweight fight. The noise coming from the room where the boxing ring was told me the other fights on the card must be going on.

"No," I told him, and started my spiel. He looked at us with detached suspicion.

"My name is, uh, Ryan Lockridge," I said, remembering that I'd used Ryan's name the last time I was in there, which I was now regretting. I gave Ryan a pleading look to play along with me. "I was here the other day to look at the gym and received these free passes. I brought along a friend of mine who could use some exercise. I'm hoping to talk him into joining with me. Can he get a free week, too?"

The guy gave me one of those fake salesman smiles. "Yeah," he said. He silently appraised Ryan's condition and handed him a form. "You'll need to fill this out," he said. I looked over Ryan's shoulder and saw that it was a medical release form. While I was in better shape than Ryan, I was surprised I hadn't had to fill one out on my first visit.

Ryan gave it a cursory reading, filled it out using my name and other particulars, and then forged my signature.

"Go ahead and look around," the man said. "Work out if you want. I don't have a trainer to help you right now. He's working in the boxing room. We close this part of the gym at nine though, so you'll need to be out by then."

I hustled Ryan back to the shabby dressing room.

"Ewww," he said. "I'm not undressing in here."

"Yes, you are," I said. Then I whispered, "And while you're at it, look up at the ceiling. It's low enough; I bet we could get up there and hide among the ceiling joists or ducts or whatever we find." I began changing into my gym clothes.

Ryan looked around nervously but started undressing. "There's no way I could get up there," he said quietly. As he peeled his shirt off and I saw how big his belly was, I was inclined to agree with him.

"All right," I said, "maybe you could hide in the back shower. It has an 'out-of-order' sign on it, and I bet no one looks in there when they close up."

"But what if they do?" Ryan said, scowling at me. He pulled on his t-shirt. "I'd be so obvious. And if I got caught, you'd get caught, too. They'd start looking for you right away."

"Maybe you're right. I wonder if they check those tanning beds."

"Great idea," Ryan said. "If I got caught, they could fry me before they grill me."

Ryan was not going to be a lot of help. But he was dressed to work out at any rate.

"Give me a boost," I said.

"What?"

"I want to look in the ceiling."

With Ryan's help, I pushed a ceiling tile up and stuck my head into the space above it. There weren't any lights up there, but enough light leaked in that I could see what I needed.

"Yeah, this is great. The builder left all the two-by-eight joists up here. And there's no demising wall, either. I could crawl right over to Richardson's office, if I wanted. Okay, let me down."

Ryan seemed a little less nervous once the ceiling tile was back in place. "Ready?" I asked him.

"No."

I pushed him out the door anyway. "C'mon, I'll get you set up on an exercise bike."

As we went through the room with the exercise machines, I silently pointed out the hallway that led to the Richardson Enterprises office. Ryan glanced at it and kept walking. When I looked up, I noticed the older man at the front desk watching us with interest. I gave him a casual smile and nodded as we walked into the free weight area. The cardio equipment was at the back of the room near the entrance to the boxing gym. I could see a crowd through that door, but there was no one in the gym. Ryan got on a recumbent bike, one where you bicycle from a seated position with your legs out in front of you instead of under you. I programmed it for fifteen minutes at a low speed and told him to look around for cameras that might be recording activity in the gym, and also for a place he might be able to hide.

I warmed up on the bench press, and then did a few sets. I looked over the floors, ceilings, and walls as carefully as I could without being obvious. No cameras mounted that I could see, although I reminded myself that cameras can be made very small. After finishing on the bench, I went into the exercise machine room and used the "pec deck," which didn't emphasize my chest the way it had emphasized the stripper's, thank goodness. I kept looking for cameras peeking out of ceiling tiles and saw none. There weren't any in the hallway leading back to Richardson's office, either. However, I *was* under surveillance from the man at the desk. I tried not to act like I noticed.

When I switched from the pec deck to the lat machine for my back, he came over.

"How long have you been working out?" he asked.

"About two years."

"Your friend?" He nodded toward the cardio room.

"I'm trying to get him started," I said.

"Do you work around here?"

"Yeah. FedEx," I replied. Federal Express has a big hub at the Indianapolis International Airport and employs lots of people. I thought I'd be safe with that one.

"You know, we have a corporate deal with FedEx. You get a reduced rate when you join. Show me your ID on your way out and I'll get you signed up. The rate's about half what we usually charge."

"You know, I'm not sure I'm ready to sign up," I said. "I haven't seen this place when it's busy. But thanks for the tip." He took up his command post at the front desk again and continued to watch me. It gave me the creeps.

Ryan finished on the bicycle and came over. "I'm done," he said, puffing.

"You can go back and change," I said under my breath. "I'm about done here. I just need to do another couple of sets to make it look good."

Ryan went to the shabby dressing room. A few minutes later, I started back there.

"Done already?" the guy at the front desk said.

"It's the first time for my friend," I said, "so I did a short workout."

"Oh," he said.

270

When we came out of the dressing room, there was no one at the front desk and no one in the gym area. Everyone seemed to be in the room where the boxing matches were taking place.

"Hmmm," I said, glancing around.

"Don't get any ideas," Ryan said. "There are still a lot of people over there." He pointed toward the boxing area.

"I was only thinking about tomorrow night." I put my foot on a strip of trim that ran around the front desk, pretending to tie my shoe. "They have another boxing card then. If there's no one around to see us leave, they'll assume we've already gone. It could work."

"I can't believe you're even thinking about it," Ryan said.

"If they're really preoccupied, I might be able to get in and out while the boxing match is going on. That would save us from having to hide out until they close. Did you see anyplace to hide?" I pretended to tie my other shoe.

"No."

"I still think the tanning booth is a good idea. How about cameras?"

"None that I could see. But the people in the boxing area kept their eyes on me. I saw your friend Chance, too."

"Really?"

"Uh, huh. He passed by the doorway a couple of times. I think he noticed me, but he seemed to be busy."

As I opened the door to exit, a chime sounded. A voice called out, "Mr. Lockridge," and we both turned to see the older gentleman who had been manning the front desk look out from the boxing room doorway. "Could I see you for a moment?" he asked, waving me toward him. Ryan looked at me, and I suddenly remembered that *I* was Mr. Lockridge.

I walked over. A wave of sticky, sweaty air hit me from

the partially open door. The crowd inside was roaring.

When I got close, he reached an arm around my shoulder and pulled me in close. He was strong. "Don't mess with us," he whispered, looking me directly in the eyes. "There'll be consequences." He held me in that position for a second then let me go. "Thanks for coming," he said aloud. He gave Ryan the fake smile and patted me on the back, propelling me toward the exit.

"Goodbye," I answered weakly.

The door swung closed behind me. "Okay, so it may not be quite that easy," I muttered under my breath.

Ryan and I got in the car. "What did that guy say to you?" Ryan asked.

"Nothing."

"He was suspicious. I could see his reflection in the mirrored wall, and he was watching your every movement."

I didn't respond.

"I'm not doing this again," he said.

The old guy had made me nervous, but I refused to be intimidated. "We'll be back," I said.

"Not a chance."

The parking lot at the adjacent N. Heat Showclub was filling up fast.

"They should be giving away memberships here to get people in the vicinity of their strip club," I said, trying to break the mood. "I'm sure that's where they make their real money."

But I was becoming more and more convinced it wasn't. The real answer, I was inclined to believe, was gambling.

But figuring out how to prove it—now that was the real gamble.

CHAPTER TWENTY-FIVE

By the time I dropped Ryan at his car downtown and drove back to Franklin, it was ten p.m. Hildy had never called, but she was waiting up, again in the leopard print nightgown. My dad was nowhere to be found. I wondered if he'd been scared off by the nightgown or hadn't been home at all.

"Did you ever hear from Judith?" I asked.

"No. I am not sure why. Perhaps she is out with friends."

"I'm sure that's it," I said, not wanting to say anything that would worry Hildy. "Has my dad been home?"

"No, but he did call. He said to tell you not to worry and not to wait up."

I asked about Stephanie and Hildy told me she was an angel. I doubted that, but I figured she'd been good.

"She misses you when you are not here," Hildy said.

"I'll go in and kiss her goodnight," I said. Of course, now I'd be on a guilt trip the rest of the night.

I opened the door and the nightlight guided me to her bed. She was sleeping on her left side, her face away from me. I bent over and kissed her softly on the cheek. She stirred.

"Goodnight, Stephanie," I whispered.

Her eyes opened just a slit, and she murmured, "I love you, Daddy."

"I love you, too, honey."

She closed her eyes again and I retreated from the room. Hildy was outside the door.

"Where did you go this evening after we talked? And where is Victor, that he is coming home so late?"

I didn't like her attitude, but she was caring for Stephanie and I appreciated that. So I answered her. "I followed up with Calvin Cahill's son, and then I checked out an establishment that may be connected to Cahill's disappearance. Where my dad is, I don't know."

She tapped her foot, crossed her arms, and frowned like she didn't believe me.

"It's true, I don't know."

"Then what is he doing?"

"Hildy, he's following up on a question I need an answer to, but didn't have time to check out myself. You don't need to know anything else. I'm sure he'll be back later tonight, like he said."

She harrumphed and went to her bedroom.

I tried, really tried, not to worry about Dad, about Stephanie, about Joan and our marriage, but I tossed and turned half the night anyway. In the next bedroom, Hildy sounded restless, too. I heard her get up at one point, and I stuck my head out in the hall. She seemed startled to see me and said she was just getting a drink of water, which she must've done pretty fast because the door to her bedroom closed soon afterward. I didn't hear her after that.

Dad came in around three a.m. I knew because I was startled from my half-sleep by some kind of commotion going on downstairs. Dad's deep voice carried into my room. I was glad to know he was home, and not wanting to wait until morning to find out if he had had any luck, I went downstairs to see what was going on.

Hildy was seated at the kitchen table, her face red, and

she had a defiant look in her eyes. The microcassette tape and tape machine from the van sat on the table in front of her. Dad, dressed in a suit and looking very dapper, paced around her. He glowered while cursing in Italian. They both eyed me when I walked in.

"She's the one who bugged your van," Dad said, pointing angrily at Hildy. "I came in quietly to avoid waking anyone and caught her changing the tapes."

Hildy looked away.

I picked up the tape. "Is this true?" I asked. I wanted to believe Dad but my brain couldn't seem to grasp the concept that Hildy would have bugged my van. Then I remembered that she'd said Cahill deserved what he got. "So that's how you knew we thought Cahill was abusive, you heard it from me!"

She drummed her fingers on the table. Finally, she said, "True." It was not apologetic.

The heat rose in my face. "For you or for Joan?"

"Joan knows nothing about it."

"What my son is doing is no business of yours," Dad said.

She turned on him. "No? When it affects the well-being of my niece and grand-niece?"

"During our last phone conversation I was honest with Joan. She knows the twists this story has taken. But you haven't told her anything yet," I said.

"Because Joan needed to concentrate on being with her mother. My plan was to tell her when she returned."

"You have *no* right to mess with our lives. You don't understand what we've been grappling with the last two years. Joan is the last person I want to hurt. Even if this investigation has gotten a little rougher than I anticipated, it doesn't mean Joan is in danger. That's one of the things I want to show her. Just because a kidnapping happened once doesn't mean it will happen again. This is real life."

"Maybe it is you who needs to realize this is real life," Hildy countered. "Joan is a real person who has fears for you because she continues to love you. To her this situation is more like being the wife of a policeman. Yes, she fears for herself. It is understandable. But she fears also for you."

I paused. That had some truth to it. I had been so preoccupied by Joan's worrying about herself that I had probably downplayed her worrying about me. Maybe it wasn't all about her.

Dr. Moore had suggested something similar once, something I'd dismissed at the time. My job is not dangerous the vast majority of the time, although the stitches above my eye spoke for the times it was. I ran my hand over them.

"It's still our business, not yours. As long as she stays in Jasper with Hugo and Janine, everything will be fine," I said. I picked up the tape machine. "Is this the only one I have to worry about, or have you hidden others around the house?"

"There are no other tape machines."

Stephanie came in, rubbing her eyes. She looked at us—Hildy sitting, me holding the tape machine, and *Nonno* pacing. "Whatcha doing?" she asked.

"Nothing for you to worry about, honey," I said. "I'm sorry we were so loud." I set the tape machine down and took her by the hand. "Let me take you back to bed."

Stephanie let go of my hand and walked to the table to look at the tape player. She touched the controls curiously, but it was clear she'd seen it before. "Did you show them your ear?" she asked Hildy.

Dad and I looked at each other. "Ear?"

"I have no clue what the child is talking about," Hildy said.

"You know, Aunt Hildy, the thing you put on the wall."

We looked at Aunt Hildy with suspicion. She pressed her lips into a sharp, downward line.

"It is called the Earprobe," she said, annoyed. "You can use it to listen through walls."

So much for thinking what I'd said in the office was private.

Dad started cursing again in Italian. I put my hand on his shoulder to quiet him.

At least I knew who'd heard my conversations. Thankfully it wasn't anyone connected with Cahill or McCutcheson. "What other devices do you have in your room?" I demanded.

"Only one other thing," she said, shedding a few tears. "A parabolic microphone. Out of doors it will pick up conversations from more than two hundred feet."

"Hildy," asked my dad, "you use these things for what? Did you buy them just to spy on my son?"

"No. We have had neighborhood situations where they have come in handy."

Dad and I looked at each other, disbelievingly. Either Hildy was the police force's best friend for reporting neighborhood vandals or she had taken being the neighborhood snoop to undreamed-of heights.

Stephanie didn't need to be listening to this.

"Look, we all need to go back to bed. I'll take Steph to her bedroom and tuck her in. Then, Hildy, I want just two minutes with you. Dad, I'll swing by your room after that." They both grumbled but said okay. After they had hugged and kissed Stephanie, I picked her up and carried her to her room, slipping her under the covers and giving her a kiss.

"Daddy, why is Aunt Hildy listening to you?"

I sat down on the bed next to her and brushed the hair out of her eyes. "Honey, Aunt Hildy is just worried about the work I'm doing right now. She thought that if she knew more about it, it might help her not worry so much."

Steph accepted that. "Okay. Goodnight, Daddy," she said.

"Love you, Stephanie," I said.

When I got back to the kitchen, Hildy was alone. She was still at the table, listening to the tape. My singing, awful as it was, was playing.

"I've known about the bug since the day after you got here, so there's nothing of interest on the tape, unless you actually like my cover of Elton John's 'I'm Still Standing.' "

"I do not."

"Don't you ever, ever, do anything like that to me and my family again."

She gave me a stone-faced stare.

"You owe me big time, Hildy. Here's what we're going to do." An idea had been taking shape in my brain, now that I knew about these snooping devices. "Tomorrow I'm going to borrow these things from you. You're going to let me have them, and you won't say a word to anyone."

Hildy did not look happy. "Perhaps."

"Goodnight, Hildy," I said.

I left her sitting with the tape machine and went to talk to Dad. He was staying in the living room, sleeping on a sofa bed. The light was on, and he was sitting in a high-back dining room chair. He motioned me in and I sat on the corner of the folded-out bed.

"Did you find out anything tonight?" I asked. He waved me off until we heard Hildy go upstairs.

"A little," he said. "Virginia Weber is a very classy woman, and I felt bad trying to get the information out of her. But here's what I know: Cahill cheated on her while they were married and she knew about it, but there was no abuse until she confronted him. I don't know whether he hit her once or if they had multiple run-ins. I didn't want to press her on the point. They divorced afterwards. Then he began working on legislation for shelters for women who had been abused."

"Guilt trip," I said. "That must be what she meant when she told me earlier that the good things he did were to make himself feel better about the bad things he did. He abused women for whatever reason, and creating shelters made him feel better about it."

"So it would appear," Dad said. "Whatever he did to her, she did not deserve. Their divorce agreement specified that she could not talk about any aspects of their marriage or she would forfeit the money he paid her monthly. It was hush money."

"That's a shame," I said.

"I did have a nice evening," he said with a twinkle in his eye.

I held up my hand. "I'm sure you did."

"Do you want me to research something else to-morrow?"

I laughed at his eagerness. "Maybe. We'll see. To-morrow could be a crowded day, and I may need you to look after Steph. *Grazie por tutti,*" I said.

"*A domani, figlio mio,*" he replied.

We all slept later than we planned the next morning. It was about eight-thirty when I woke to a ringing phone. I fumbled with the receiver, managing to croak out a hello.

"Nick Bertetto, please."

"Speaking."

"This is Claire Hurst from the Indianapolis Police Department. We've decided to let you and Ryan Lockridge view the tapes from the Federal Club. Can you meet us today at ten o'clock?"

I glanced at the clock.

"I can be there. IPD headquarters?"

"No, we want you to watch the duplicate tapes, the ones the Federal Club has."

Good, I thought. "Have you contacted Ryan?"

"We've tried, but we're not getting an answer at his house or office."

I had a bad feeling and hoped it didn't mean trouble. "Let me try. I'll see you at the Federal Club at ten."

Ryan wasn't at the office, so I left a message there and called his cell phone. He almost always answered the cell. Nothing. I left another message, but it bothered me that he hadn't picked up.

It would take me half an hour to drive from Franklin to downtown Indianapolis, so I had no time to waste. I showered, shaved, dressed, and woke Stephanie so we could have breakfast together. Feeling guilty because I had to once again leave her with *Nonno* and Hildy, I made muffins from a mix—strawberry, Stephanie's favorite. We ate together. I was glad the phone hadn't awakened the others.

Before I had figured out how I was going to tell Stephanie I had to go to work, she brought it up.

"Daddy, I want to go to the park with you today," she said.

"Honey, you know that I would really like to stay home with you. If I didn't have to get this story done so quickly, I would."

"Why do you have to work so hard?"

Good question, but hard to explain to a four-year-old. "You know how you and Mommy count on me to make dinner since I work here at home?" She nodded. "Well, there are lots of people who are counting on me to get to the end of this story. And I want to do it, because then I'll have it done, and I can spend more time with you and Mommy. These kinds of stories don't come along very often, so I know things will settle down after it's done."

"Don't go, Daddy."

I smiled and ran my hand over the top of her head. "I wish I could stay here with you. I know how you feel. Really, I do, but I have to go. *Nonno* and Aunt Hildy are here. I know you'll be fine. Now, while you finish your muffin, I'm going to get *Nonno* up."

Dad was already awake and making up the sofa bed when I went into the living room.

"Smells good. What have you made for breakfast?" he asked.

"Muffins. There's plenty of them. You'll need to get breakfast yourself, though. I have to be in Indianapolis at ten."

"I can do that," he said.

It was best to leave Dad with simple things when it came to making meals. Since Mom died three years ago, he mostly ate out or was invited over to the homes of attractive widows interested in his company. I went back upstairs and heard Hildy banging around in her room. I knocked on the door and told her about the muffins, too.

Half an hour later I was headed for the Federal Club. Since it was a Saturday, traffic was light. I parked in the attached garage and walked around to the side entrance, where two unmarked police cars sat. Claire Hurst got out of hers. She was in uniform today.

"Thanks for meeting us here," she said, shaking my hand.

She looked over the bruises on my face. "Looks like the traces of your 'mugging' are starting to fade. Does it still hurt?"

"Only when I touch it."

"Still think it was Chance Marston?"

"Uh-huh."

She got down to business. "We've looked at these tapes over and over again, and we don't see anything. We're hoping you might. Where's Lockridge?"

"I don't know. I couldn't get hold of him. I did leave a message, though, telling him to meet us here."

"I'll ask one of the other detectives to stay down here in case he shows up," Hurst said. She went over to the second car. A large, overweight policeman got out. He nodded as she spoke to him.

I followed Claire into the Federal Club. "Where's Smallwood?" I asked.

"He's not on duty today, which is just as well. You know he doesn't like you, don't you? He wouldn't be happy if you found something."

We took the elevator to the third floor. When we got out, we walked past the windows that looked out on the roof of the second-floor athletic center. I stopped Claire.

"Do these windows open?" I asked. "I don't see a way for them to open, but I'm sure people must be able to get out onto the roof somehow."

"We asked about that. None of the windows open, but a door off the security room leads to the roof." She pointed to a set of windows on the right. I saw the door between the last window and the corner where the roof overlooks the street.

"Have you been out there?" I asked.

"No, but I've checked the door. There's no way to get to it but through security."

We turned left into a hallway that ran to the security room. Claire knocked on the door, announced us, and we were admitted.

Hildy would like this setup, I thought. Though the room was small, there was quite a bit of equipment, and it looked sophisticated. A bank of four color televisions was mounted across a main desk where two security guards were stationed. Their backs were to the door. A VCR was attached to each television, and they were actively recording. The guards scanned two televisions each, back and forth and back and forth. It looked like a boring job. The TVs were trained on four entrances: the main entry, the side entry, the loading dock, and the back entry. There wasn't a lot of action; a few people were coming and going.

Claire introduced me to one of the guards.

"Nice to meet ya," he said. "The tapes you're looking for are over there." He indicated a gray metal table in the corner by an outside window. The window was covered with opaque film.

"It's dark in here," I told Claire as we moved to the table, which held a nineteen-inch television and VCR. Claire turned them on.

"They keep it dark to cut down on the glare," she said.

"Be too easy to sleep, though."

I pulled a chair with rollers away from the desk and sat down. Claire picked up the tape labeled "Front Entry," then slid it into the tape deck. She pressed Play, and soon the events of that day unfolded before my eyes. I recognized the movers and shakers of the city who were members of the Federal Club.

"How long are the tapes?" I asked.

"The tape you're looking at starts at six a.m. and goes to two p.m. That probably covers the time when whoever killed Cahill came in or went out, or both," she said.

"And I have four of them to watch?"

"Fast forward until you see something you want to look at. That's what we've done. I'll stay as long as you need. We're hoping you'll see something we didn't." She pulled up another chair and sat.

I viewed the "Front Entry" and the "Side Entry" tapes. Each one took an hour, even at high speed. I slowed the tapes a couple of times for people I recognized. The only notable entry was Calvin Cahill, who showed up on the "Side Entry" tape at ten thirty-three a.m. I noted the time and looked at Claire.

"Does Cahill's arrival time match what you'd been told?"

"It checks."

The "Back Entry" tape was more interesting. Most people using the back entrance were either employees or people making small deliveries. I watched Chance Marston come in at seven, and stopped the tape. "He's here rather early, isn't he?"

"Marston? He's here legitimately. They get calls at breakfast for Bloody Marys and Mimosas. Someone's got to make them. He puts in a full day by mid-afternoon."

"Okay," I said. I went back to the tape. At eight twenty-four a buxom woman walked into view and I stopped the tape. "Who's that?" I asked.

"IPD is not a dating service," Claire cracked.

"Seriously. I've seen her before."

"We asked about all the employees. I'm fairly sure they told us she's in housekeeping. I don't remember her name, but we could find out."

"Would you, please?" I asked. "And did they mention what her hours were? I saw her one afternoon working out at Marston's gym. Not that she couldn't have had that day off, or worked shorter hours, but something may not be right there."

I went back to the tape again. Because of the way the camera was placed, you could see all the faces of the people coming in, but only the backs of the people going out. Matching up the people coming in and going out later would be a nightmare. Not only would it cross tapes, but it would cross entrances. People who went in the front entry might well have gone out the side or the back. I asked Claire if the police had made that effort yet. She said they had made an initial try but were short of manpower and hadn't gotten back to it.

At one forty-five p.m., Frank McCutcheson came in the back entry. He passed a woman dressed in a kitchen uniform who was leaving. After she passed him, he turned around to say something to her. It was as though he recognized her. Then he shook his head and moved on. I backed the tape up and watched it again.

"McCutcheson's time checks out with his alibi," Claire said, before I could ask. "He was at a Goodwill Industries benefit luncheon before he showed up here. At least a hundred witnesses place him at the luncheon."

I frowned. "But he did show up that day, and he's one of the dead."

"We don't know if the two deaths are connected."

"They need to be," I said. I smiled.

"Would be easier if they were," Claire replied. "One killer instead of two."

"Do you know who it was he passed in the hall? We can't see her face."

285

"Management doesn't know. From the uniform, she looks like someone who helps in the kitchen, but they can't place who it is. We've tried tracking it, but we keep coming up to a dead end. We've questioned the kitchen staff, too. There's no one on staff not accounted for, and they don't remember her."

Starting the tape from where I'd backed it up, I watched the woman a little more closely. She had darkish hair, but it was under a hairnet. The bulky shirt hid her shape. She couldn't have been tall, because McCutcheson, who was about five foot six, looked taller. It could have been someone I'd met, but if it wasn't, I wouldn't be surprised either.

"Well, I don't know who she is," I finally admitted.

It was after noon and I was thinking that I needed to get something to eat when the kitchen sent up several club sandwiches, potato chips, raw vegetables, and drinks. Claire said that the Federal Club had been very hospitable to the police while they'd been investigating Cahill's disappearance.

I removed the bacon from the club sandwich, ate the vegetables instead of the potato chips, and had water instead of soda. I noticed Claire did the same, so I didn't feel quite so conspicuous.

Ryan still hadn't called. I tried his cell phone again but got no answer. Tired of leaving messages, I hung up.

Claire put in the "Loading Dock" tape. I had no idea that so many companies made stops at the Federal Club. Flowers, baked goods, seafood, meats, vegetables, uniforms, furniture, and more came and left. The names of the vendors were by and large recognizable names in the Indianapolis area, but one I saw caught my attention. I stopped the tape as a bright green truck pulled up.

"Hadley Wholesale Produce Wagon," I said, turning to Claire. "He's the same guy Elijah Smith claimed picked him up outside Peoria."

"And he denied it, remember? We know it's the same guy. But that company's had an account here for a long time, well before Paul Hadley bought into the company. They make two regular deliveries every day, one in the morning and one in the afternoon. There was nothing unusual in what they did."

"It seems like a small company to be providing services to the Federal Club," I said.

"The guy legitimately delivers to them every day," she insisted.

This was the morning delivery, nine thirty-seven a.m. Paul Hadley and two associates, both male, opened the back of their truck and delivered produce. There was already a meat truck unloading, with four people wandering around. That truck partially blocked Hadley's from the camera. Soon there were nine people on the dock. Some were from the kitchen, some were from the meat truck, some were from Hadley's truck. A third truck pulled up and was waiting for a spot to open. The driver got out and came to the loading dock as well. With so many people moving around and in and out of the dock area, it was difficult to keep track of who belonged to what truck. I spotted the mysterious woman from the kitchen, moving away from the camera. Again, we couldn't see her face. Claire pointed her out, too. Eventually Hadley and his people got in the truck and left. The other truck pulled up.

"How many people did Hadley bring?" I asked.

We backed up the tape. Claire sat up and we started counting, trying to establish who was with Hadley. It proved to be impossible because his truck was partially blocked. We could count three who belonged to Hadley, and three left with Hadley, but we couldn't account for everyone on the dock. Plus, the camera was far enough away that we couldn't clearly see faces.

"Could he have brought the extra kitchen person?"

"No way to tell from the tape. I'll have an officer check with Hadley directly."

We moved on. Hadley's afternoon delivery must have come after two p.m., because it wasn't on the tape. Claire requested the next dock tape and we watched it. Hadley's second delivery came at three thirty-five p.m. Hadley had two associates and himself. A uniform truck pulled up, but not until Hadley's delivery was finished. The same three individuals got in Hadley's truck and left.

"If Hadley dropped off the extra person, she didn't wait around until the afternoon to get back in," Claire said.

I looked around the security room. "Can I get out on the roof?" I asked the security guard.

He yawned. "Why?"

"I want to see how to get out there. Will an alarm go off or anything?"

"No. Just open the door in the corner. It leads to the outside door."

The door was mostly out of sight of the security guards, behind them to the right. It opened out. There was a small landing beyond it, with another door that opened out onto the roof. Once you went out on the roof, the door closed behind you with no way to get back in, so I held onto it while Claire followed me out. I found a large rock to jam in the doorway. It was the only rock around, so I guessed it had been used for that purpose before. I walked to the edge of the flat roof and looked down.

"That seems like a long drop," I said. Below me was an

alley with a few trucks parked illegally, partially blocking the narrow passage. Across the alley was a brick building I recognized as recently restored condos.

"It is," said Claire. "You couldn't jump without breaking something."

"And they couldn't have pushed Cahill's body over to pick up later, or there would have been extensive damage to the cadaver." I backed up. Being that close to the edge made me nervous.

"They could have lowered it over the edge, if they'd had a cot or something."

"Would have been pretty obvious from the street, though, even late at night," I said.

"But not impossible. We've never asked the people in the condos across the way if they'd seen anything. A lot of people won't volunteer information unless you ask them directly. I'll have someone knock on the doors over there."

"You know, even if Cahill's body did go out this way, whoever did it would still had to have the cooperation of security."

"True."

Back inside the security room, I asked the security guard if they ever went outside.

"No," he said, "we're not supposed to."

"What about the guards on the other shifts?"

He looked at the other security guard as if for confirmation. The other guard shrugged. "As far as I know, none of us go out," he replied. "We do our jobs well."

"I didn't mean to imply you don't. We're just trying to figure out if someone could have gotten past you and been out on the roof long enough to lower something to the ground."

"I don't see how. There's two of us on the day and evening shifts. Be hard for someone to sneak past us."

"What about the night shift?"

"I suppose it would be easier. There's only one guy on the night shift. But we are really conscientious."

"I'm sure you are. Thanks for the help."

Claire and I went back downstairs. It was now almost four p.m. I wondered how Hildy, Stephanie, and my dad were doing, and whether Joan was home yet.

"I'll have someone go knock on doors at the condos, see if anyone who faces the Federal Club saw anything on the roof that night," Claire said.

"Sounds good. I'm sorry I wasn't more help. Wish I would have found the clue you needed."

"You may be on the right track with Hadley Produce. We'll see what we can come up with."

Claire went out the side door to her car, and I went out the back entrance to the van. On the way out, I turned and looked at the camera. "Not very well placed," I muttered to myself. "Or maybe they need two, one that catches faces as they come in and one to catch them as they leave."

As I exited, I went through a cloud of smoke. Two employees dressed in kitchen attire were puffing on cigarettes. They were still there when I drove the van down from the second floor of the parking garage, so I looked at them, mentally comparing them to the back of the person I'd seen pass McCutcheson in the tape. Neither had the right hair or skin color. But as I drove out, I kept them in the rearview mirror, studying them. Something about them was nagging at me, but I couldn't put my finger on it. Maybe my subconscious had already figured something out, but the rest of me was missing it.

CHAPTER TWENTY-SIX

I was thinking of Hadley Produce, and the suggestion of food made my stomach growl, although I'd eaten a club sandwich not all that long ago. Mark Zoringer lectures me on eating enough to support a bodybuilding diet, and his advice is to eat something like a protein bar between meals when my stomach's hungry. My stomach, which has gotten used to this, growls at me rather vocally now for no apparent reason. I don't so much mind it when I'm at home and food is just a walk down the hall, but when I'm away it can be a problem.

I hadn't restocked the van with protein bars, so I walked over to Circle Centre Mall and bought some at a health food store. I returned to the van and ate a chocolate–peanut butter bar while using my cell phone to dial Ryan. He answered on the first ring.

"Where have you been?" I asked.

"What?"

"Didn't you get my message? Claire Hurst and I just finished looking at the films from the Federal Club's security cameras. Why didn't you show up?"

"Are you just now getting done? I figured you'd finished a long time ago and didn't find anything, or you would have called again. I didn't get your message until an hour ago."

"So what have you been doing?" I asked.

"Does that mean you didn't find anything?"

"Stop answering my questions with a question. Are you

291

avoiding telling me what you did?"

"Not on purpose," Ryan said. "You first. What did you find?"

"A woman who works out at the same gym as Marston showed up on a tape. Supposedly she works in house-keeping at the club. Claire is checking that out. There's also a possibility more people came in on the Hadley Produce truck than left, which means they might be involved. Other than those things, not much. One tape showed Cahill coming in. I also saw McCutcheson. McCutcheson looked like he recognized someone he passed in the hall, but we couldn't see her face from the angle of the camera. It looked to be a woman who worked in the kitchen, but without her face we haven't got much. No one knows who she is. Also, remember we wondered whether the body could have been smuggled out from the roof on the third floor? The only door to the roof is through security, so it's unlikely."

Ryan didn't say anything. I prompted him. "Now it's your turn," I said. "What have you been doing?"

"I don't think this is the right time to tell you."

"It's okay, Ryan. My cell phone isn't tapped. I found out last night that Hildy's the one who was bugging the van. She's been doing my office, too. You should see all the eavesdropping equipment she has."

"Aunt Hildy?"

"Uh-huh. And I've got a new idea on what we can do with those devices."

Ryan was quiet for a moment. "Well, I'll tell you one of the things that I did. I went to visit your friend Eli at Wishard. He's sticking to his story about the angels and all that. The guy may be nuts, but he's sincere. I can see how you would like him. Did you know they're releasing him to the shelter tomorrow?"

"How can they do that? I thought he was there for protection."

"Money. They've got more people there than IPD wants
to pay for, and they've deemed him the easiest one to move.
That's not what they said; that's how I read it. You should
go see him. He mentioned your name a dozen times. He
wants to see you soon."

"I could do that before I head home. Did you get any information on the people who'd checked into Room 632
around the time Cahill was killed?"

"No word yet. Let me call her again and I'll get back to
you."

He hung up. I finished the protein bar and a bottle of
water I'd also bought at the health food store. After
throwing the rest of the bars in the glove compartment, I
started the van and drove west on Michigan Street to
Wishard Hospital. I had to park far away from the main entrance, adding to the frustration of the day. Before getting
out, I grabbed a notebook in case Eli decided to reveal
more of what he knew.

I bounded up the stairs to the secure area, asked for Eli,
showed identification, and was allowed in. When I got to
Eli's room, the bed was made and the room looked empty. I
stopped a nurse in the hall.

"Excuse me," I said. "The man in that room, Elijah
Smith. Is he still here?"

She looked in. "I don't think they've left yet." She
pointed to a box in the corner of the room. "No, those are
his things. He must be visiting some of the prisoners. He's
so good with them. Talks to them about his own mistakes
and how people can change. If he stayed here much longer,
he'd probably convert them all."

Just then Eli walked out of a room two doors down. He was wearing clean jeans and a Dale Earnhardt, Jr. NASCAR t-shirt; his head and face had been shaved, and he stood taller somehow. I crossed the aseptic hall to greet him.

The smile on his face when he spotted me was huge and genuine. When he talked, he had that same intelligence that I'd become used to over the past few days.

"Eli, you look much better now. Does your head still hurt where they hit you?"

"No, I've got a hard head, I guess. Are you doing okay? Let's go sit down." He walked me back to his room. "Did you know they're releasing me?"

"Ryan Lockridge said you were being released to-morrow."

Eli sat on the bed. I sat in the chair, the notebook on my lap. "They've moved it up to this afternoon. I was just saying goodbye to a couple of friends."

"Where is the angel you were working on?"

"Packed in that box. It's almost done. It's a present for you. I'll have it ready the next time you come to the shelter."

"Have you heard the angels lately?"

"No, they're away doing other things."

"Other things?"

He looked out the window. "Other things."

"I hope they're working to stop someone I know from dying," I said, reaching for my notebook. It had been sitting on my lap, but now it fell to the floor and slid over to where Eli sat. I rose to pick it up, and when I bent down, my necklace fell out of the shirt. I tucked it back in as I came up with the notebook in my hand.

Eli stood next to me and pulled the necklace out. "What

is this you're wearing?" he asked.

I reddened slightly. "It's called a Miraculous Medal. It was given to me by a friend."

Eli grinned. "I can tell by your expression that there is more to the story."

"It was about a year ago. My friend believes she is receiving messages from heaven, from Mary the Mother of Jesus. She gave me this medal."

"Go on."

"Supposedly I have been granted a favor, that whenever I require special help, it'll be given to me if I ask."

"Really?" Eli said. There was no sarcasm in his voice. "Tell me," he said, leaning in and softening his voice, "what is it that you want more than anything?"

Eli's question stopped me. I closed my eyes for a moment while I tried to think out what to say. "I want things to be the way they were before my wife was kidnapped—when she loved me and trusted me and believed in me, and I believed in myself, and I could be what I am without feeling as if I am letting her down every time I go out to investigate a story. And she could be happy and secure."

Eli patted me on the shoulder. "Maybe it will happen," he said.

A Franklin policewoman I didn't recognize came in. "Time to go, Mr. Smith."

"There's my ride," Eli said to me.

He picked up his box. I walked out behind the two of them, but we split up when they went to the police car parked in a no-parking zone right outside the building. I had a much longer walk to mine.

I got home at quarter past five. The kitchen smelled strange, like spices that didn't quite go together. Stephanie ran in to greet me.

After returning her warm hug, I asked, "Steph, what is Aunt Hildy cooking for dinner?"

"Wiener noodles."

"Hot dogs?"

"No, wieners."

I clicked on the oven light and looked through the glass. It took me a few seconds to put it all together. "Wiener schnitzel," I said.

Stephanie nodded.

"There's something else I'm smelling." I looked in another pot on the stove.

"*Nonno* is making spaghetti."

"*Nonno* is?" He must be getting better in the kitchen, I thought.

"Uh-huh."

"To go with the Wiener schnitzel?"

"*Nonno* says he doesn't like wiener noodles."

"I bet that went over big," I said to myself. "Where is *Nonno* now?"

"He and Aunt Hildy are listening to the neighbors."

"And what were you doing?"

"Helping."

"Are they in Aunt Hildy's room?"

Stephanie nodded.

"Why don't you watch cartoons while I go up and tell them I'm home?" I said. She took my hand and we went to the family room. I turned on the television for her, then went upstairs.

Hildy had the window open and was pointing what looked to be a small, handheld satellite dish at the neighbor's house directly behind us. Dad had a headset on, and the expression on his face was one of wonderment.

"It sounds so close," Dad said. "Like I'm standing right next to them."

"What are they saying?" Hildy asked.

"The man who is barbequing asked his wife if she could get him a beer, and she said in a not-very-nice fashion that he could get his own damn . . ."

"Ahem," I said.

They both spun around.

"Hello," said Hildy, just a bit guiltily.

I went to the window and snatched the dish from her. "I can't believe you're spying on my neighbors," I said. I was especially angry at my dad. He should know better.

"We were only testing it out," Dad said. "You should try it. It's amazing."

I looked out the window. "I don't think we need to listen in on what's happening at the Stackhouses' barbeque," I said. From the upstairs window I could see across into the next neighborhood. The house where Melissa the Motor-mouth lived was easily visible. I pointed it out. "Is that how you knew Melissa's parents had split up? You eavesdropped on them?"

Hildy shrugged.

I firmly took the headset away from Dad. "I'm sure there are good uses for these, but finding out what the neighbors are saying is not one of them. Why don't we go downstairs and finish making dinner?"

Hildy looked at her watch. "Shouldn't Joan be home by now?"

"Has she called to say she's on the way?" I asked. I guess I had expected she would, but I'd hoped she would change her mind.

"My brother called about half an hour ago, checking on her. He said she left about two."

"Three hours would be about right," I said. It was five-thirty. "She probably just ran into some traffic." I tried her cell phone but didn't get an answer; that wasn't unexpected, she often turned it off unless she needed to use it. We held dinner another fifteen minutes, then decided to eat. I fixed a plate for her and put it in the oven.

Forty-five minutes later, after an unusual but tasty dinner of Wiener schnitzel and spaghetti, I began to worry.

"The Wiener schnitzel was good, Hildy," my dad said. "Maybe I have misjudged German food."

"And your spaghetti was better than I expected, too," Hildy replied.

"I'm going to call Hugo," I said, going into the kitchen and pressing the memory button on the phone for Joan's parents. Hugo picked up on the first ring.

"Hello?" he said.

I told him it was me and asked about Janine. When he'd given me the latest, I asked, "Did Joan change her mind and come back to your house?"

"No, she's not here. You mean she's not there?"

"She's not, and it's starting to worry me. Did she have her cell phone with her?"

"I didn't see her put it in her purse, but I think so," he said.

"I'm going to call it again," I said. I promised to call Hugo back.

There was no answer on the cell phone. When I called Joan's parents again, Janine answered.

"It's Nick," I said. I asked her how she felt, and we exchanged quick pleasantries about how Stephanie and Hildy were. Then I asked for Hugo.

"He left right after you called. Said he had to go out for a little while. Is everything all right?"

A dilemma. Do I tell the mother of my wife, who just went in for a heart procedure, that we're worried about her daughter? Especially when her husband didn't tell her?

"Things are fine. Please have him call me when he gets in," I said.

We hung up.

Dad, Hildy, and I sat together in the family room, playing Chutes and Ladders with Stephanie to stave off the nervousness. I debated whether I should take the van and drive the route at least part way to Jasper to see if she had had an accident and was off the road. The phone rang and I snatched it up.

"Hello?"

"Ken Roth, Nick. Have you called a tow truck yet for Joan's car?"

"What's wrong with her car, Ken? Is Joan there? Is she okay?"

"She's not around. That's why I called. Her Malibu is parked on the right side of route 44 coming in from I-65. Doesn't appear to be anything wrong with it, but she's not in it. Another officer ran the plate check and when it came up with the Bertetto name, he called me. It's like I've got everyone watching you. Tell me what's going on."

"I don't know, Ken. She was coming back from her mom and dad's in Jasper. She's late and I'm worried."

He paused. "There aren't any signs of a struggle. I won't tell you not to worry because this is unusual and you have a knack for being involved in things you shouldn't. Why don't you come out here and bring your extra set of keys? I'd like to check this out."

"I'll be right there," I said.

I asked Hildy to take Stephanie upstairs for a bath. Hildy shot me a look, and I said, "Later." Stephanie began to protest but Hildy whisked her up the stairs anyway.

I told Dad what Ken had found.

"I'm going out there," I said. "I'll let you know when we know anything." I grabbed my keys and wallet and left.

It was a wrenching drive to State Road 44. My hands were shaking as if electricity ran through them; I gripped the steering wheel to try to stop it. Instead, the shakiness went into my arms.

I spotted Joan's car, with Ken Roth beside it. I pulled off onto the shoulder, waited for traffic to clear, and crossed the road.

"You got the keys?" Ken asked.

I nodded and hit the unlock button on the keyless remote. Ken heard the door unlocking and opened the passenger door. He checked over the seat before he climbed in, then sat and examined the two front seats, the console, and the glove box. Joan's purse was missing, but the cell phone was not. It was in the console. He asked me to get in and start the engine, which I did. It started fine.

"Doesn't look like she left unwillingly," Ken said. He stared at the nearby apartment complex. "We could check in there, but at the moment nothing suggests she's in danger."

Tears stung my eyes. "She must be, Ken. Why would she abandon the car and not call me? She's already in the Franklin city limits here."

"I don't know the answer to that. But if you know something about why she would disappear, now's the time to tell it. Is there a new development in the Cahill story you're holding back?"

"I wish there were. I'm working with the Indianapolis Police Department. We've got suspects, but no hard evidence. This doesn't make sense."

Ken got out of the Malibu. So did I. "You want to drive the car back to your house? At the moment I don't have enough cause for us to keep it or take fingerprints or do analysis. But keep it in the garage, okay? Just in case."

"I'll drive it home and leave the van here for now. My dad will bring me back for the van."

I sat in the car and breathed in Joan's scent. With my eyes closed, it felt just as if she were there. I started the car and wound through the streets of the nearby apartment complex. Nothing. I drove the surrounding neighborhood. Still no sign of Joan. I drove home.

When I arrived I told Hildy and Dad the truth, that she'd just disappeared. Hildy cried, then I started losing it, too. I went to get tissues for everyone. I could feel the emotions pounding at my heart.

I had Dad drive me back to State Road 44. He didn't say much on the way over. When I got out of his Park Avenue, he said, *"La trovi."* 'You'll find her.'

"Si, papá. I have to."

I hadn't been in the van for more than a minute when the cell phone went off. It was Ryan.

"Got the names of the people who stayed in Room 632. One of them you'll recognize. Gus Richardson."

"Of Richardson Enterprises?"

"The very one."

"Ryan, yesterday I was threatened before we left the gym."

"Really?"

"I didn't tell you about it because you were already freaked. I didn't want to make it worse."

"The old guy?"

"Yes. He told me not to mess with them. That there would be consequences."

301

Ryan got very quiet.

I made a snap decision. "It's time to pay a visit to Richardson Enterprises, Ryan. I'll meet you there as quickly as I can. Wait for me outside."

I hung up before he could object.

When I arrived home, I threw open the door and called for Hildy. She came running.

"I need all your listening devices," I told her.

"What for?"

"I'm going somewhere I might need them. I don't have time to explain. Please just get them for me."

Hildy left the room, and Dad, who had also come running, began to pressure me. "Don't you think you ought to wait here and find out what happened to Joan?"

"Dad, trust me, I'm going to find out more about what happened to Joan by doing this than by sitting here. You and Hildy need to be here for Stephanie and in case the police call. You can reach me by cell phone if you need to."

Hildy brought me the devices and I left, with both Dad and Hildy objecting.

My drive to the west side of Indianapolis was an angry, aggressive one. I broke speed limits big time and cut in and out of traffic. It was eight-fifteen when I pulled into the N. Heat Showclub parking lot. The Squared Circle gym lot was already full because of the boxing match. Ryan wasn't there.

I didn't know how long I would be able to wait, but while I did, I scanned the lot. The lights inside the West Washington Street Coin-Operated Laundry next to the gym were on. I could see two women folding clothes. Something nagged at me. Why? It had happened at the Federal Club, too, when I'd seen two uniformed staff people outside smoking. What was the connection?

My subconscious must be ahead of me, I thought. I leaned back and took a deep breath. I stared at the sky. Then I closed my eyes and tried to clear my mind to let whatever was in my subconscious come through. Nothing. These things don't often come when you call.

I thought about it again. Cleaning, smoking. No. Folding, smoking? Cleaning, employees? No and no. Cleaning, what? And then it hit me. Cleaning, uniforms. Did Richardson Enterprises own the uniform business I'd seen picking up clothes at the Federal Club? When Ryan had mentioned some of the legitimate ways they made money, he mentioned cleaning.

I spotted Ryan's Saturn and waved him down.

"Explain," he said, through his open window.

"Joan's missing. Her car was found locked and empty along State Road 44 on her way home from Jasper."

"You think Richardson or Marston had something to do with it?"

"I was threatened here just yesterday, and we know Marston and Richardson Enterprises are connected with Cahill's death. We don't know how. And Ryan, I figured out how Marston could have taken the body out. Do you know if Richardson Enterprises owns the uniform business that services the Federal Club?"

"Off the top of my head, no."

"Do you have your notes with you?"

"Yes, but . . ."

"Get them out. If I'm right and Richardson owns that business, they took the body out the dock wrapped up with the uniforms. It's so simple."

Ryan jumped out of the Saturn, opened the back door, and began rummaging through his stuff. It took him several minutes, but he found the answer I was expecting.

"They own Uniforms Unlimited," he said. "Is that the one?"

"I'm sure it is. It sounds familiar. I wish I had known it when I looked at the tapes earlier today. Then we'd be sure."

"You're not really planning to break into Richardson's office."

"I don't think so. Not unless the situation presents itself. But I'm going to go up over the ceiling to Richardson's office and find out if Joan's in there. If she isn't, I'm going to plant this wireless mike." I pulled out of my gym bag the little microphone Hildy had planted in the van. The tape recorder was also in there.

"What about Marston?"

"If I see him, I'm going to confront him."

"I don't feel good about this."

"You don't have to. All you have to do is play lookout for me." I threw him a tiny walkie-talkie, also courtesy of Hildy. "We'll be the only two in the gym. It'll be just like last night. Everyone is here for the boxing match. Ride the bike. If you see anyone coming toward the changing room, hit the send button. Mine will buzz and I'll know to hustle back."

Ryan was scared and I practically had to yank him out of his car. I put his gym bag in his hand and nudged him toward the door. "Joan's life is at stake, and the gym is only open another half hour," I said. "We've got to hurry."

As predicted, there was no one in the exercise area. We gave our passes to the person at the door, this time the woman who had been there the first visit I'd made. We went to the changing room and put on our gym clothes.

"Give me a boost, Ryan, I need to get into the ceiling."

"What about the lady at the front desk? She'll notice

you're not with me when I go out."

"No, she won't. I'm telling you, everyone's more interested in the boxing matches. She won't think anything about it."

Ryan cupped his hands and I stepped up on them with one foot, balancing myself against the wall. "You're heavy," Ryan said.

"I'll work fast." I was already removing the ceiling tile above me. "Once I'm up here, you can hand me the gym bag and then you can go on out." I found a joist I could hang onto and was just pulling myself up when Ryan said, "Uh-oh." A second later I heard him say "Ugh," like he'd been hit.

Someone grabbed my leg and yanked it hard. Losing my grip, I tumbled out of the ceiling and into the arms of Chance Marston.

CHAPTER TWENTY-SEVEN

Marston didn't look nearly as surprised as I did. He was ready when I recovered and tried to punch him in the face. He dropped me. I scrambled up off the floor. Legs flexed, I was ready to run or grapple with him as needed. Ryan was bent over in pain.

"Oh, yeah, attack me, Bertetto," Marston said. He pushed the long sleeves of his black Squared Circle Fitness t-shirt up his arms. His biceps looked like thick steel cables. "Give me a reason to finish the job I started a few nights ago."

I glanced at Ryan. With his bulk, the two of us might be able to overpower Marston, but Ryan was still recovering from Marston's punch. I circled Marston to buy time.

"You son of a bitch," I said. "Where's my wife?"

The two of us were doing a dance, eyes locked on each other. I circled and he shifted his position to counter me. He seemed relaxed and confident.

"I don't know anything about your wife. Should I? Is she worth looking at?"

I wasn't about to let him egg me. In a moment his back would be completely turned to Ryan.

"Don't lie to me, Marston. I know you killed Cahill, and you've been trying to stop me from getting to the truth ever since. You tried pinning the murder on Eli, and now you've taken Joan. That was one step too far."

I neared the door and glanced at it to throw Marston off-base, hoping to make him think I would run. As soon as he saw my eyes shift, he bought it. He rushed me.

"Ryan," I yelled.

It was as if I'd slapped Ryan in the face. He came to just as Marston realized he'd fallen for a deception. He turned to look at Ryan. I rushed him from behind, trying to knock him to the floor. He was an experienced boxer, but if he wasn't upright, it wasn't an advantage.

Ryan jumped on him and the two of us wrestled him to the floor. The victory was short-lived. The old guy who had been running the counter yesterday stood in the doorway. He was holding a gun, trained on us.

"Get up," he said.

"Let me handle them, Mr. Richardson," Marston said, scrambling to his feet. "I'll see to it they never bother us again."

I cocked my head toward the older man. "You're Gus Richardson?"

"Yes, Nick, I think it's time we officially met. I've been curious about your investigation ever since you registered as Ryan Lockridge. Yesterday I tried to warn you off, but you came back. And now you've accused one of my employees of murder and kidnapping. I'd like to know what you think is going on." He looked at Marston with suspicion. "Stay with Lockridge, Chance, but don't hurt him. Just keep him here.

"Let's go," Richardson said. He nudged me with the gun. We walked out the door and down the hall into his office.

I was now in the one place I'd wanted to be, but under far different circumstances than I'd hoped. Worst of all, Joan wasn't here.

"Sit down," he said, indicating a brown leather chair

across the desk from him. His appearance grew harder and more menacing, or maybe it was because I now knew who he was. His eyebrows, gray and black, protruded from his forehead. Hawkish blue eyes focused on me like prey. "Don't try any heroics. The gun I'm placing on the desk is still within easy reach. Don't mistake my age for ineptness."

I wouldn't underestimate him, but I hoped he would underestimate me. "I want my wife back," I said.

"So I heard. Why do you think we have her?"

"You're trying to stop me from proving you had Cahill killed."

"I barely knew the man. I'm curious why you think I would do that."

"He double-crossed your interests in the new gambling legislation."

Richardson shook his head. "While I have some interest in both getting a new casino boat in Cartersville City and pull-tab machines at the horse tracks, it would certainly not be worth killing anyone over."

"So you say."

He slapped his hand on the desk. "Don't contradict me," he said sharply. "You have a lot of nerve, marching in here to plant bugs in our ceiling and accuse us of kidnapping." He settled back into his desk chair. "What makes you think Chance is involved in anything illegal?"

"Oh, come on. He's running your prostitution business at the Federal Club."

"No. It's not *my* business. We stationed Chance at the Federal Club because we occasionally need to influence people, and that's what I pay him to do. If he uses prostitution, that's his initiative. He's also a bouncer, and I don't tell him how to do that job, either. What does any of this have to do with Cahill?"

I was angry, nervous, and desperate. It was difficult to think. I didn't like the way this was going. And I had to admit that maybe, just maybe, I'd been wrong.

"I don't believe you. You had to know about this. Cahill was one of the clients Marston was supplying prostitutes to. The signal was a red handkerchief Cahill wore. After Cahill was killed, Marston got him out of the building—I'm not sure how, but I have an idea—and later tried to use the dead body to frame a friend of mine for the murder."

Richardson leaned back in his chair. "You're either pretty good at what you do or you have a vivid imagination." He looked at his watch. "This is damned inconvenient of you, to show up right now when we have a boxing card going on."

Richardson picked up the gun and walked past me to the door. He opened it. Marston was standing outside in the hall. He had Ryan's right arm twisted behind his back. "Listening to the conversation, Chance?"

"I had nothing to do with Cahill's death," he said.

"Come and sit down," Richardson said. "You, too, Lockridge."

Marston forced Ryan into a chair next to me, but instead of sitting he stood behind us. The confidence he'd displayed in the locker room was gone. Shuffling nervously, he looked like a schoolboy facing the principal after being caught cheating.

"You've been with me for a couple of years, now, Chance. I gave you the job at the Federal Club because I wanted someone there I could trust. I don't want to believe you've violated that trust, which would be very damaging to our relationship. I want the truth. What do you know about Cahill's death?"

Marston took a deep breath. "When you asked me to remove Dexter from the job, I found out he had this prostitution service set up. It was what he was using for influence. He was making money on the side, but I know you don't have a problem with that, as long we get the job done. And you never said how to do it. So I kept using what worked." Marston was chattering nervously. He glanced at Ryan and me. "You sure you want me to continue with them here?"

"Don't worry about them. I have plans," he said.

Marston continued. "Cahill was a pussy hound, and he made it clear he wanted to continue what Dexter had arranged for him. Cassandra seemed like a good choice. A week ago she showed up to service him, as usual, but when she got there, he had a bullet hole through his head. She was scared and didn't know what to do, so she called me. We usually use empty rooms, but during big weeks I reserve a suite in your name, since you have a membership, and then pay it in cash at checkout. We couldn't just leave him there. I stuck him in the refrigerator and smuggled him out later in a laundry bag through your uniform service. At the Showclub we stuck him in a deep freezer until we could do something with the body."

"Why didn't you tell me?" Richardson demanded.

Marston had a look of panic on his face.

"Chance?"

"I . . . I didn't want you to know we'd screwed up. I thought I could handle it."

"A big mistake," Richardson said, his voice cold.

He looked from Chance to Ryan and me, but his mind was focused on what to do. Then he cocked one eyebrow at me. "But I think we can yet fix it."

He turned back to Marston. "Who else would know that Cahill was going to be in that room?"

"I've been trying to figure that out. We never let anyone

know who our clients are."

"Is McCutcheson one of your clients?" I asked. Whatever Richardson had in mind, I still wanted to get to the truth. Joan was out there somewhere.

Marston looked to Richardson to see if he had to answer. Richardson nodded.

"I'm surprised you have to ask, since you caught us talking at the Federal Club," Marston said to me. "We got to him recently, but after the first time, we couldn't get him interested again. He always had a guilty look on his face."

"Did you have him in Room 632?"

"Maybe; 632 is in a dark corner tucked back at the end of a hall. There's not much traffic. We use other rooms, too, though."

"Who else are you working on to get the gambling legislation passed?" I said.

Richardson gave me a hard look. "I'll do the questioning," he said. After thinking a moment, though, he asked, "So are there any other legislators we have to worry about?"

"One or two others. I'll tell you, but not in front of Bertetto."

Ryan suddenly sat up. "What about Judith Blackard?"

Marston squirmed a moment. "Yeah, but she doesn't count, since she never had a vote and has quit now anyway. We did her to smooth out some relationships. And she came on to me anyway."

"Judith?" I said. "I can't believe that!"

"Took care of her myself. She was exhausting. Got a sex drive to rival a porno star."

I sat there in shock. Joan's cousin Judith. How had Ryan guessed?

"Why did you attack him?" Ryan asked, indicating me.

311

"We'd gotten a tip that he knew about the red handkerchief. Until we got rid of the body, I couldn't have anybody snooping around. Unfortunately he had a guardian angel that day." Marston rubbed the ribs where he'd been whacked with Hildy's tire iron. "But Bertetto's involvement put us onto the fact that the police were questioning a homeless guy, so we decided to set him up. Which would have gone a lot more smoothly if Bertetto here hadn't shown up again. At least we got rid of the body that night."

Richardson crossed his arms. "And you swear to me you did not kill Cahill?"

"I thought about it a couple of times when he punched Cassie around, but I didn't."

"Do you believe him?" I asked Richardson.

Richardson turned to me. "Don't you?"

"But what about my wife?"

"What about her?" Richardson asked.

"She's missing. Her car was found abandoned on State Road 44 in Franklin and there's no sign of her."

Richardson looked at Marston, but Marston shook his head. "We don't have her."

I stood up. "Someone does."

In a quiet voice, Ryan said, "Yes, Nick, but it's not them."

I looked at him. "You know who?"

"Maybe."

"Ryan, if you know something . . ."

He threw me a look just as Marston began to rant.

"We're not going to let them walk out of here, are we?" Marston said to Richardson.

"I want to talk to Bertetto," Richardson answered. "Alone. Take Lockridge back to the dressing room and let him get their things together. Make sure they take all their bugs."

As they left, Marston looked unhappy but Ryan looked relieved. I didn't know what to think.

"Please sit down," Richardson said, which I did. "You and I each have something on the other. You know what my organization is doing at the Federal Club, but by the time you try to prove it, I'll have it covered up. Nonetheless, I know you could make it difficult for me.

"For my part, I have a clear case of you attempting to bug a legitimate business. And I have it on tape. You obviously don't know how small they make cameras now. We have them all over the gym. I could have you arrested. Or I could have Chance remove you permanently."

Richardson paused for effect. "But I'm not without sympathy. Your wife is missing, you're desperate, and I think you could be useful. I think we should come to an arrangement. I will let you and Lockridge walk out of here unharmed and unaccused of a crime in exchange for your silence."

I hesitated, but my fear for Joan had been ratcheted up another notch. I needed to get moving. If she wasn't here, I needed to find out where she was.

Richardson sweetened the deal. "I'll put feelers out to find your wife. If someone really does have her, I may be able to find her faster than you."

A deal with the devil. "Okay," I said. "But I can't make the deal for Ryan."

"You already have," he said. "It will be your responsibility to keep him quiet as well. Now I'm going to let you go, and I wish you luck in finding your wife."

He put the gun in the top drawer of his desk. "Come," he said, and he put his hand on my back the way my father did. "I can see you're a good reporter. Not many would have gotten this far. We may find our paths intersect again, and I want you to know I am a businessman who cares about his friends."

He walked me out to the front desk. Marston was there, and so was Ryan, now back in his street clothes. I could hear the rowdiness of the crowd in the next room and the bell clanging for the start of another round.

"Goodbye," Richardson said, shaking Ryan's hand and then mine. "If I hear anything," he said to me, "I'll be in touch."

And with that we left the light of Squared Circle Fitness for the darkness of the parking lot.

"They let us go," Ryan said, surprised.

"It's part of a deal I made. A bargain to keep quiet. But I still don't know where Joan is."

"I have an idea," Ryan said. "Assuming that this is not some random kidnapping, or that she suffered some calamity, maybe we've been concentrating too much on trying to make sense of the clues. Maybe we should be asking: Who knew that Joan was in Jasper and when she would be coming home?"

"Judith?" I asked, tentative. "But how would she . . ."

"From Hildy, of course. Hildy may even have told Judith without her asking. Hildy may not know anything about Judith's connection."

"All along I've been thinking that it was Joan who suggested Hildy stay with Stephanie and me. But maybe it wasn't. Hildy never said it was. Maybe it was Judith."

A police car turned into the drive for the N. Heat Showclub, then crossed the parking lot and halted about four feet outside our lane. Its headlights washed over us, blinding us momentarily. Then the lights went out and a figure opened the door. I was confident it would be Claire Hurst.

"You look all right, for being in there that long," she said. "I came as soon as I could. We got a call you might be in trouble."

"We're okay," I said.

"The name of the woman in housekeeping you thought you recognized is Cassandra Wicker, called Cassie. She works a different schedule weekly, so we would have to trace back to find out if she was supposed to work that day. Also, we went in a roundabout way to get the employee list for Hadley Produce. No one unusual came up. But we did discover that Paul Hadley's middle name is Blackard."

"Blackard," Ryan said.

"I don't know her father's side of the family," I told Ryan. "How is he related to Judith?" I asked Claire.

"Cousins, we think," she said. "We're checking on it. Problem is, it doesn't prove anything. We want to question her further, but we've tried calling her residence, and no one answers. I had a policeman check it out, and it looks like no one is home."

"Okay," I said. "Thanks."

"I don't know what you were trying to do at Richardson's gym, but don't be stupid, Nick. We have a deal. It's our investigation."

She got into her patrol car and drove away.

"But it's my wife," I said quietly.

Ryan put his hand on my shoulder. "I didn't tell you earlier, Nick, because I didn't want you to know unless I turned out to be right, but this morning when you couldn't get hold of me, I was watching Judith's place."

"Find anything?"

"It was dark, but here and there I could see into the

house around the curtains. It looks like she's packing up to go somewhere."

The blood drained out of my face. "You know the way there," I said, opening the car door to his Saturn and throwing our gym bags in the back. "You drive. And hurry."

CHAPTER TWENTY-EIGHT

As Ryan sped north, I tried to put it all together.

"Okay," I said, "I don't know why Judith would do this to Joan, but she certainly had the opportunity to snatch her. All she had to do was call Hildy or Joan's parents to get the approximate time Joan would arrive in Franklin. She could have anticipated Joan coming in on I-65 and waited near the exit. My guess is she faked a car problem, knowing Joan would stop for her. But how did she force Joan in the car against her will?"

"It may not have been against her will," Ryan said. "She may have made up a story that something happened to you or Stephanie. Joan had no reason not to trust Judith. But at some point I guess she would have to force Joan to cooperate." Ryan turned to me suddenly. "Nick, maybe I forced Judith's hand. I hung around her condo this morning. She might have spotted me and decided she needed to do something to stop us. I'm sorry."

"Watch the road," I said, as Ryan swerved to avoid going onto the shoulder. "What I want to know is, what did Judith hope to gain by taking Joan hostage? Was she going to threaten us? Blackmail me?"

"Call your dad," Ryan said. He pulled a cell phone out of his pocket. "See if he's heard anything."

I dialed the number. Dad picked up right away.

"*Dios mio,*" he said, when he heard my voice. "Nick, have you heard anything from Joan?"

"No, Dad, I was hoping you had. Anything new from the police?"

"One of your friends on the force came over and looked at the car again. He took a few pictures of the inside. I think he may have taken some hair samples from the seats. Anyway, they said they've talked to people at the apartments. Someone said they saw a woman there earlier with car trouble, but not Joan's car. That was it. No one knows anything else. The police are still trying."

"Okay, Dad, keep up the vigil. Ryan and I have another place we want to try. The last one was a bust. Is Hildy there?"

"No, she left more than an hour ago. Said she had to go back to her house for something."

"Have her call me when she gets in."

I gave him Ryan's cell phone number and hung up.

"Hildy might be able to help us talk sense to Judith," I said to Ryan. I glanced at the interstate exit signs we were passing on I-465. Speedway/Crawfordsville Road. Ryan was making good time, but we still had twenty minutes or so before we reached Judith's condo in Nora, even at eighty miles an hour. He jerked the car into the slow lane, sped up and passed three cars, then changed lanes again. A car honked at him.

Ryan ignored it. "Okay, keep going backwards," he said. "Judith shot Cahill. Why?"

"I don't know. I was surprised to learn she liked sex with strangers. She doesn't strike me as the type to approach Marston looking for sex."

"If she knew Marston could supply it, maybe she knew about Cahill."

"All along I suspected she knew more about the red handkerchief than she was letting on. McCutcheson knew

318

about it, too. And we know McCutcheson went for the prostitutes once, at least according to Marston."

"Marston described Cahill as a pussy hound at the same time he described Judith as exhausting in the sack. You don't suppose . . ."

"That Judith and Cahill were having an affair? They may well have been. Judith seemed to alternate between affection for him and distancing herself from him."

"Why did she give us the clue about the red handkerchief?"

"If she killed him, and she was cleared by the police, she might have wanted us to discover the connection to Marston. He had the body. It would have firmly set him up for the murder."

We rode on in silence, lost in our thoughts. I prayed that Joan was still alive. Somehow I still couldn't see Judith as either a kidnapper or a murderer.

"Why did she kill McCutcheson, then?" Ryan asked.

"On the tape I watched, when McCutcheson came in the back entrance, he looked like he recognized someone going past him. Someone in a kitchen uniform. Judith could have come in on the Hadley Produce truck undetected, then left in disguise. If McCutcheson recognized her—and he'd seen her a lot, since she's the secretary for the Ways and Means Committee—he might have threatened to tell the police he'd seen her there."

"Coming in on the Hadley Produce truck makes Paul Hadley an accomplice," Ryan said. "He had to have suspected something was wrong. Maybe not at first, but certainly after Cahill turned up missing and then dead, he should have guessed and called the police."

"He'll have to be questioned, assuming we're right about Judith." I was glad Ryan kept talking, asking questions. It helped me not to think too hard about Joan, about what we might find when we got there. "I still don't know what she would hope to accomplish by kidnapping Joan."

"You said that Judith joked at dinner the other night she might retire and sip margaritas all day. Maybe she's planning to leave the country, and she wants to stop us until she's gone."

"It's not working," I said.

"No, but it might yet. The kidnapping has slowed us down, made us wary. She might be out of the country even now."

"All I care about is getting Joan back."

Ryan slowed a bit as we rounded the corner where I-465 makes the transition from west to north. The Michigan Road exit loomed ahead. Meridian Street was a few minutes beyond it. From there, we would turn south on Meridian and take 86th Street east to Nora. Ryan changed two lanes at once and suddenly we were in the fast lane again going eighty.

When we got to Meridian, Ryan spoke again. "I still don't get how Elijah Smith fits into the whole thing. How did he know about the red handkerchief? How did he get the photo of Room 632?"

"I don't know. He's very evasive about it."

"Who took the photo originally, though? Who had it?"

"Here's what I think," I said. "If McCutcheson knew about Cahill's sexual bribes, then Cahill probably knew about McCutcheson's one and only liaison. Cahill's son said that Cahill was going to give him something that would help stop the gambling expansion bill. We know that McCutcheson felt remorse afterwards. Cahill probably thought that McCutcheson would respond to the threat by backing off his support of the gambling legislation. But the photo never got to Cahill's son."

"The biggest problem we have is, we have a pretty good story but with no corroborating facts and nothing concrete that ties it directly to Judith."

"I can't worry about that now," I said. "I have to get Joan back."

We covered the last few minutes of the drive in silence. Ryan pulled into the winding, outside road back to Judith's condo, built into a small grove of trees that provided some seclusion. There were no lights on that we could see from the street.

"I'm going to knock on the door," I told Ryan, "and if I don't get any answer, I'm going to try to pick the lock. You stay here and be my backup."

"Take the mike," Ryan said. He rifled through my gym bag and pulled out Hildy's listening equipment. The wireless mike he gave to me. The tape recorder he kept for himself. "I've got a headset in the glove box. Hand it to me."

I pulled it out and gave it to him. He plugged it into the tape recorder.

"I'll be able to listen in as well as record what happens."

I hooked the mike in the waistband of my shorts. "If I need help, you'll know."

I got out of the car. The air was cool and humid, not unusual for a mid-May Indiana night. I was still in my gym clothes. My hands were cold and clammy from nervousness. All I could think about was Joan. I couldn't believe that Judith would hurt Joan, but then I couldn't see her as a murderer, either.

The doorbell rang a melodious chime, but no one came to the door. I rang it over and over again. Finally I knocked. Getting no action, I pulled out my lock picks. The lock in the doorknob was no problem, but the deadbolt took a few minutes longer. My hands shook. I held my breath. The deadbolt turned over. Easing the door open, I went in.

The entryway was dark. I wished I had brought a flashlight, but there was no turning back to see if Ryan had one in his car. I didn't want to lose momentum.

As my eyes became accustomed to the dark, I saw a bluish light coming from a doorway on the right down a short hallway. I'd been in Judith's condo a couple of times, but not enough to navigate well in the dark. I took small steps as I crept toward the light, trying not to make any noise and going slow so I wouldn't trip over anything. After what seemed like hours, I reached Judith's kitchen. The blue light came from the time display on the stove. It gave off just enough illumination to navigate in the kitchen. I was about to turn on the light switch when I heard a click. I had heard a click like that before. It was not a good click.

"Judith?" I said.

"So you did figure it out," she said. "I was afraid of that. I guess I'll have to use my bargaining chip now."

I knew who she was talking about. "Where's Joan?" I turned toward her.

"First bedroom in the back."

Judith was holding a gun on me. I couldn't tell what kind it was in the dim light, but it looked real enough to convince me. "I want to see her. Now."

"Exactly what I had in mind."

"Is she all right?"

"She's fine. And as long as everything goes smoothly, she will continue to be fine."

"I'm going to turn on the light, Judith."

"No, you're not."

I hit the switch, and light flooded the kitchen. "Yes, I am."

Both of us stood shakily as our eyes adjusted to the light. The kitchen was clearly visible now, leading to the family room. There was a hall off to my left that led to the back. Judith stood in the family room, her arm straight out with the gun pointed at me. It was a petite lady's handgun, so small it almost looked like a toy. But I knew it wasn't.

I put my hands up. I had been through this drill several times recently.

"Why have you done this, Judith?"

"If it means anything, Nick, I wish I hadn't. Cahill was a bastard who deserved to die for what he'd done to me. But now I think it would have been better to have made his life a living hell, to have exposed him for what he was."

"You had a relationship?"

"He and I had been occasional lovers for a long time. Now turn around. I want you in the back with Joan." She nodded toward the hall while keeping the gun trained on me. "Let's go."

I moved out of the kitchen and into the hall, taking slow, deliberate steps. I turned backwards so that I could face her. I wanted to make sure Joan was okay, but I also wanted to evaluate the situation, see if I could get the gun away from Judith. I watched her closely, but she stayed well out of arm's reach.

"What kind of relationship could you have had with Cahill? He was going to prostitutes and he married a stripper."

"You don't understand what we had. I loved him but I loved my career, too. If we had gotten married, it would never have worked. We both knew it. What was important was I knew he loved me; the others were just about sex. We were together a long time."

"Until he started hurting you."

Silence. She didn't take the bait. I needed to keep her talking. When she was talking, she was more likely to make a mistake.

"You told me that he had gotten to where he needed special sexual stimulus. That was true?"

"He was exciting to be with, Nick. Okay? Then the prostitutes and the rough sex got out of control. He beat me pretty bad a couple of weeks ago. I'd had enough."

We reached the bedroom.

"Open the door slowly," she said, "using one hand to turn the door knob but your foot to push the door open. I want both hands back up where I can see them as soon as the knob is turned. No heroics, Nick. I don't want to shoot you or Joan."

I did as she asked. There was a nightlight in the bedroom, and I could see Joan sitting on a paisley print upholstered chair near a window with the shades drawn. She sat very still. "Joan, are you all right?"

"I'm okay, Nick," she said flatly. Relief flooded through me at the sound of her voice.

"You can go over to her. Just be slow about it," Judith said.

Hands still raised, I went towards Joan. When I got close, she stood up and embraced me. I kissed her and we stood there holding onto each other, both of us a little shaken.

"I'm so sorry, Joan," I whispered. "It's all my fault."

She held me tightly. "No, it's not, Nick. It's Judith's fault. And maybe a little of mine. You asked me to stay in Jasper."

All of that sounded so good, and so normal. But the situation was still desperate. "I'm trying to figure out how to get us out of here alive."

"Judith is counting on me to fall apart, like the last time I was kidnapped, and for you to cave in because of me."

"You're not afraid?"

"Of course I'm afraid, but I'm not hysterical. It's Judith. I don't believe she can really bring herself to kill us."

Knowing that she'd killed twice and that she didn't particularly like me anyway, I wasn't so sure about my chances. But I didn't tell Joan.

"Stop whispering!" Judith demanded, her voice on edge.

Joan began pleading. She sounded convincing, but I could tell it was an act. "Please let us go, Judith. Please don't shoot us. You've always been nice to me. Don't change now. Please let us go."

"Quiet," she said. "Both of you sit down on the bed." We did.

"Why did you kill McCutcheson?" I asked. "Because he recognized you at the Federal Club?"

"Everyone thought I was back at the Statehouse. I had an adequate alibi, but under too much scrutiny someone would have spotted the hole in it. You know, if you had just tracked everything back to Marston before he dumped the body on that homeless guy, I think Frank would have been okay with it. He didn't like Marston and I think he would have been relieved if Marston had been nailed with killing Cahill."

"Sorry." I let my voice ooze sarcasm. "How did Marston know about me? Why did he attack me?"

"I phoned him an anonymous tip. Then I sent Mom to watch out for you. I didn't want you dead, I just wanted you to know Marston."

Joan blurted out the next question. "What are you going to do with us?"

"Well, that depends. I'm getting on a plane for the

Virgin Islands tomorrow. There's a private little island I know about where I have a reservation. I've parked enough money in an offshore bank that I should be comfortable in my retirement. It's not what I particularly wanted to do, but it'll have to do now.

"If you try to escape before I leave, I'll have to kill you. Otherwise, I'll tie you up and let someone in the family know where you are once I arrive on the island."

I thought of Stephanie, of what would happen to her if Joan and I died. I was willing to be tied up to save our lives, but with Ryan outside listening to this, I doubted it would be that simple. Had Ryan called the police, and if he had, how would that affect the outcome?

And could Judith be trusted to do what she said? Why the hell hadn't she left already? Why kidnap Joan?

"If all you needed to do was get to the Virgin Islands, why didn't you take an earlier flight? You didn't have to drag Joan into this. You could have gotten one out of Chicago or Cincinnati, if you couldn't get one here."

"Nice idea, but I'm being picked up by a boat late tomorrow night. If you had figured it out before then, I'd have still been in the Virgin Islands and could have been extradited to the States."

"Judith, you're not going to get away with this," I said, thinking again that Ryan was outside. "Why don't you turn yourself in? Cahill beat you. You can find a sympathetic jury. With a good lawyer, you can probably plead temporary insanity on McCutcheson's death."

The look on her face told me Judith wasn't even going to contemplate my suggestion. Before she could say anything, though, there was the sound of a door banging open and people coming in. The door slammed shut. I prayed it was the police.

Instead, it was Ryan who pushed through the door of the bedroom, followed by Hildy. Hildy was wearing Ryan's headset and had a gun trained on him. She flipped on the light.

Judith's mouth opened wide in disbelief. "Mom!"

"We have to hurry, Judith. Nick's friend has already notified the police," Hildy said. "I destroyed the tape he was making."

"You weren't supposed to know about this," Judith said, almost shouting. There was a hint of whining in her voice.

"But I do. Mothers know these things. I have been afraid since that first legislator disappeared that you were involved. When the second one died, I knew it was you. No one else made sense. Now, you take my gun and give me yours."

The two did the exchange, keeping us under watch. Judith had a puzzled look on her face.

"Wipe that gun clean with this rag, and then hold it on them so I can clean this one."

"Okay," Judith said. They wiped the guns of each other's prints. "Now go put it away," Hildy said.

"But . . ."

"Just put it away. And hurry." Hildy held Judith's gun on Joan, Ryan, and me.

Judith did as Hildy ordered. I suppose she always had.

"What do I do about the police?" Judith asked, sounding like a scared little girl now. For the first time, she sounded unsure of herself.

"Let's just all take a deep breath," I said. "Why not be reasonable about this? There's no way Judith will be able to escape."

They both looked at me, Judith in anger and Hildy with understanding.

"You are correct there, Nick," Hildy said. "There will be no escape. Someone will have to go down for this."

Silence gripped the room. We all looked at each other.

Judith was the first to understand. "Mom, no!"

"I have it all set up," Hildy continued in an even, knowing voice. "Here is my confession." She held up a letter. "It states that I knew Cahill was hurting you, that I took matters into my own hands. I know how you did it, Judith; you see, after you persuaded me to call Joan about helping out at their house, spying on Nick to protect Joan, I bugged your condo as well. I am sorry, but as I said, I was afraid you had done this."

"I should never have let you see me with the bruises."

Hildy gently caressed her daughter's face. "Oh, no, my dear. Who else could you go to but your mother? I love you so much. That is why everyone will believe I killed him to protect you. And killed the other legislator to protect you again. You and I look enough alike that with a disguise on, he mistook me for you. I had to eliminate him to protect the both of us, since your alibi was weak. You will say you knew nothing about it.

"And Nick, though you are not my main concern, this will solve your problem, too. You were not the one who put the police onto Richardson. It will be me."

I looked at her, astonished. "How did you know about that? That just happened."

"You have been carrying a listening device on your person since you discovered the one in your car. It's in your pen. I had to know what was going on. I had to protect Judith."

We heard sirens outside. Hildy began to cry.

"Judith, I love you," she said, through her sobs. "But as long as I am alive, I am a danger to you. They will have to prove the case against me. I will ransom my life for yours."

She put the gun to her head. Both Judith and I saw it coming at the same time. "No!" we both screamed, and we rushed at her.

But we screwed up the chance to stop Hildy. As if in slow motion I saw Judith reach Hildy at the same time I did, both of us grasping for the gun and knocking each other away like opposing basketball players colliding under a hoop.

There was a shot. I felt warm drops hit my face. Hildy's body dropped away. I looked at my arms, sprayed with red.

"Ohmigod," I said, sinking to my knees. "Ohmigod."

I started to cry. And then I realized we were all crying— Judith, Joan, me, even Ryan. Judith threw herself on Hildy's body, sobbing and screaming out, "Mom! Mom!" The rest of us crowded around, trying to figure out if we could save her.

The police burst in with guns drawn. "Don't move," I heard Claire Hurst say. "Don't move."

EPILOGUE

The police pulled Judith off Hildy and did what they could to save her, but she was beyond medical help. Judith confessed to everything. There was a lot of confusion when the police read Hildy's letter, but Ryan, Joan, and I supported Judith's version. Later it was not difficult to prove Hildy's innocence. Phone records from her house and mine, as well as a scan of her computer, yielded enough information to show she was neither at the Federal Club nor at the Statehouse at the times Cahill and McCutcheson died. Her interest in buying listening devices over the Internet ironically prevented her from fulfilling the plan she had developed through eavesdropping.

Ryan and I used Judith's confession to tie in Marston, using Hildy's earlier suggestion. Richardson was implicated but not convicted of a crime. Marston took the dive for his boss.

Hildy's sacrifice ultimately did what it was supposed to do: redeem her daughter. Judith gave the confession willingly to save her mother's reputation. She went to jail, but jail was not the highest price she paid for her crimes. Her responsibility for her mother's death would be a horrible burden that she would have to deal with the rest of her life.

Though Hildy's letter of confession did not contain the truth, defining truth as reality, it contained a different kind of truth, one that continues to awe and inspire me. Parents love their children so much that they are willing to lay down their lives to save them, no matter what they may have done. As a father, I know this instinctively. After we arrived home, Joan and I looked in on Stephanie and cried again, not knowing why, only that it was out of love somehow. Deep love.

I saw that same depth in my father. We told him what had happened when we got home, and he shed a few tears for Hildy, though he didn't know her well. I believe he understood how she could do it even better than Joan or I.

We learned a lot of other things from Judith's confession. For example, we discovered that Judith had taken the photo of Room 632 from Cahill's pocket because it was the room where she and Marston had had sex, and she didn't want the police to have it when they found Cahill's body. I believed it was also the room where Frank McCutcheson had his one and only liaison with a stripper, one he forever regretted. It explained why Cahill believed it could be used to make McCutcheson drop his support for the gambling legislation. Judith must have dropped the photo in the Hadley Produce wagon, where it was picked up by Paul Hadley and dropped again in the cab of the truck he had driven to and from Peoria for Yellow Freight.

How Eli got hold of it, like Hildy's truth, depended on how you interpreted things. In one version, Paul Hadley lied when he said he didn't pick up hitchhikers. He had indeed picked up Eli, whereupon Eli found the photo on the floor of the cab and kept it for whatever reason.

The second version is understandable only after hearing what happened later that morning after Hildy died.

I had lain on the bed next to Joan, watching her sleep. We had held each other a lot through the night. We hadn't talked much, but one memory stood out. She had told me she loved me. I had heard it before, but not for a long time, not that way, and I told myself that one "I love you" meant more than any other she had ever said. She finally fell asleep at six a.m.

I wanted to have that kind of release, but there was too much on my mind. Before the evening began I had said I wanted everything to be the way it was. With a second kidnapping I feared it might never be. But Joan had been strong through the ordeal, at least as long as the rest of us had, until Hildy died. So time would tell. I was hopeful.

Joan didn't stir as I got up. I put on a robe and went to the office with the intention of recording as much of tonight as I remembered. Soon Ryan and I would have to write the story for the *Standard*, and I knew I needed to get the facts down on paper while they were fresh in my mind.

The mystery of Elijah Smith still bothered me. I could account for everything except him—how he'd gotten the photo, how he'd known about the handkerchief. Maybe Paul Hadley had heard about the red handkerchief from Judith, but how could a hitchhiker, even if he had been picked up, have learned about it? It was unlikely that Hadley would have mentioned it to a stranger.

And how had Eli's angels correctly predicted that someone I knew would die?

Stephanie came into my office at eight o'clock. She held the door open and looked into the hall expectantly as she pretended to let others in.

"I see you've brought your fairy princesses with you," I said.

She put her hands on her hips. "You can't see them, Daddy."

"Sure I can."

"No you can't."

"Why not?"

332

"Because you have to *be* a fairy princess to be able to see one."

I thought about that for a moment. "Oh, my God," I said. "Oh, my." I turned to Steph. "Is *Nonno* up?"

"Yes."

"I have to run out for a moment. Would you let him know?"

I dressed quietly and managed to get out of the house without waking Joan.

Driving on a Sunday morning in Franklin is a pretty laid-back affair. Only people headed for church seemed to be out, and they were not in a big hurry. I crossed downtown Franklin on my way to Yandes Street, headed for the shelter at Good Shepherd Lutheran Church. The early service had already started, and I had a difficult time finding a parking spot on the street. A block or so away, I finally found one.

The manager answered the door when I rang. "I tried to stop him," he told me right away, "but he was so determined to leave."

"Eli's gone," I said, not so much a question as a statement.

"Left about half an hour ago. I tried to call you, but I couldn't find your card."

I felt hope drain out of me.

"But he did leave something for you," he said.

I followed the manager into the hall. He indicated something bulky, about a foot tall, wrapped in brown paper sitting on the dining room table. I picked it up and unwrapped it.

Inside was the angel Eli had promised me. I stared at the face and was again struck by the remarkable detail Eli was able to put into his statues. He'd managed to produce another convincing argument for his ability to see angels. I recognized the face immediately. Eli had looked into a mirror to create it.

I glanced around me. The air suddenly seemed to close in, comforting me like a warm blanket. "Thank you," I whispered.